Lost in the Black Hologram

Novels and Short Fiction
by Tom McKay

WEST FORK

ANOTHER LIFE

THE OLD GUARD

JUNK TO THINK ABOUT:
SHORT AND SHORTER STORIES

FINDING THEIR WAY:
SHORT AND LONGER STORIES

Lost
in the
Black
Hologram

TOM McKAY

RIVER LIGHTS PUBLISHING
Dubuque, Iowa

River Lights Publishing
1098 Main St.
Dubuque, IA 52001

Copyright © 2023 by Tom McKay

All rights reserved including the right of reproduction in whole or part in any form. No part of this publication may be reproduced or transmitted in any form or by any means without permission of the author.

This book is a work of fiction. All of the characters, names, incidents, organizations, and dialogue in the stories are either products of the author's imagination or are used fictionally.

Printed in the United States of America.

ISBN: 978-1-7342780-5-7

Acknowledgments

The road to the ultimate publication of this novel began with the willingness of Tracy Williams to read a stranger's manuscript with an open heart and open mind. Her encouragement along the way has been invaluable. Her contributions through the Questions for Discussion have added depth and meaning to a challenging story.

Many others have contributed to the shaping of this book. Clayborn Benson, Anita Johnson, and Debbie Kmetz invested their time and talents in the "Finding Jobs" project at the Wisconsin Black Historical Society and Museum. That project helped establish a base for the content of this story. Similarly, the "Coming to Madison" project with Angela Whitmal at the State Historical Society of Wisconsin contributed further perspective. Deep gratitude is due to members of an older generation of African American residents of Milwaukee and Madison who opened their homes and apartments to share their knowledge and experiences. A younger generation of African Americans helped gather that information in each project. Lonnie Bunch was one of the consultants for "Finding Jobs." I have learned more than through years of friendship and collegiality with Lonnie than I can possibly acknowledge in full.

Writers grow through the critical assessment of peers. For nearly two decades, members of the Thursday Writer's Group in Madison, Wisconsin have provided that support for me. Special thanks go to Zach Elliot, Gypsy Thomas, Sarah Moeser, Joanne Colby, and

Ingrid Kallick. Angela Whitmal and Jamila Benson are recent readers who offered words of support and insight.

The publication of any book requires a team of talented people. Ingrid Kallick is a superb artist and illustrator who produced the cover art. Sara DeHaan's skill at interior design has enhanced the novel. Robert Replinger's engagement with the story and careful copyediting helped create a finished product. Special thanks go to River Lights Publishing for providing an avenue to bring this novel to the public.

As always, I am grateful to my wife Joyce for her patience and encouragement. I hope *Lost in the Black Hologram* makes the support from so many people worthwhile.

CHAPTER 1

June 2000

Emma Jean Whitcomb bent over and jiggled the key in the sticky lock on her mailbox. She had lived in The Manor for two weeks, and the occasionally uncooperative mailbox was her only complaint, though it would have been nice to see another black face besides her daughter, Shaikera, around the historic mansion that had been converted into apartments. So far, that hadn't happened.

The apartment Emma Jean and Shai shared on the third floor of the old Second Empire-style house offered more than enough room. Although tucked up under the Mansard roof, dormer windows on all sides filled their living space with light. The Manor perched on a bluff above the rest of Iowa City, and the living room and Emma Jean's study offered perfect views of the Iowa River and the university campus to the west and south. Shaikera had protested that her mother took the best room for a study, but Emma Jean and Shai both had beautiful bedrooms in the sprawling apartment that occupied the entire top floor of the historic house.

The real estate agent's showing to Emma Jean included more information about the old mansion than any tenant ever needed to know. E.L. Lowery, its first owner, used the third floor as a huge, open ballroom to host parties for Iowa City's nineteenth-century elite. He had the house built in the 1870s with money from a fortune gained by investing in short-line railroads—not statewide railroads, not national railroads, just local short-line railroads. Emma Jean's history courses in college never mentioned short-line railroads. Somehow, they had made E.L. Lowery very rich. White folks, it seemed, had always known how to make money.

One of Lowery's nephews converted the huge house into apartments in the 1930s and christened it The Manor. Emma Jean paused at the irony of a city-born black woman and her daughter living in a place called The Manor. With all of the hubbub when the calendar turned to the year 2000 in January, she would have been happy if they had renamed the place The Millennium. Obviously, that hadn't happened. She arched her back to her full six-foot, two-inch height and let out a deep breath. At least they didn't call the place The Plantation.

The mailbox lock gave in to her persistence, but the open door revealed no mail. She snapped the door shut and briefly pondered the small, white slip of paper identifying the adjacent box for apartment 6. It read "W. Whitcomb." On the day she moved in, Emma Jean had noted the apparent existence of another occupant of The Manor who shared her last name. A part of her was still wondering if by coincidence W. Whitcomb also could be black. It didn't seem likely in a place as white as Iowa City.

Whoever W. Whitcomb was, Emma Jean had seen no activity indicating that anybody lived in apartment 6. That unit occupied a loft in the mansion's former carriage house. The first floor of the building contained storage areas for The Manor's tenants. Emma Jean made several trips to her storage space during the week that she moved. W. Whitcomb failed to show his or her face during any of the forays to the carriage house.

She turned from the mailboxes in the vestibule and opened one of the massive double doors entering into the grand hallway. Despite the conversion into apartments, virtually all of the rich architectural elements of the historic mansion had been preserved. On either side of the hallway, broad arches of cherry woodwork reached almost to the fourteen-foot-high ceiling and framed pocket doors that had been permanently closed to create the two first-floor apartments. A burgundy carpet ran down the center of the wide hall, leaving exposed on each side the elaborate oak and walnut parquet pattern built into the edges of the hardwood floor. A grand staircase ascended to the two apartments on the second story.

Emma Jean walked to the end of the hallway and reached for a smaller oak door barely noticeable next to the grandeur of the main staircase. Opening the door revealed a passageway that gave servants from the days of E.L. Lowery access to a small elevator. Through this passage, the hired help once brought food from the basement kitchen to be served in the first-floor dining room or evening coffee to the railroad entrepreneur in his library across the hall. In some place other than Iowa City, Emma Jean might have envisioned black people carrying those trays. That would have made The Manor a place too uncomfortable for her to live, but Iowa City seemed so white that her mind's eye saw only immigrant girls in gray uniform dresses and crisp white aprons tending to the needs of E.L. Lowery. Regardless, the era of cooks and maids had ended decades ago. Today, the elevator served Emma Jean and Shaikera as the private entrance to their apartment.

Emma Jean thought of what an odd pair she and Shai made at The Manor. Dr. Isaacs, a woman in her late fifties who taught in the university music department, occupied the larger of the two first-floor apartments. The sound of her grand piano frequently migrated through the locked pocket doors into the central hall. A retired classics professor, Dr. Tremaine, lived on the opposite side of the first floor. His shock of pure white hair and slow, halting gait made him seem as ancient as the texts in his field of study.

The Hubers, one an English professor and the other in the history department, lived on the second floor. Already, they had invited Emma Jean and Shai twice for drinks to get acquainted. The selection of mango, kiwi, and guava juices on hand to offer Shai provided conclusive evidence that the Hubers had never had children. Conversations revealed that they had spent the past thirty years devoted to each other, their research, and the beautiful antiques that filled their home. Mrs. Riddell, widow of yet another university professor, lived in the smaller of the two second-floor apartments.

The Hubers' apartment wound through several former bedrooms on one side of the second floor and included a small square alcove at the front of the house. Mrs. Huber used the little room as her retreat to write poetry. Ann Huber's acclaimed work as a poet had, in fact, made her one of the stars of the university.

Emma Jean knew that she, too, had been recruited to the University of Iowa to be a star professor. Unlike her faculty neighbors in The Manor, Emma Jean did not hold a Ph.D. She did, however, bring the distinction of being an award-winning, Broadway-produced, black, female playwright.

Emma Jean's status grew from her success as the author of *The Black Hologram*. She completed the searing and controversial play within months of finishing college. Every ounce of her anger over the racism she experienced growing up in Milwaukee flowed through the keyboard of her computer and onto the pages of the play. The first literary agent she contacted took her on as a client and found a producer with a speed Emma Jean had been told in school was impossible. When the play opened in New York, fame, admiration, and hostility became her rewards in equal measure.

Emma Jean's fame proved more than sufficient to attract the attention of a Big Ten university anxious to build a more racially diverse faculty and even more highly motivated to compete for status with other major research universities. The people at Iowa considered its creative writing program to be one of the jewels in the university's crown. To add her luster to this gem, Emma Jean received a healthy six-figure offer to leave Howard University and come to Iowa City. Only Emma Jean knew that the professional lure of a larger university took second place to escaping unhappy personal memories in Washington. The opening of the elevator door saved her from lapsing into those thoughts.

"Hi, Sugar, I'm home," Emma Jean yelled. "Where are you, baby?"

"Watching TV, Mama."

Emma Jean walked down a hallway toward the second room on the left. Lord knew they had plenty of space: a living room, a dining room, the kitchen, Emma Jean's bedroom, Shai's room, a guest room, three baths, a study, and the room where they kept the television. Emma Jean couldn't bring herself to call it the den. She had come far enough from inner city Milwaukee to be able to afford the $2,100-a-month apartment, but not so far that she would have something in her home called a den. Dens were for the white folks in all the rich suburbs that surrounded every city in the country.

"Whatcha watchin'?" Emma Jean asked as she slid down onto the sofa next to Shai.

"Basketball," Shai answered softly. "Daddy's on."

"Who's playing?"

"Come on, Mama. It's the championships. Los Angeles and Miami. Wanna watch?"

"I don't think so, Sugar. I never got this basketball goin' on in June. I don't care if it's playoffs or championships or whatever. Basketball's for winter."

"I just want to listen to Daddy for a while."

"You go ahead, Sugar. I've got some work I'm gonna do in the study."

Emma Jean walked to the study and settled in at her desk. She knew it was good for Shai to see her father on television. Marcus

Williams had become a broadcaster when he retired from the NBA's Washington Wizards, and after three years, he landed a spot on the number one network broadcast team. Marcus was something to listen to: charming and articulate, but always with enough of an edge to suggest that sparks might fly.

Once, that edge had seemed infinitely harder. That was the Marcus Williams Emma Jean had listened to—not some television sportscaster. They met at Northwestern University when Marcus was an unquestioned superstar on a less than mediocre team. His individual brilliance carried the team to winning records far beyond any reasonable expectations and, more important to Emma Jean, created a platform for Marcus to speak out about the lives of black people in America.

He did not shy away from commenting about poverty in the inner cities, the racism of measuring safety in suburbs by the absence of black faces, the justice system that swallowed ever increasing numbers of black men into ever increasing numbers of prisons, and especially about the exploitation of young black athletes by old white men who ran America's universities. Though Emma Jean had her own strong voice, she listened with pride when Marcus Williams showed the courage to confront the so-called journalists who covered sports with those issues.

Others listened differently—with feelings of anger, resentment, and even hatred. By the time of his All-American senior season, Marcus Williams had become one of the most controversial athletes in the country. He paid little attention to the hate mail. He had known of the sickness that led to such letters long before he began receiving them. The attacks on him as a player that filled the sports pages wounded Marcus much more. Instead of recognizing him as a great athlete who carried an inferior team against far stronger opponents, columnists painted Marcus as a selfish, arrogant star whose teams could never win the big games.

The criticism cut deep. Marcus didn't expect better of white sportswriters than the rest of white America, but basketball was a game with clear rules and measurable results. Scores and statistics and records offered a tangible basis for fairness. It was black and white in the best sense of the words. Box scores proved how many times he led both his team and the opposition in scoring. Records showed that the only winning seasons posted by Northwestern in two decades were the four years that he played on the team. Yet the negative opinions about Marcus Williams persisted on America's sports pages.

As his basketball career wore on with a steady rumble of criticism, Marcus turned more and more to Emma Jean. Sportswriters, hostile fans, narrow-minded coaches, or self-righteous athletic directors meant nothing to her. In Emma Jean, he found a match—another black and bold person possessing exceptional talent. They married in their senior year at Northwestern, during the basketball season. Several media outlets carried ridiculous commentaries about the timing of the wedding as a distraction to Northwestern's team. Somehow, the vows of marriage became another sign of a selfish ballplayer.

Emma Jean reached over and touched her Northwestern University mug filled with pens and pencils. It sat in the place where she once kept the small framed picture of her and Marcus on their wedding day. The movement of her hand seemed to summon the ringing of the telephone that shared space on the desk.

"Hello."

"Jeanie, it's Lu."

Emma Jean smiled. The only person who ever called her Jeanie was her big sister.

"It's your mother," Lu said. "I'm worried about her health."

Emma Jean's smile faded. "What's wrong? She sick? Somethin' happen?"

"Not yet, but I think I'm gonna kill her."

"Uh, oh. Mama bein' Mama?"

"Like always."

"Better tell me," Emma Jean said.

"You bet I'm telling you. Then maybe you can go an' tell her how to behave."

"Our Mama?"

"Sylvia and I went over to Glen Oaks to see her. So, Mama wants to sit in the common area an' have coffee."

It had been Lu's idea to move their mother from Milwaukee to the assisted living facility in Iowa City six months ago. Lu had lived in the town for twelve years coaching basketball at the university.

"Anyway, we're sitting there an' Mama starts talking about the banquet."

"Right, Shai an' I are taking her."

"That's not the problem. She thinks she has to tell me how to act. She tells me not to wear pants."

"What?"

"She says 'You can't wear no pants to be gettin' no big award.' Like I'm eight instead of thirty-eight."

Emma Jean laughed.

"It's not funny, Emma Jean. She got worse."

"How bad?"

"How about she says, 'I know you got thank you's to say, but mind how you say 'em. It ain't no place to be talkin' 'bout no wife.' Mama in her loud voice right there in the common area."

"Damn, Lu."

"I know, an' Sylvia sittin' right there. I never call her my wife. She never calls me her wife. You ever hear us say that?"

"No, I know you don't."

"An' what if we did?"

Emma Jean shifted in her chair. She almost never heard her big sister get mad. Always being in control was part of what made her a successful coach.

"You still there?" Lu snapped.

"Sorry," Emma Jean said. "Don't be angry, sweetie."

"Angry? I'm not angry. I'm mad as hell."

"Mama's old. She's got her old ways. Prob'ly saw somethin' watchin' one of those daytime talk shows."

"She doesn't need the TV to get her talkin'."

"No, but prob'ly this time. You know Mama loves you. She loves Sylvia, too, in her own way."

"Still," Lu sighed.

"What did Sylvia say?"

"Nothing at the time. You know Sylvia."

"Afterwards?" Emma Jean asked.

"She said Mama speaking her mind was part of how you and I learned to be independent."

"Maybe she's right," Emma Jean said. "Feel better?"

"I feel better that you and Shai are here, Jeanie. I didn't mean to go off."

"Prob'ly be my turn next."

"Prob'ly, but thanks. I better go. I'm cookin' supper tonight."

"Bye, sweetie."

"Bye."

Emma Jean stared at the phone as she hung up the receiver. For an instant, nothing in her world made sense. It didn't seem possible that she could be teaching at the same university where her sister coached basketball. Emma Jean's affection for the ethereal white woman who had been Lu's partner for fifteen years felt just as unreal. In Emma Jean's marriage, basketball and white women had created very different emotions.

When Marcus began his pro basketball career, very little changed from college except for the huge money. Drafted by a last-place Sacramento franchise, his high scoring couldn't turn them into a winning team. The newspaper columns about the selfish superstar moved with him from Northwestern to the NBA.

Four times in his eleven-year career, Marcus was traded to losing teams seeking his talents as the savior for their failing basketball fortunes. Emma Jean, not a follower in any other part of her life, loyally followed Marcus to each new town. Over those eleven years, Marcus never averaged less than twenty-two points a game, but only once made the All-Star game. During that same span, Emma Jean never repeated the success of *The Black Hologram*. Were Sacramento, Memphis, and Indianapolis cultural outposts that held her back, or had she spent all her emotional capital in her one great play? She didn't even know how to search for the answer.

Marcus played the last four years of his career in Washington. The move to the nation's capital opened up the opportunity for Emma Jean to teach at Howard and placed her in a city alive with cultural activity. Neither revived her playwriting career.

At the beginning of their marriage, Emma Jean, the bold playwright, and Marcus, the activist athlete, found support in each other. Yet, Marcus seemed to take less and less notice as *The Black Hologram* moved Emma Jean to the forefront of young playwrights. He showed more interest in messages from agents and stockbrokers than the messages of a black aesthetic and assertiveness that filled theaters during performances of her stunning play. When she struggled to sustain her success, it barely registered with Marcus.

The pain of watching money and the professional basketball lifestyle diminish Marcus' public conscience hurt Emma Jean. Coming to understand that his private conscience had always been weak hurt her even more. At Northwestern, she knew that the attention of young women whose heads were turned by a handsome and intriguing black man had fed Marcus' powerful ego. Emma Jean told herself that those women mattered little. She thought of the occasional charming wink he bestowed on them, particularly the white ones, as his private game to put them down. Emma Jean had a bond with Marcus that a thousand women could not break.

By the time he reached Washington in his eighth year of pro ball, Emma Jean wondered if there had been a thousand women. All the wives in the league knew that professional ballplayers who chose to didn't need to look far in any city for the company of beautiful women. Emma Jean surprised herself with how quickly she fell into the position of so many other players' wives—professing trust in her husband while holding in her constant doubts.

Marcus' tenderness when Shai was born rekindled Emma Jean's hope, but eventually the doubts far outweighed the trust. A professional basketball team was simply too small for many secrets. The looks from other wives, a stray comment not intended for Emma Jean's ears, and the feeling of distance rather than closeness when Marcus returned from a long road trip all pointed to the same conclusion. Emma Jean endured and hoped, but for reasons completely unclear to her and totally unlike her, she never confronted Marcus. Finally, though she did not *know* all, she *understood* more than enough. Yes, there were women. Worse, there were many women. Worst, most were probably white women. When Shai was seven, Emma Jean filed for divorce. Marcus did not contest.

CHAPTER 2

"Whatcha doin', Mama?"

Shai's voice startled her mother. Emma Jean had been lost in a swirl of painful memories.

"Just writing down some ideas," she said. "You know what I tell you. I gotta grab an idea on paper before it gets away from me."

"You writin' a new play?"

"No, just catchin' ideas before they're gone, Sugar. But what about you? I thought you were watchin' your daddy."

"It's halftime, a bunch of other people are talkin'," Shai said as she gazed out the window of her mother's study.

"How's the game?"

"It's okay. Daddy keeps sayin' they gotta play harder for a playoff game. He said you gotta be a man in the playoffs."

"That's your daddy."

She wanted Shai to be proud of her father, but she also wanted her to be proud of real things. Emma Jean wondered if the line from Marcus about being a man was genuine commentary or just part of his outspoken image that the network and advertisers thought would sell beer or automobiles to television audiences this year. If playoff games were about manhood, Marcus had played in precious few of them during his own career. Emma Jean kept her thoughts to herself.

"I don't like the suit daddy's wearing."

"What's wrong with his suit?" Emma Jean asked through a laugh.

"It's just a plain ol' suit," Shai answered. "Daddy's way handsomer than those other guys he's on TV with. He don't need to be wearin' no plain, ol' suit. He needs a good lookin' suit like him."

"Your daddy's a handsome man," Emma Jean agreed. "He also speaks better than all this wearin', talkin', and lookin' mess you're givin' me."

"Just like you talk," Shai said.

"At home."

"We are at home, Mama, and it's still a plain suit."

Emma Jean shook her head. She knew that Marcus always calculated the image he wanted to project. If he wore a plain suit, it was probably a strategy to wrap his supposedly outspoken comments in a conservative package. Viewers could see that he wasn't afraid to criticize highly paid basketball players who were mostly black while not appearing too threatening to highly paid television executives who were, after all, very white. Basketball wasn't the only game Marcus Williams could play, and he was obviously reaching for the same star status in a broadcast booth that he once possessed on the basketball court.

While Emma Jean stayed lost in her thoughts, Shai turned her attention outside. Watching through the north window of the study, she saw a man walking out of the old carriage house. He was white like everyone else at The Manor, but younger. Shai thought he might be about her mama's age. Tucked under one arm, he carried a basketball. She watched as he began taking shots at a hoop mounted along the apartment building's driveway. He didn't look tall enough to be a real basketball player. Not like her daddy.

"You want a snack while you watch the game?" Emma Jean asked. "I bought some grapes and some of those crackers you like at the store yesterday."

"No thanks, Mama. I think I'm gonna go outside for a while."

"Okay, Sugar." She didn't add the words *be careful*. Living in Washington, Emma Jean used those words in any situation where Shai wouldn't be in the immediate vicinity of her mother. In things both good and bad, calling Iowa City home promised to be a different life.

―――

Shai opened the door to the elevator then pushed the button to go down. The big old house was a funny place to live, but she did think that having their own elevator was pretty neat. On the first floor, she stepped out, slipped through the narrow passageway and walked down the wide, formal hall. As usual, she didn't see anybody else around. That felt weird after their neighborhood in Washington where she saw people all the time. Not just old people, either, but kids her own age.

She made her way around to the side of the building on a long curving walk that hugged a row of boxwood bushes trimming the house. Down the driveway, the man from the carriage house lofted leisurely shots at the basketball hoop. He seemed kind of skinny in his T-shirt and shorts, and his brown hair bounced a little every time he shot.

Shai looked over at the flower beds, trying not to watch the man too much. She saw some bits of mulch that had escaped onto the blacktop drive and nudged them back where they belonged with the toe of her sneaker. She looked at the man again then bent down to pluck a blade of grass that the lawn service had missed. Gradually, her movements inched her toward the basketball hoop at the end of the drive.

A misfired shot bounced off the rim and rolled in Shai's direction.

She took a few loping strides down the driveway and retrieved the rolling ball. With an awkward underhand toss, she sent it back to the man walking toward her from the basket.

"Thanks," he said.

"That's okay," Shai answered as he moved a couple of steps closer.

"Are you here visiting?" he asked.

"No, I live here. Up on the top floor. Me and Mama moved in three weeks ago."

"Well, I live here, too, but my apartment's in the carriage house. I just got back from vacation. I didn't know anybody was moving in, yet. We don't see too many kids around here."

"I know that's the truth," Shai said.

She saw a smile cross the man's face as he asked, "What's your name?"

"Shaikera," she said. "Shaikera is my real name, but everybody calls me Shai."

"Well, Wesley is my real name, but everybody calls me Wes. You wanna shoot some baskets?"

"I guess so," Shai answered.

Wesley handed her the ball and retreated under the basket. Her first shot came up well short and missed the rim completely. Wes caught the ball and casually tossed it back. Her second try hit iron, and by her fourth attempt she banked the ball through the hoop. Although she shot without much confidence, Shai moved with tall and slender grace as Wes tossed the ball back to her after each try.

"What grade are you in, Shai?"

"Eighth. I start eighth when it's time for school."

"Do you play basketball?"

"No."

"I'd say you look pretty good for someone who doesn't play. There's lots of good chances for girls to do sports in Iowa City. I know your school will have a basketball team."

"I play tennis. Mama had me take tennis lessons the last two years."

"The high school has a tennis team," Wes said. "I'm not sure about junior high. Anyway, I guess you like tennis better than basketball."

"I like basketball, too," Shai answered quickly. "Mama just doesn't think it's good for me to play."

"Really?" Wes said. "I guess you could hurt a knee or an ankle or something, but I don't think too many kids get injured in basketball."

"No," she said, "it's because of my daddy. Mama thinks everybody will put pressure on me."

"You know what? I don't quite get what you're saying."

"My daddy's famous. He played in the NBA."

"Wow. You better tell me who he is."

"My daddy is Marcus Williams," Shai said proudly. "Because he's so good, Mama says everybody will think I should be that good, too."

"He was awful good," Wes agreed. "He's on TV today, doing the playoffs."

"I *know*," Shai giggled. "Whadda ya think I was just watching?"

Wes laughed and hoisted a shot up to the basket. The ball cut through the net with a swish.

"Well, I suppose your mom knows what's best about you and basketball," Wes said as he watched Shai pick up the ball.

She didn't answer but sent her own shot through the rim for her first swish of the day.

"Good shot!" Wes said.

Shai turned toward him. "I kinda would like to play on a team."

"Maybe you should talk to your mom."

"I don't think Mama's gonna change her mind."

"Never know. You just moved here. Your mom could think things might be different in a new place."

"It's different here *for sure*," Shai said. "We used to live in Washington, D.C."

For a second, Wes was lost in the sound of Shai's voice, transfixed by the distinctive emphasis she placed on her words.

"There you go," Wes said. "I'll bet people are a lot more relaxed in Iowa City than Washington."

"She'll probably think Iowa City's worse. My aunt Lu lives here, and she played basketball in the Olympics!"

"Your aunt is Lu Whitcomb?"

"*Uh, huh*," Shai answered with a decisive nod of her head.

"She comes into my restaurant once in a while," Wes said, thinking of the tall, elegant coach of the women's basketball team at the University of Iowa.

"You got a restaurant?" Shai asked.

"I actually own two restaurants. One called the Red Door Café and one called City Streets."

"Man, two restaurants."

"Two restaurants isn't much compared to your family," Wes said. "You've got two famous *people* in your family."

"More than that." Shai smiled. "My mama's famous, too. She wrote *The Black Hologram*."

Shai's declaration caught Wes off guard. Ten years ago, every conservative, tub-thumping radio talk show host and every ambitious, right-wing politician in the country had vilified the author of *The Black Hologram*. Wes remembered the uproar. Alarm raised over the play's intense anger. Shock expressed about its raw language. The furor over its indictment of life in America.

Wes also remembered that *The Black Hologram* won enough awards to make a lot of people mad all over again. It stayed in the news for months as conservatives used it to warn about the threat to America from the liberal media and the entertainment industry. It probably stayed on Broadway long enough to make lots of money, too.

"I remember that play," Wes said.

"Did you like it?" Shai asked.

"Well, I didn't actually see it. I remember reading a lot about it in the newspaper."

"I think more black people like to see the play than white people," Shai said with genuine innocence.

"I'm sure it's a good play. I just don't go to plays very much. You want to shoot a couple more baskets?"

Shai took the ball and had a nice, soft shot bounce gently on the rim and drop through the net. As she began alternating shots with Wes, her awkward dribbling and mistimed rebounding clearly showed that she had little experience with a basketball. Still, she moved with such natural grace and her shooting improved so quickly that it was fun to watch as more of her shots connected.

As they continued, Shai also watched Wes closely. When she was younger, she had gone to the basketball courts with her daddy a few times. Watching Wesley was nothing like watching her daddy. Her daddy did everything so easily, and it seemed like *he* never missed a shot. Still, Wes did pretty good, and he wasn't like some fat, old clumsy guy running around after the ball. When Shai watched basketball on television, she saw almost all tall, athletic black men, but Wes didn't seem too bad for a regular white guy.

"I'll bet the game's getting close to over," Wes finally said as he remembered the playoffs on TV. "I think I'll go back inside."

"Me, too," Shai answered.

"See that little box over there?" Wes pointed toward the multi-car garage.

Shai nodded.

"In the winter, it has salt in it for melting ice, but it's empty in the summer. If you want, I'll put my basketball in there, and you can use it any time you feel like it."

"I'd like that," Shai said with the distinctive rhythm that rose in her voice.

"Okay, just be sure you put it back when you're done shooting."

"I will."

―――

Emma Jean had looked out from her study window to see Shai shooting baskets with some white man. He didn't fit the age bracket of the other residents at The Manor. She wondered if he was some visiting nephew or second cousin. Emma Jean had kept her eye on the situation and saw Shai give the man a little wave before heading back toward the house.

"Shai, come in here please," Emma Jean called down the hall when she heard the elevator door open.

Shai bounced down the hall toward the study without answering her mother.

"Didn't you hear me?" Emma Jean asked as Shai entered the room.

"I heard you."

"You heard me, but you didn't think you needed to answer?"

"I'm sorry."

"And what were you doing outside?"

"I was shooting baskets with this white man."

"I *know* you were, girl. I saw from the window."

"I was shootin' good, Mama, and he says I can use his basketball anytime I want."

"First off, slow down," Emma Jean said in a firm tone. "You know what we've talked about with you and basketball."

"Please, Mama. I just want to shoot. He put his basketball in a box just so I can use it."

"Listen up. You best forget about shootin' basketballs until you tell me who this man is."

"He's Wesley," Shai answered.

"You mean he's Mr. Wesley?" Emma Jean asked.

"No, Wesley is his first name, but he says everybody calls him Wes. Anyway, he lives in the other building."

"Wesley," Emma Jean whispered under her breath. Shai had met the W. Whitcomb in the carriage house. "*Wesley* Whitcomb."

"You say something, Mama?"

"I'll tell you what I'm gonna say. Just because you know somebody's name don't mean you know him. If you wanted to be shootin' baskets with him, you should have had me come down and meet him."

"Mama, he lives here. That's all it was, just shooting baskets."

"Girl, you know what I mean."

"Sorry."

"I'm not gonna fuss about it anymore, but we're in a new place. You don't know everything about everybody here. Just remember that."

"I will," Shai said. "Can I go see the end of the game? When it's over, Daddy will be on talkin' all about it. He could be on right now."

"Okay, Sugar, you go on ahead." Emma Jean rose from her desk. "I think I'll go start some supper."

CHAPTER 3

The exhaust fan from the Red Door Café whirred loudly as Wes pulled into his usual parking space off the back alley. The simple sound welcomed him back—back from vacation, back to Iowa, back to the routine he had created for himself with the two restaurants he owned. Inside the Red Door Café, Suzie Bosch would already be at work.

Eight years ago, Wes hired Suzie as a waitress, and she immediately fell in love with the unique way he ran his hole-in-the wall restaurant. Soon, she was slicing, mixing, cooking, and baking right alongside him. When he opened his City Streets restaurant three years later, Suzie's role at the Red Door grew larger. At age fifty-four, she had twenty years on Wes. A tiny woman with completely gray hair, she always claimed she was twice as old as Wes and half his size. While neither claim was precisely true, the pair presented a curious picture working next to each other in the close quarters behind the café's lunch counter. Now, customers saw that picture less and less as City Streets demanded more and more of his time. The Red Door Café still operated in virtually the same way as it had the day Wes opened for business, but now it seemed almost as much Suzie's restaurant as his.

He entered the back door, picked up an apple peeler, and reached into a cardboard peck of apples. After washing his hands and the fruit, he began peeling and slicing apples to fill the four pie plates that Suzie had already lined with crust. He dropped the apple slices in a huge bowl and measured and mixed in sugar, flour, and spices.

Wes smiled as he began to fill one of the Red Door Café's "Always Apple" pies. He started his restaurant with the idea of making things from scratch. It wasn't so much a philosophy as simply the way he liked to cook. To him, making a pie meant starting with a piece of fruit, not a can of filling, though he didn't know how to classify his love of making raisin pies since that required starting with fruit from a box.

One day, Wes had explained to a customer that he sometimes made rhubarb pie, sometimes peach, blackberry, or even green tomato pie, depending on what was available, but always apple because apples were always available. The next day, the same customer asked for a piece of the "Always Apple" pie. Nickname magic had been worked, and the restaurant's number one dessert became known as "Always Apple" pie.

"There's a chocolate mayonnaise cake in the oven," Suzie chirped as she walked through the swinging doors that separated the small kitchen from the main part of the restaurant. "I just finished making the donut batter. You want to finish the pies or bake donuts?"

"That's some greeting for a guy who's just back from vacation." Wes feigned annoyance.

"Well, *sorry*, Mr. Traveling-Man. I guess I'm just kind of busy. While you've been wandering around half the country, I've been here working my butt off."

"Now that is a shame," Wes said. "Particularly since you didn't have much of a butt to begin with."

"Careful, Mr. Big-Shot-Restaurant-Owner," Suzie bantered back, "or I'll sue you for sexual harassment and end up owning this place myself."

"Heck, you may as well own it," he said. "You already make more money out of it than I do."

Suzie laughed an easy laugh, though they both knew the truth of his last comment. As City Streets grew, Wes relied on Suzie to make the Red Door Café run.

She ordered the food, scheduled the waitresses, kept the place organized, and opened and closed on most days. He paid her well to take over, but the little restaurant didn't handle enough money for two people to do well. The profit he made on the Red Door no longer amounted to even half the salary he paid Suzie.

The money didn't matter. The success of City Streets far more than made up for his small take at the Red Door. What did matter was that Wes loved the Red Door Café and he loved Suzie Bosch. He couldn't imagine teasing back and forth with some other person about the size of her salary or her butt. In fact, he probably wouldn't even say the word *butt* to any other woman. Wes had a way of cruising through life without stopping much to think about things. He hadn't really thought about whether he had a best friend. If he did, it was Suzie Bosch.

"Hey, snap out of it, Mr. Vacation-Boy," she said. "Why don't you tell me about your trip and then go bake those donuts. I'll make the pies and the cinnamon crisps. You know, it's seven-fifteen already."

"Oh, the trip was really good. Of course, I drove to Cleveland first for the restaurant expo. Stayed there two days. Didn't see too much at the show that was new, but it's probably good to go to the thing once in a while. Anyway, the city's nicer than I expected."

"Did you go to the Rock and Roll Hall of Fame?"

"Actually . . . no." He knew that would have been Suzie's first stop. "I saved my hall of fame visiting for later."

"Baseball," Suzie said, nodding her head.

"Yeah, I drove the interstate to Buffalo and then sort of wandered across New York until I got to Cooperstown. I did the state highways and a few back roads. I'll tell you what, there's some really pretty lakes and little towns, especially Cooperstown."

"You trying to tell me you actually did something other than the Baseball Hall of Fame?"

"The truth is, I walked all over town. Even went to some other museums. Of course, I did spend almost a full day in the Hall of Fame."

"I'm surprised you weren't there longer than that."

"Well, you see, I had to save some time for the card shops down the street. You know, baseball cards. I got a really good Harmon Killebrew, a Rod Carew, and an old Nellie Fox."

"I have no idea what you just said." Suzie leaned on the work counter. "Did you eat in any good restaurants?"

Wes answered her traditional question with his customary response, "None as good as the Red Door."

She smiled and gave him a little shove. "Then go make some donuts. The batter's ready. It's gonna be nine o'clock before you know it."

Wes stepped out of the kitchen into the front of the restaurant. A long lunch counter stretched down one side of the room. A few feet from the front door, the counter curved to close off the space behind it from the customers. A dozen stools provided the seating, and six tables for two filled the opposite wall of the narrow building. The left side of the main door had a table with four chairs next to a front window.

He plugged in two electric donut bakers and opened the small under-counter refrigerator for the batter. He breathed in the aroma of the café around him and shook his head at the thought of owning a restaurant at all. He had come to Iowa City to attend the University of Iowa. After being a good student in high school, college seemed his natural next step just as it had been for his older sister. Ann's business degree had carried her out of little Princeton, Iowa, and into a good job with a large publishing company in Des Moines. She began her career earning more money than their father would ever see as a mechanic in the Princeton's Ford garage. Wes figured college could do the same thing for him.

College may have been the logical next step for him, but once Wes got there, he discovered that he had no idea of what path to follow. The university portrayed itself as a place of discovery and reflection. With two years of classes under his belt, Wes reflected on his university life and discovered that he was a good student with little genuine interest in any academic area. At the beginning of his junior year, he finally declared a communications major. Every student had to have a major. What Wes didn't have was anything he particularly wanted to communicate or anyone he particularly wanted to communicate with.

His college career unfolded in a pattern possible only at a large university, mixing the outward appearance of success with the inner truth of disinterest. His sense of responsibility and knack for getting good grades saved him from any negative attention. At the same time, he rarely engaged any professors and stayed nearly anonymous even to those in his major department. Each summer he happily returned home to Princeton for a job cooking at the Riverview Inn. In those summer months, he put the University of Iowa completely out of his mind.

Princeton sat perched on the banks of the Mississippi River halfway between Davenport and Clinton. Every weekend in the summer, its normally sleepy streets swelled with boaters and fishermen from the larger towns. After a day on the water, many of the weekend crowd drifted in for dinner at the Riverview, a rundown tavern with a simple, square dining room on the back. From scuffed linoleum to yellowing tape holding together worn menus, the place offered a down-at-the-heels ambience capped by the irony that the river couldn't be seen at all from the dining room. It also offered the best steaks and catfish dinners in the area. The Riverview Inn's customers cared more about the food than either the tavern's appearance or its mythical view.

Wes began bussing tables and washing dishes on Saturday nights during the summer after his freshman year in high school. The tavern's owner took an immediate liking to him, and before Wes graduated from high school, he had become the right-hand man on weekends—preparing homemade hashbrowns and coleslaw and gradually learning the secrets of how to age steaks properly. After college graduation, Wes wasn't sure what he knew about communications, but he was confident he knew how to prepare food for the public.

"Hey, Wes," Suzie shouted from the kitchen, "I think four dozen will be enough today."

"That's what I figured," he answered. "A dozen cinnamon and sugar, a dozen vanilla, and two dozen chocolate."

"Just like always," Suzie said.

Wes shook his head again as he recognized the comfortable predictability of his little restaurant's operation. On a normal day, the biggest decision was choosing whether to make four or five dozen donuts. In this part of June, with the university out of session, things slowed down a little at the Red Door. That fact gave him the opportunity to take a ten-day vacation. It also made the choice of four dozen donuts instead of five pretty easy.

His earliest decisions about the Red Door Café had not been so simple. He didn't go to college to become the owner of a rundown restaurant, but nine years ago he had made exactly that decision. With $15,000 inherited from his grandmother, he put a down payment on Art's Hamburger Haven. Arthur Lewis owned the place that college students just called "The Haven" for almost fifty years. If ever a restaurant lived up to the name "hamburger joint," Art's was it. He did little else than sell hamburgers, fries, and malts. For its last few years of operation, the restaurant did little enough of that.

Art Lewis also had done little enough cleaning toward the end. When Wes took possession of the restaurant, a film of hamburger grease and frying oil clung to everything in the premises. He found only one exception: the vent hood and its fan had not a *film* but thick *globs* of grease and oil. Short on money and long on second thoughts, Wes scrubbed and cleaned by himself for more than two weeks. Washing away the grease uncovered tables, chairs, and stools in surprisingly good condition. Scraping and steaming the mess out of the vent hood led Wes to uncover something else: a new conviction about the restaurant business. He would sell no hamburgers and serve no french fries. He sold the fryer for thirty-five dollars and used half of the money to buy a gallon of bright red paint for the beat up wooden door on the front of the building.

Almost a decade had passed since a gallon of red paint and his revulsion at hamburger grease helped to shape the unique profile of the Red Door Café. Deciding that frying bacon and sausage conjured up the same ills as hamburgers, Wes opened the Red Door as an establishment for lunch only. In his mind, the concept of a noontime café began with a daily special. He created his roster of specials and the rest of his menu by following his consistent rule of cooking what he liked.

Specials:

Monday—Meatloaf and mashed potatoes

Tuesday—Tuna casserole

Wednesday—Boiled dinner (ring bologna, green beans, and potatoes or ham, cabbage, and potatoes)

Thursday—Sauerkraut and spare ribs

Friday—Two specials, salmon loaf and scalloped potatoes and ham

Saturday—Beans and wieners

Sandwiches

Grilled cheese

Grilled ham and cheese

Cold roast beef

Cold turkey breast

Cold ham

Egg salad

Liverwurst

Hot dog

Salad Plates

Curried chicken salad with green grapes

Bowtie pasta with ham cubes, black and green olives, and artichoke hearts tossed in oil, vinegar, and parmesan cheese

Oasis salad with chick peas, chopped fresh spinach, chopped green peppers, sunflower seeds, and diced oranges tossed in oil, vinegar, tarragon, and honey

Soups

Chili

Chicken lemon rice

Desserts:

Always apple pie

Fresh fruit pie

Chocolate mayonnaise cake or pineapple upside-down cake

Donuts

Cinnamon crisps

Every week, the Red Door Café roasted four turkey breasts, two boneless hams, and two rounds of beef, saving the beef drippings for Monday's mashed potatoes and gravy. Specials came with fresh vegetables or applesauce, sandwiches with potato chips and sweet pickles. The café's routine included regular trips to the Mennonite community south of Iowa City for loaves of fresh bread and jars of homemade pickles.

Maybe the whole thing shouldn't have worked, but somehow it did. Almost from the beginning, an odd mix of university secretaries, tradesmen, students, and people wondering what was behind the bright red door filled the little restaurant at lunch time. In nine years, only one significant change occurred. Suzie added the cinnamon crisps. Within a month of hiring her, Suzie had made fussing over the owner another of her duties in the restaurant. Just before closing one afternoon, she surprised him by baking an extra piece of pie dough sprinkled with cinnamon and sugar. Over cups of coffee, Wes, Suzie, and a lingering customer shared the simple treat that generations of mothers had made for their children. One of the threesome—Wes and Suzie both took credit—said the cinnamon crisps would be great with morning coffee. The next afternoon, Wes bought two electric donut bakers at the neighborhood hardware store, and the following Monday, the Red Door Café began opening at nine a.m. with homemade donuts, cinnamon crisps and coffee.

This Monday morning, Wes finished spreading the chocolate frosting Suzie had made on the last of the donuts and stepped back into the kitchen. He saw her busy at the sink washing rhubarb.

"So what are you staring at?" she asked without turning around.

"I'm surprised you found good rhubarb this late in June," he said to her as she began chopping the red and green stalks into small pieces.

"Me, too. I stopped at the farmer's market first thing Saturday morning and Ed Elwin said he still had some good rhubarb that was real tender. He was right, so I figured I better buy it."

"You want me to mix the meatloaf?" Wes asked.

"Sure."

He opened the refrigerator and pulled out two large packages of ground beef, three onions, and six eggs. From a high shelf on the wall he took down a sleeve of soda crackers to crumble.

As he grabbed an oversized mixing bowl, Suzie spoke again, "When did you get home?"

"It was about nine o'clock Saturday night. I stopped up at my parent's house in Princeton. Mom made me dinner."

"How are they?"

"They seem fine. I think Dad's ready to retire, but he's got a ways to go."

"How old's your dad?"

"Sixty-one. He needs to get where he can draw his full Social Security and Medicare."

Suzie nodded and turned the conversation in another direction. "Everything in one piece when you got home?"

"Yeah, I asked Mrs. Riddell to check my apartment a couple times while I was gone," he said. "I do have some new neighbors."

"Are they nice?"

"I only met the little girl. I was shooting baskets and she shot around with me for a little while. She seems like a nice kid."

Suzie turned around. "A kid at The Manor with all those stuffy university people? I don't know why *you* live there. It sure doesn't seem like a very natural place for a family."

"Not a family," Wes said. "Just a mom and a daughter."

"Oh." Suzie arched an eyebrow. "Maybe you should meet the mom. Know anything about her?"

"They're black," he answered. "The mom actually does teach at the university."

Without Wes or Suzie noticing, the mention of Emma Jean's skin color put an end to any suggestion of Wes pursuing her.

"What's she teach?" Suzie asked.

"She's in the theater department, I think. She's a famous playwright, anyway."

"And her name?" Suzie, a reader of celebrity magazines, asked immediately.

"Emma Jean Whitcomb."

"I'll be darned, same as yours, but if she's so famous, how come I never heard of her?"

"She wrote that one play a few years ago," he said. "You've heard of it, *The Black Hologram*."

"You mean the one against white people?"

"I think it's a play about blacks, more than against white people," Wes said.

"Well, when it came out, all I remember is TV and the papers goin' on and on. Black rage, black anger, white discrimination. I got sick of that in a hurry. I'm glad I forgot about her. I never heard that much about a play, 'cept maybe *Sound of Music*."

Wes shrugged. "The daughter's nice. I never saw the play. Only read about it in *Time* magazine and stuff."

31

"Time!" Suzie blurted. "It's twenty minutes to nine. I better make the coffee."

"Go ahead," Wes said, watching her shove two rhubarb pies into the oven. "I'll finish mixing the meatloaf and start peeling some potatoes."

CHAPTER 4

Emma Jean pulled her black BMW smoothly into a diagonal space in one of Iowa City's downtown parking garages. Shai practically jumped out of the passenger side and quickly closed the door with a solid thump. She was already around to the driver's side as Emma Jean got out and locked the vehicle with the remote-entry device. Emma Jean hesitated ever so briefly as she turned to walk toward the street with Shai. The simple moment felt too precious to describe, watching a daughter who was clearly growing up but still young enough to be so eager for their special shopping trip.

"Slow down, girl," Emma Jean said as Shai practically skipped down the ramp. "I can't keep up with you."

"Oh Mama, hurry up a little," Shai answered. "Anyway, you're so tall you could catch me in one step."

"Well, I'm still not lookin' to race you, Sugar."

"Why not? You got running shoes on," Shai teased.

"I put on some tennis shoes and my jeans to be comfortable, not to be chasin' after you."

"Now where?" Shai asked as they reached the street.

"There's a store down and around the corner a ways." Emma Jean motioned to cross the street. "Mrs. Huber told me about it. You gotta have somethin' special to wear when your Aunt Lu gets her award."

"So is this like a really top award?"

"It's the Governor's Distinguished Citizen Award." Emma Jean smiled. "They only give out three a year, and you and I and your gramma are gonna be sitting at a table right up front with Lu."

"Who else won?"

"Don't know," Emma Jean answered. "Forgot to ask, but Lu did tell me the banquet is in the Governor's Ballroom at the Des Moines Hilton. I don't suppose it gets much fancier than that in Iowa. We gotta show these Iowa people what two classy ladies look like when we walk in the door."

Shai giggled.

"You go ahead and laugh. I'm dead serious."

"So Aunt Lu is gettin' this award for having basketball camps?"

"They're a lot more than basketball, Sugar. Your Aunt Lu takes her camps right into the neighborhoods. Ones where the girls need help the most. She calls 'em Life and Learning Sports Camps."

"I know."

"I know you know. It doesn't hurt you to know a little more."

"I didn't mean anything, Mama."

"That's okay, Sugar, but when you go to the banquet you should understand how much your Aunt Lu does. She's got four camps she puts on in Iowa. Lu told me Davenport, Des Moines, Sioux City, and Waterloo. She does those through the university. But then, she does one every year in our old neighborhood in Milwaukee. That one's on her own. Raises all the money herself."

Emma Jean fell silent as they walked past the coffee shops, specialty boutiques, gift stores, and sports bars lining a city street that had been paved over with red bricks and turned into a pedestrian mall. She felt a bittersweet emotion wash over her as she realized that her daughter's life in university towns and upscale apartments would never allow Shai to truly understand the "neighborhoods."

It was obvious that the old neighborhood remained an unchanging part of Lu, even after eighteen years as head coach of the University of Iowa's women's basketball team. At twenty-seven, Lu Whitcomb had become both the youngest head coach in the Big Ten and the first black woman in the conference to serve in that position. Nearly two decades later, she and her teams had six league championships to their credit. Lu spoke with pride about her teams for good reason. Emma Jean loved that she heard the same passion in Lu's voice when she talked about her camps, especially the one in Milwaukee.

Lu organized the camps to live up to the "life and learning" part of their name. The girls played basketball every morning, but they also learned about sports as recreation, trying their hands at softball, ping pong, badminton, and even chess in the afternoon. After dinner, special guests—role models ranging from grandmothers to successful writers—spoke to the girls about respecting each other, respecting their bodies, and respecting themselves. Every evening, the campers wrote in journals that Lu gave them. Clearly, Lu had never forgotten how her own journal had been a private friend as she grew up in inner-city Milwaukee or how she had started her baby sister writing with the journal she gave Emma Jean for her ninth birthday.

Pride filled Emma Jean as she thought of her sister's success—and her courage. Women's athletics had changed dramatically in Lu's years as Iowa's coach, and only one of Lu's championships had been achieved in the last decade. In conferences like the Big Ten, basketball camps for girls had evolved into money-makers and recruiting tools. Emma Jean knew enough to understand that. She also knew from her sister that the Life and Learning Sports Camps uncovered an occasional gem for the University of Iowa, but it hardly served as a basketball pipeline in the way camps for other schools did.

Whispers that the college game was passing Lu by were no secret, not even to Emma Jean, who held the whole subject of basketball at arms' length. Even so, Lu never wavered in making her camps serve the girls first and basketball second. Emma Jean saw the Governor's Distinguished Citizen Award as her sister's victory for big ideas over small minds.

"There's the store." Emma Jean pointed to her left as they came to the end of the block. A 1950s sign with small neon tubes in script lettering identified the Misses to Mrs. Shop.

"This place looks *old*," Shai said. "They gonna have anything I like?"

"Now you listen up, girl. You ain't dressin' up to be on MTV or someplace. This is a fancy banquet where your Aunt Lu gets honored. You're gonna show 'em a proper young lady when you walk into that ballroom. You hear what I'm sayin'?"

"Okay, Mama. I was just asking." Shai could tell from Emma Jean's voice not to push. Whenever her mother got on edge, her words started coming out a lot more like Shai's grandmother than a college professor. There was enough of Gramma in Emma Jean's voice now for Shai to keep any more comments about the Misses to Mrs. Shop to herself.

A small brass bell mounted on the door frame rang as Emma Jean and Shai entered the shop. The only people in the store were two immaculately dressed and carefully made-up women standing behind a counter near the cash register.

"May we help you?" one of the women asked coolly.

"We'd like to look a moment," Emma Jean answered. "My daughter needs a nice dress."

"Oh, I see. Our misses' section is toward the back. You will notice that all of our *prices* are clearly marked." The women maintained their positions near the register, but their eyes stayed fixed on Shai and Emma Jean walking back to the misses' section of the store.

Mother and daughter made their way to a small clothes rack hung with long evening dresses. Somehow, the number of sleeveless gowns with skinny, little shoulder straps caught Emma Jean by surprise. They seemed so revealing for a thirteen- or fourteen-year-old girl. Her eyes fell on a silk-blend dress with short sleeves and beautiful brocaded flowers running across the bodice and down one side of the skirt. Shai reached for a sleeveless black velvet gown with tiny, sparkling beaded florets.

Emma Jean looked at the price on each dress—$230 for the silk brocade, $180 for the black velvet. The extra fifty dollars struck her as worth the money to keep Shai covered up a little better. Still, she couldn't help but notice that her daughter had excellent taste. The two clerks approaching from the front of the store had also noted the selections.

"I'm not sure that either of those will fit," one woman commented to Emma Jean. "Your daughter is quite tall."

"She's five-eight and still growing." Emma Jean gestured to her own six-foot, two-inch stature. "She might even catch me someday."

"Perhaps so, but the items here in misses are probably too short," the second clerk chimed in, "and the gowns up front are cut for a woman."

"I think this one is long enough," Emma Jean said, holding the silk brocade up to Shai.

"I shouldn't say the question is length alone," the clerk said. "The young lady is quite high-waisted. We pride ourselves on our service. We won't sell a dress that doesn't have the proper fit."

"Maybe she's right, Mama," Shai said. "This one with the straps might fit me better."

"Of course, I hate to contradict a customer, young lady, but the same problem could—"

Emma Jean cut off the clerk in midsentence. "I think my daughter is right. I'd like to see how you look in that dress, Sugar. Why don't you try it on."

"I'll unlock the fitting room," the first woman said, resuming her cool tone. "We *do* limit customers to only one of the better dresses at a time in the fitting room."

The clerks moved away while Emma Jean stood near the fitting room door. She could hear the sounds of Shai changing clothes in the small dressing area. She could also hear the stage whispers of the two salespeople.

"You try to be delicate, and it doesn't help," one woman murmured.

"I'm just glad she tried on the sleeveless gown," the second woman said. "We might well have had to dry clean the perspiration out of the other."

As fury grew within Emma Jean, Shai emerged from the dressing room. She was every inch a beautiful young woman as she stood before her mother. Much more important, Shai's face revealed no indication that she had overhead the two bigots staring back from the front of the store.

"You're lovely, Sugar," Emma Jean said softly, "but that dress shows an awful lot of shoulders and back. I have to think about whether you're ready for it."

"But Mama," Shai said.

"Now, I said I have to think about it. Besides," Emma Jean raised her voice, "I don't think this place lives up to its reputation for quality."

Shai's shoulders slumped as she stepped back into the dressing room. Emma Jean turned and glared at the two women who stood frozen by one of the clothes racks near the front door. Finally, they moved to another rack of dresses and pretended to busy themselves.

Shai opened the door of the dressing room and held up the dress. "What should I do with this?"

"Just leave it in there," Emma Jean answered. "They can take care of it."

"Is something wrong, Mama?" Shai asked as they walked past the clerks.

"There are a lot of things wrong in this world, Sugar."

Emma Jean walked briskly to the car with Shai at her side. Less than a half-hour earlier, she had worried that Shai was shielded from knowing about the neighborhoods of Emma Jean's youth. Now, she was reminded that there were too many times when she couldn't protect her daughter enough. She would have to talk to Shai about the Misses to Mrs. Shop, but not now. At the moment, she only wanted to change the subject.

"I need to go to the supermarket," Emma Jean said as they settled into the BMW. "I invited the Hubers for dinner tomorrow night. They've already had us over twice to visit."

"Okay," was all Shai said.

"I think I'd like some music." Emma Jean reached into the console next to the driver's seat and pulled out a CD by Wynton Marsalis.

She knew next to nothing about good cooking and not much more about where to shop for food. She simply headed the car toward the supermarket nearest The Manor, one that claimed its customers would always find "friendly stores inside our doors." She definitely wanted something friendlier than the Misses to Mrs. Shop right now.

She planned to fall back on her old standard for disguising a lack of cooking skills—a prime rib roast. Surround the roast with potatoes to oven brown, steam some broccoli, choose a good red wine, buy dessert at a bakery, set the table nicely, and all she had to do to produce an elegant meal was read a meat thermometer correctly. Most times, Emma Jean could pull that off.

Shai grabbed a shopping cart for her mother as they entered the supermarket. After a brief stop in the produce department for potatoes and broccoli, they headed toward the meat case. A quick scan of the beef cuts revealed chuck roast, rump roast, blade roast, but no prime rib roast. Emma Jean turned to a young man passing by, sporting a friendly smile and a store apron.

"Where do I find a standing rib?" she asked.

"Down at the other end," he answered. "We've got country ribs and spareribs, both."

"Spareribs!" Emma Jean exploded. "I didn't ask for spareribs."

"I thought . . ." the young man stammered.

"You thought that all we eat is spareribs and maybe some chittlins or collard greens. Come on, Shai," Emma Jean stalked away, leaving the cart with its bag of potatoes and stalks of broccoli standing in the middle of the grocery aisle.

"Mama, what's wrong?" Shai asked plaintively as they reached the car.

"What's wrong is that this is just a backwards Iowa town. The university don't mean nothin'. I didn't ask for no spareribs!"

"I don't think he understood," Shai said with a true look of distress.

Emma Jean collected herself as she saw the anxiety on her daughter's face.

"Sugar, you didn't hear what those women in the dress shop said." She sighed and leaned against the car. "They didn't want us in there because we're black."

"I know, Mama."

"You heard them?"

"Sometimes you don't have to hear. All that stuff about high-waisted. I don't even know what that is. I could tell they didn't want us in there, and I don't want their stupid dress."

"We're gonna get you the nicest dress in Iowa, Sugar." Emma Jean hugged her.

"But what about that boy in there?" Shai asked.

"I don't know if he meant anything or not by what he said, but I ain't gonna apologize to no white boy today. His people made this mess. I guess it's on him to live with it this time. We better go find that prime rib someplace else."

CHAPTER 5

Three dozen tiny tart shells spread out before Wes on a flat metal tray as he stood at a gleaming stainless steel counter in the kitchen of his City Streets restaurant. One of the cooks had baked the tart shells while Wes made the fillings: glazed fresh strawberries, whipped chocolate mousse, and a sinfully rich orange pudding. Wes didn't spend much time cooking nowadays. His position as owner of a large and successful restaurant such as City Streets had become more like the captain of a ship commanding a crew that stretched from stem to stern. Still, he enjoyed the chance to make one of his specialties, and orange pudding tarts were a specialty.

He discovered the pudding recipe in a colonial cookbook reprint. He bought it for fifty cents at a flea market. While flea markets didn't interest Wes very much, his antique-hunting parents loved them. When he visited, it always made them happy if he tagged along on one of their antiquing excursions. The orange pudding recipe was an unexpected bonus from a sale during Big River Days in Princeton. He had mastered making the pudding, even though the directions in the cookbook left much to the imagination: "Mix yolk of six eggs, grated skin of oranges, butter to cover the bottom of a porringer, and the same of sugar. Bake between two crusts until sufficiently brown and pudding is smooth."

Wes decided to try making the pudding in a double boiler and using it to fill tart shells. Patience and plain old dumb luck eventually led him to the right proportion of sugar in a dish where too little left the pudding runny and too much made it grainy. What he never figured out was how to transfer his knack for making the dessert to his cooks. Orange pudding only appeared as a City Streets special when Wes was moved to make it. Tonight, he was so moved. Tonight, his new neighbors were coming to dinner.

Almost three weeks had passed since he met the graceful, young black girl who had moved into The Manor apartments with her mother. Since then, he had talked to Shaikera twice as she shot baskets with the ball he left for her to use, but her mother was nowhere to be seen either time. With his schedule revolving around two restaurants, he often went a couple of weeks without seeing any particular neighbor. Even so, he was curious to meet the famous woman who lived next door. He filled the last tart, washed his hands, and headed toward the dining room for a word with the hostess.

"Hi, Jan. How ya doin'?" he asked as he approached the hostess station.

"Can't complain. It looks like a pretty busy night for a Tuesday."

"Yeah. I wanted to talk to you about one of the reservations."

"Which one?"

"It's right here." Wes touched a line in the reservation book. "Dr. Carson."

"Okay."

"He's a theater professor, or maybe English," Wes said. "I'm not sure which. Anyway, when Sarah took the reservation, he said it was a welcoming party for Emma Jean Whitcomb."

"Oh," Jan answered. "I see she put Whitcomb Party in parentheses in the book. A relative of yours?"

"No, actually she's a new professor. She's a playwright. Sorta famous. You remember *The Black Hologram*?"

"Remember it. Never saw it."

"Well, that's her," he said. "She wrote it. Anyway, she lives in The Manor now."

"So you know her," Jan said.

Wes shook his head. "No, I've just met her daughter, but I want tonight to be nice for them. Where do you plan to seat them?"

"Well, the reservation says fourteen people," Jan explained. "I'm having two long tables pulled together on Dodge Street."

"Sure, that's good," Wes said. "Here's the thing. When they finish their dinner, I made a little tray of tarts for dessert. It's kind of a surprise. You know, since she's a neighbor."

Jan nodded.

"Well, when you see they're finishing their meals, come find me," he said. "I'll bring out the tarts. Got it?"

"I'll keep an eye on 'em."

"Thanks."

Wes retreated to his office, and nearly two hours passed before a punctual Dr. Carson presented himself and a colleague at the hostess station at six fifty-five for a seven o'clock reservation.

"Two for dinner tonight?" Jan asked.

"No," the professor replied stiffly, "you should have a reservation in the name of Dr. Carson at seven o'clock. We will have others joining us. There should be fourteen in all."

"Right," Jan answered. "That's what I have here in the book. If you'll follow me, we have you set up on Dodge Street."

She walked briskly toward the opposite end of the restaurant with the two professors trailing behind. City Streets had been built in 1914 as an automobile repair and parking garage. Wes bought the two-story, brick building with the aid of a generous historic preservation loan. Originally, much of the first floor had provided covered parking for the not-very-well-covered cars of the teens and twenties. A walled-off corner of the large building had enclosed space for the automobile service area. In the opposite corner, was a lift originally constructed to hoist cars to the second floor for winter storage in an era when many automobile owners found it wise not to brave icy or snow-covered roads in cars of marginal—or less—reliability.

Wes acquired the building with his restaurant motif well in mind. He painted the concrete floors with white and yellow lane markings and completed the City Streets theme with the only thing he learned as a communications major that he ever put to practical use: photomurals. Contractors mounted huge photos of Iowa City street scenes on guide wires that stretched from floor to ceiling to divide the open expanse into "streets." Dodge, Clinton, Washington, and Dubuque Streets all became seating areas of the restaurant. A scattering of lamp posts, streetlights, and traffic signs completed the décor.

"Here you are," Jan said as she showed Dr. Carson and friend to the paired tables already set with silverware, napkins, condiments, and glasses of ice water.

"Ah, next to the streetcar," he said. "Would that I had lived in Iowa City in those days."

Jan gestured for them to sit. "Kyle will be your server. If you care for a drink, I can send him over."

"No thank you," Dr. Carson replied. "We'll wait until the others arrive."

Emma Jean Whitcomb's new colleagues appeared at the hostess station in timely succession, and the table filled quickly. Just after seven, Emma Jean and Shai entered City Streets.

"Look, Mama," Shai said. "This is Wes's restaurant."

"I know, Sugar." Emma Jean smiled.

"Look at all the old pictures." Shai turned in a circle. "It's all streets like the name says. Come on."

"Slow down, girl. Someone has to seat us."

"Wes might do it."

"I imagine he's pretty busy with a big restaurant like this."

"Mama, you gotta meet Wes. He's really nice."

"I will, Shai. I will."

"Maybe you'll meet him tonight. We've already lived here a whole month, and you don't even know him at all."

"If you don't calm down, I don't know if I want to meet him," Emma Jean teased. "You're makin' an awful fuss over some short, little white man."

"He's not short," Shai answered back. "You're just tall."

"I'm only kidding, Sugar. I'm sure we'll meet in due time."

Their exchange ended as Jan returned to the hostess station. "May I help you?"

"Yes, I'm Emma Jean Whitcomb. We're meeting a group here for dinner."

"Of course," Jan said. "Right this way, please."

They followed the hostess to their table with Shai adjusting her stride to step on each of the dashed lines painted in the middle of the "street." Emma Jean smiled at the mercurial shift between little girl and young woman in her eighth-grade daughter. The young woman reemerged as they approached the gathering of university professors. Dr. Carson rose at the head of the table.

"Welcome, Professor Whitcomb." He extended his hand enthusiastically, having adroitly negotiated the fact that, unlike the others at the table, Emma Jean had no "Dr." to put before her name. "And this must be your daughter."

"Yes, this is Shaikera."

"Well, welcome to you, young lady," Dr. Carson said. "Professor Whitcomb, I know you have met most of your colleagues already, but perhaps I should introduce you around the table again."

As he moved through the introductions, their waiter approached to take drink orders. Emma Jean decided on a gin and tonic. Shai surprised her mother by foregoing her usual Pepsi and asking for a ginger ale. With the waiter dispatched for drinks, the entire table turned its collective attention to the menus. Except for Emma Jean and Shai, everyone at the table had eaten at City Streets before. They shared compliments about its eclectic offerings and unanimous agreement that "everything is good."

The menu at City Streets reflected Wes's interest in food and the talents of Brian Hennesy, the classically trained but relentlessly innovative young chef who was the first hire for the restaurant. A scan down the listings showed not only frog legs sautéed in butter and garlic, veal ala Oscar, and salmon with dill sauce but also medallions of pork with apricot compote, grilled portabella mushrooms and sweet red peppers topped with sun-dried tomatoes and provolone cheese, and braised breast of goose with wild rice and a raspberry white wine reduction sauce. A light appetite could find pecan-encrusted sea bass, while the bold eater could select the Bavarian dinner combining chunks of smoked pork chop and German sausages, pan-seared, and then cooked slowly with apples, onions, sauerkraut, and dark beer.

Like any good Iowa restaurant, a selection of hand-cut and aged steaks buttressed the rest of the menu. The art of aging steaks that Wes had learned in Princeton at the Riverview Inn still helped pay the bills. Brian Hennesy, though he loved the forum that City Streets provided for his creative cooking, could never quite get over the fact that the Classic Cut Ribeye was still the number one seller on the menu.

Emma Jean pondered her choice as she sat surrounded by an extremely white and oddly quiet table. An inner awkwardness gripped her as she considered what to choose for dinner. In university seminars, faculty meetings, or association conferences—all created by a white cultural power structure—she never cringed at being big, bold, or black. Whatever was deeper than pride, stronger than courage, and more enduring than love—life's most profound and least knowable essence—came to Emma Jean from being black.

Being big was different, especially at a dinner table filled with strangers. At six-two and 220 pounds, she projected an imposing presence that few women anywhere could match. Unlike being black, being big represented only the surface of her person. Behind whatever façade she could present, her size created daily moments of uncertainty and embarrassment that she tried to hide from the world. She studied the menu in her hand with just such a feeling.

The Bavarian dinner sounded intriguing, but Emma Jean's quick inventory of the group around the table confirmed that she was not only the biggest woman but also the biggest person, period, in the party of scholars. Ordering a dish of pork, sausages, and beer accompanied by German fried potatoes felt like a recipe for heaping embarrassing extra attention on the fact of her size. Had she come to City Streets to eat with just Shai, Bavarian dinner would have been the choice. Now she vacillated. She grew up in Milwaukee. Maybe she could order the Bavarian dinner and deflect attention from her man-sized appetite with a glib reference to her childhood home.

Remaining uncertain of her choice, Emma Jean looked around the table again and thought about the new setting she had entered. The university had spared little in its efforts to attract her to Iowa City. Her salary more than doubled the money she had earned at Howard, and her joint appointment in the theater and English departments gave her a special status on the faculty. Tonight, the theater professors had gathered to welcome her. The occasion only reinforced to her how much men, all of them white men, dominated the department. With Suzanne Peters out of town, Dr. Roberta Engle, the third and final woman in the department, seemed almost as out of place as Emma Jean among the gathering at the table.

Emma Jean had chosen her own seat carefully and managed to maneuver Shai between herself and Dr. Carson. Although too little time had passed for Emma Jean to know the department members well, Dr. Carson's precise demeanor and prissy mannerisms had already become annoying. She felt certain that he would be disinclined to waste time making conversation with a child—a belief that assuaged her guilt at placing Shai in the position of buffer zone.

Kyle returned to the table and efficiently delivered the proper drinks to each member of the party. That duty complete, he produced a pen and pad to take food orders. By the time he reached Emma Jean, selections had ranged from orange-glazed duck, veal ala Oscar, and pork medallions to the evening special of Greek pasta with black olives, tomato, feta cheese, and scallions. No one had ordered the Bavarian dinner.

"And what will you have, ma'am?" Kyle asked.

"It all sounds so good," Emma Jean said. A faint frown formed on her lips when she heard her words sound just as white as the dish she ordered. "I'll have the lemon zest tilapia."

"What would you like, miss?" the waiter asked.

Shai pointed at her menu. "I want the coconut-fried shrimp."

Emma Jean had presumed Shai would order one of the dishes made with chicken breast. Chicken was her favorite. She always ordered chicken in a nice restaurant. Was it possible that she interpreted Emma Jean's choice of tilapia as a social cue to order some kind of fish? That question dissolved in the realization that shrimp coated with coconut sounded a lot better than tilapia dusted with lemon zest. Still, Emma Jean couldn't be sure if coconut shrimp was the innocent choice of a child or the more calculated selection of an adult. Perhaps her only certainty was the bittersweet swell of emotion at her daughter moving so quickly into adolescence—that and the fact that she wished she had ordered the Bavarian dinner for herself.

Warm popovers and a crisp salad that tossed endive and watercress into an exceptional mix of greens deflected Emma Jean's attention from regrets about her dinner selection. The tilapia arrived surrounded by rosettes of mashed sweet potatoes, and the pure pleasure of the delicious fish removed any remaining regrets completely. Shai seemed to find equal delight in her shrimp. Emma Jean knew that the company and conversation had to be a lot less delightful to her daughter.

Shai sat quietly and politely through drinks and dinner as talk dragged along from reawakening interest in Greek tragedies to staging Shakespeare in-the-round to questioning whether the "new classics" truly were classics. Only her mother's annoyance during talk about the last topic gave Shai any relief from her intense boredom. The succulent shrimp did bring a smile to her face. She just knew Wes would have a good restaurant. Her shrimp proved it, but as the conversation around her carried on, she kept wishing that it was Wes and not a bunch of boring professors sitting at the table with her and her mother. That thought had passed through her mind for at least the hundredth time when she looked up and saw Wes approaching with a large glass tray in his hands.

"Hi, Shai," were his first words as he reached the table.

"Hi, Wes." Shai grabbed her mother's wrist. "This is Mama. I told her you'd be here."

Wes nodded to Emma Jean and placed the tray in the center of the table.

She stood to shake hands. "Hello, Mr. Whitcomb. It's very nice to finally meet you. Shai sings your praises."

Wes froze for a moment, transfixed by the woman who rose up beside him. It wasn't just that she loomed a good four inches, or more, taller than he did; she had a big presence in every way. She stood erect, making no attempt to minimize her height or her imposing breasts. Her body seemed thick—not fat—with a prodigious, round backside that more than balanced her top half. The cut of her short-sleeved blouse revealed strength in her arms, and Emma Jean's skin carried a blackness so deep that it seemed to glisten. Styling gel held her straightened jet-black hair in place like an ebony crown.

"Nice to meet you, too." Wes answered with his hand in a firm grip from Emma Jean. "Please, call me Wes."

Emma Jean had seen him from her window, but standing close she was quick to take his measure: average height, sandy brown hair, smallish hands, ordinary build, really an ordinary man in every way. Except for the eyes. Emma Jean always studied eyes carefully. There was something honest or kind or serious—something of substance—in his soft green eyes.

"I can do that," she said. "If you'll call me Emma Jean."

Wes smiled, but felt the presence of another person next to him. His attention shifted for a moment. "You must be Dr. Carson."

"I am, indeed. Yours is a most delightful restaurant. I must say the food was delicious tonight."

"Thank you, Dr. Carson. And thank you for choosing City Streets. It's especially nice that you thought of us since Shai and her mother are new neighbors of mine."

"It was our pleasure."

Heads nodded in agreement and compliments on the food came from around the table. An odd table it was, with the formal and conservative Dr. Carson at one end and a colleague at the other in a denim work shirt with the sleeves rolled up and the front unbuttoned a third of the way down to reveal a graying, hairy chest. Such was the result of a theater department combining scholars of Shakespeare with theorists in set design.

"I'm glad you enjoyed your dinner," Wes said. "Since you managed to get my new neighbors to the restaurant before I did, I thought the least I could do was make dessert. I hope everyone will enjoy tarts and coffee, compliments of City Streets."

"Indeed. Why, thank you very much, Mr. Whitcomb," Dr. Carson answered amid the murmured thanks of the others in the group.

Wes looked over at Shai, certain that she didn't want coffee and equally convinced that she must be tired of the company that surrounded her.

"Shai," he said, "how would you like to see the rest of the restaurant with me?"

She smiled and stood with a quick, "Okay."

"Great," Wes said. "I'll have the kitchen box up a few tarts for you to take home."

Shai suddenly realized that she should have asked her mother for permission before rising from the table. She looked to her right and Emma Jean gave a simple nod of approval.

"Let's walk down Washington Street." Wes motioned to his left. "It's my favorite."

Shai walked by his side. "This place is big."

"Whadda ya think of it?"

"I like it," she said.

"Good."

"You figure it all out by yourself?" she asked.

"You mean the pictures and everything?"

"Yeah."

"Yep, it's all my idea. Come on, let's go in the kitchen."

Shai had never been in the kitchen of a big restaurant, and everything being so busy surprised her. People in white coats were working everywhere—reaching into giant refrigerators, chopping vegetables at shiny, stainless steel counters, and grabbing pots or frying pans that hung on racks overhead. Steam escaped from a dishwashing machine at the far end of the kitchen, while food sizzled and simmered in pans on the restaurant stoves in the middle of the room.

"Is it always like this?" she asked.

Her eyes widened when Wes said, "Nope, on Fridays and Saturdays it gets really busy."

"Man," she said.

"Come on this way. I want to show you the banquet hall. It's upstairs." He led the way to an industrial-sized steel door at the back of the kitchen. "This is our service elevator. It's how we take the food up to the second floor. That whole space is just for special events."

"Man, this is big."

"Yeah, it used to be for cars," Wes said.

"Cars," Shai giggled.

"I'm serious. Years ago, they stored cars in this building. This was how they got them up and down to the second floor. Like I said, now the upstairs is for special events."

"Like sports banquets and stuff?"

"We do all kinds of events," he said. "Could be sports, Jaycees, college reunions, you name it. The restaurant is called City Streets, so the upstairs is County Park. You'll see."

The idea for County Park came to Wes when he was picking out pictures for photomurals. A search through the files of the Johnson County Historical Society turned up lots of street scenes, but he couldn't resist exploring other folders, including the one marked "County Parks." He loved the old photographs of gazebos, swimming beaches, and picnic grounds, but they didn't fit the City Streets theme. That's when he decided to have his County Park.

The clear span roof rafters of the old parking garage created one huge, open room on the second floor. He had the entire area covered in green, indoor/outdoor carpeting to mimic grass then lined the walls with photomurals of his favorite pictures from the county park file and filled the room with plastic patio tables and chairs. Against the front wall, a recreated bandstand served as a stage. A merry-go-round and a jungle gym, both salvaged from the playground of a closed parochial school, occupied opposite corners in the rear of the room. Even if all the things used to create the County Park banquet hall didn't really belong together, none of that bothered Wes. The customers never seemed to mind, either. In fact, he always sensed that playing make believe was part of being successful with a restaurant theme.

"This is County Park," he said as they stepped off the elevator.

"Man," Shai said for the third time on her tour of the restaurant.

Wes wondered how she could get so much inflection into a one-syllable word. "I guess that means you like it."

"Uh huh."

"You can have a picnic up here any time of the year," he said.

"But it's for banquets."

"Right," he said. "The picnic part is the food: meatloaf, ham, fried chicken, potato salad, baked beans, coleslaw, three-bean salad, chocolate cake, blueberry and cherry pie, pickles, veggie tray. We even make deviled eggs."

"So it's a picnic banquet," she said as she walked toward the jungle gym.

"That's exactly what it is."

"And that's all you do up here?"

"Just about. We can do a hog roast, but that costs a little more. Most people go with the picnic."

Shai twirled around. "This whole big place just for picnics?"

"Well, where else can you have a picnic in January or February? It's pretty successful."

Wes understated the truth. With its reputation for fine food, City Streets did well, but the County Park side of the business was like a license to print money. The food was ample and good, but simple to prepare. Banquets with guaranteed preregistrations made costs easy to manage, and the hall was used a lot. Where else in Iowa City *could* you have a picnic in January?

"I'm glad it's not winter," Shai said as she began climbing the jungle gym. "I don't like it cold."

"Nah, me neither." Wes watched her go up another rung. "I gotta say, you look right at home on those monkey bars."

Shai froze on the second level of the jungle gym, then retreated down to the floor in two steps. "I think we should go back downstairs. They're probably done with dessert."

Wes could almost feel his foot planted firmly in his mouth. Teenage girls probably didn't want to be complimented for their monkey bar climbing.

Shai stood with her arms crossed.

"You're right," he said. "Let me show you one or two of the pictures, and we'll head down."

"Okay."

Wes pointed out a few details in the photos as she stood by politely. After he tried a couple more awkward attempts at conversation, they took the elevator back to the first floor.

"How was your tour, Sugar?" Emma Jean asked as Shai and Wes came to the table.

"All right," Shai answered.

"Thank you for giving her a look around," Emma Jean said.

"And thank you for the lovely tarts." Dr. Carson stood and offered his hand.

"My pleasure." Wes shook hands then turned to Emma Jean. "I'm really glad you could come to the restaurant tonight. You getting to know your way around town?"

Emma Jean laughed. "Big campus, small town. Just the opposite of Howard and D.C."

"I suppose so."

"But thank you for asking. I think I've managed the basics." Emma Jean counted things off with her fingers. "So far, I've found a tennis club, somebody to change my oil, and a place to buy groceries."

"Tennis is a basic?" he asked.

"I get into it pretty good." She laughed again.

"It's a fun game," Wes said.

"So, you play, too?"

"A little. I like the exercise."

"If you have time tomorrow afternoon, why don't you join me at my club," Emma Jean said on impulse. "I found a regular Thursday afternoon partner, but she had to cancel this week. I'm looking for someone to play."

"Sounds like fun," he said. "Afternoon's a good time for me."

"It's set, then. Three o'clock at Maplewood Country Club. I can return some of your hospitality and your kindness to Shai."

"Does that mean I'll have a good chance to win?" Wes joked.

"No promises there."

Amidst a chorus of goodbyes and thank-yous, Emma Jean didn't notice the scowl on Shai's face until they reached the parking lot.

"What's the matter, Sugar?"

"Nothin'."

"Well, it must be somethin' 'cuz you got your lip stickin' out to here, girl."

"You don't have to tease me, Mama."

"Now, don't be tellin' me about teasin'," Emma Jean said as they got into the car. "If there's somethin' wrong, you just say it."

"You don't have to play tennis with him for me." Shai turned her head and looked out the car window.

"What? You embarrassed 'cuz I used your name?"

"No."

"What then? You're the one always tellin' me how nice he is. Wes this and Wes that."

"He called me a monkey, Mama."

"What! He called you what?"

"A monkey."

"He said 'Shai, you're a monkey'?"

"Not like that."

"All right, like what? I wanna know what he said."

"We were upstairs," Shai said. "He's got a picnic place up there."

"Huh?"

"It's not really for picnics. It's for banquets, but they have the same kinda food as picnics. The whole room has those plastic tables for outside and big pictures of parks and playground stuff—"

"I don't care about all that. When did he call you a monkey?"

"We were by the playground stuff," Shai answered, "and he said, 'You look right at home on those monkey bars.'"

"So, he didn't really say you were a monkey."

"No."

"Did he say it that way?" Emma Jean asked. "You know what I mean."

"Maybe not." Shai sighed. "It's just when he said it . . ."

"I know, Sugar." Emma Jean touched Shai's hand. "He probably didn't mean anything. Like you said to me about that boy in the grocery store the other day."

"I thought Wes was my friend. He coulda thought about what he was sayin'."

"Sometimes white folks don't have any sense," Emma Jean said. "If he's as nice as you been tellin' me, he didn't mean anything by it."

"I still didn't like it."

"I understand. Sounds like he just talked without thinkin'. How about this? Just to be on the safe side, I'll beat his butt real bad in tennis tomorrow."

Shai giggled. "Okay, Mama."

CHAPTER 6

The Maplewood Country Club hid from Iowa City in an odd triangle of land north of the interstate highway. At the time Maplewood was built, a rural location separated it from the everyday lives of the town's ordinary citizens. In the 1960s, construction of the highway cut off the possible extension of city streets from the south. A crook of the river had always blocked any approach from the other directions. Two ravines with thick stands of trees muted the whining rush of traffic on the interstate. With only a narrow road leading to its gate, the country club remained the very private retreat of bank owners, top attorneys, and university presidents—Iowa City's version of the elite.

The university president had nominated Emma Jean for membership in Maplewood. She asked about a country club membership as part of the package that brought her to Iowa. If the university wanted to point to her as a faculty star, she expected the trappings of that status in return. At Maplewood, the eighteen-hole golf course crawled over wooded knolls and circled little gullies long ago reshaped into manmade ponds. The layout formed one of the two championship-caliber courses in Iowa. It mattered not to Emma Jean that she had never picked up a golf club in her life and never intended to. She found out from her sister that the football coach received a membership in Maplewood. If a fat, white football coach rated a membership, Emma Jean figured a tall, black playwright deserved just as much. The university foundation went along and paid for her dues.

Luckily for her, Maplewood had added new indoor tennis courts three years ago. The four courts nestled into the side of a knoll under an asymmetrical roof designed to take advantage of the topography. With three-quarters of the new tennis building enveloped by earth, the stately, white-colonnaded original clubhouse shielded the rest of it from view as members entered the grounds along a wooded drive. The courts, a concession to younger members, blended almost seamlessly into the Maplewood's tradition-rich environment.

Emma Jean waited for Wes on a varnished oak bench inside the entrance to the tennis building. She smoothed the short skirt of her favorite tennis outfit over the top of her thighs. The pale, margarita-green tennis dress had tiny lavender and yellow bands accenting its neckline and sleeves. The designer of the outfit repeated those colors in the waistband of the matching panties that went under the skirt, although Emma Jean wondered who was supposed to see those additional accents tucked so far out of sight. The *LBH* monogram on one sleeve represented a common brand of tennis apparel, but Emma Jean, as always, had special-ordered the outfit from a catalog. Even the largest pro shops and sporting goods stores in Washington didn't carry tennis wear to fit a six-foot two-inch, 220-pound woman. She would have preferred playing in the kind of shorts she *could* have purchased in any store for large and tall women, but she thought maybe the fluted tennis dresses made her behind look a little less prominent.

An effort to reduce the size of her behind had helped get Emma Jean interested in tennis in the first place, though not until she reached her mid-twenties. Growing up, she dreaded stepping onto an athletic field of any kind. Being Lu Whitcomb's younger sister wasn't easy. Another two inches taller than Emma Jean, Lu presented the picture of sinewy strength and grace on a basketball court. Emma Jean saw in her own body only an awkward bearing and undeniable girth. As a teenager, she sometimes slipped into the bathroom and poked at her thighs and stomach. They weren't fat or blubbery, but they seemed so thick compared to the long, taut muscles that graced Lu's arms and legs. Emma Jean wondered how two sisters could receive bodies so different. Whatever the explanation, she hated gym class, declined to play even the simplest games at family picnics, and left the athletics to Lu.

Life with Marcus eventually changed that, but it wasn't watching him play basketball that brought Emma Jean to the tennis courts. Both understood while they were dating at Northwestern and after they married that she had no interest in playing sports. Then, Shai came along and half the weight Emma Jean gained during pregnancy claimed a permanent home around her waist and hips—especially her hips.

Even before Shai was born, Emma Jean became aware of the procession of beautiful women who found their way to NBA arenas. In their early years together, Marcus and Emma Jean made love with an intensity that locked their bodies together in a fierce physical passion. When she began to suspect that Marcus was spending his passion on the road, Emma Jean yearned to reshape her body. The weight gained with Shai pushed that desire even further.

A single Saturday morning spent shopping for exercise equipment convinced Emma Jean that she would never have a useful relationship with a treadmill or stationary bike. Two weeks later, she arranged a trial tennis lesson at an expensive Georgetown club. She purchased a membership the same day.

With the money Marcus earned, she could afford lessons from a top-notch teaching pro. Tennis placed an unbreakable hold on Emma Jean, even if it didn't help her hold onto Marcus. Within a year, she mastered a smashing serve, learned a powerful forehand, turned fifteen pounds of fat into twenty pounds of muscle, and divorced Marcus Williams. Everything changed except her dress size.

She never expected the physical exertion of sports to seduce her, but it did. The feeling only grew stronger as she routinely emerged a winner on the tennis courts. None of the women she played with recreationally could stand up to her powerful game. Occasionally, she and three male colleagues from Howard got together for doubles matches. No matter how they divided into teams, her side always came away victorious. Now, seated on a bench at the Maplewood courts, she expected nothing less as she saw Wes enter through the front doors dressed in a pair of khaki shorts and a gray T-shirt that read "Burlington Riverboat Days."

"Hi." Emma Jean stood to greet her neighbor.

Wes answered with a wave and a smile.

"Have you been here before?" she asked.

"First time. Thanks for having me."

"I thought with all the people you meet at the restaurant, maybe you'd been to the club."

"I serve 'em dinner, but I guess you could say I don't run in their circles." He said, oblivious to the fact that Emma Jean's club membership made her part of "Their circles."

Her face scrunched in a reflexive scowl.

"Is this all right?" Wes touched the hem of his shorts and nodded toward the doubles players on the far court.

Emma Jean glanced in the direction of the doubles match and took notice of the four men in blazing white tennis shorts and matching pullover shirts. Each outfit sported a designer logo and a swatch, circle, or patch of tasteful trim. She unconsciously smoothed her own designer tennis skirt again.

"Oh . . . yeah," she said. "There's no dress code or anything. I think it's just what people are used to."

Her halting attempt to reassure Wes didn't seem to help. She could see his ears blush red as he lowered his head and unzipped the vinyl cover on his tennis racket.

"Let's volley," Emma Jean said simply. She reached into a custom sports bag for her racket and a new can of tennis balls.

"Okay."

They moved to the court and took positions on opposite sides of the net. Emma Jean bounced a ball on the court and stroked a firm forehand toward him. He answered with a low, flat return in easy reach of her racket. They settled into a comfortable rally, broken after half a dozen returns when one of his shots tipped the net and dribbled onto her side of the court. She took another ball and started the warm-up routine again.

After a back and forth to the forehand, she pulled a ball crosscourt to his backhand side. He made a short punch with his racket that floated the ball safely over the net. Emma Jean returned it with the smooth, strong backhand stroke she had learned in Washington under the guidance of her tennis pro.

No tennis lessons there, she thought to herself as Wes poked another poor backhand shot in her direction.

She switched the rally back to the forehand side as the poverty of his backhand began to annoy her. After all, *he* wasn't poor. Owning a successful restaurant had to provide him with a comfortable, middle-class lifestyle. He could afford both lessons and tennis clothes, if he wanted them.

She picked up the pace of her shots as she thought about her own lifestyle. It was, she knew, much more than comfortable or middle class. Marcus Williams may have screwed lots of women, but that was in bed. During the divorce, his attorneys arranged ample child support for Shai and offered a generous settlement to Emma Jean. Her own six-figure salary plus the trickle of royalties from *The Black Hologram* would have been enough for her and Shai, anyway. The education trust that Marcus set up for Shai had allowed Emma Jean to funnel much of her own money into a series of successful investments. Marcus even had his financial advisors help her. By the standards of most Americans, Emma Jean was rich.

With each stroke, she grew more agitated at Wes' lousy backhand and khaki shorts. Somehow, this white guy aroused an aggravating sense of guilt in her about her money. She reminded herself again that he was far from poor. Besides, whites never *gave* black people anything. The money in her life came from the talents of a gifted black man and a smart black woman. She narrowed her eyes and slammed a sizzling forehand that glanced off the frame of his racket.

"Nice shot," he said.

"How about a set?" she asked without acknowledging the compliment.

"Sounds good," he answered while trying to understand the abrupt end to their warm-ups. He jogged back to the fence to retrieve the vanquished ball.

Wes thought back to high school when he and his best friend plunged into tennis. Neither knew enough about the sport to give much thought to warming up. Tennis for two small-town Iowa kids was grab a racket, head to the court, and start a game. Somehow, that didn't seem like Emma Jean. Serious tennis players warmed up and warmed up and warmed up. From her club membership to her tennis clothes to her blazing forehand, Emma Jean seemed every inch a serious tennis player.

"Rally for serve?" she asked.

"Ladies first," he said.

"Okay." She gave him a blank smile. From what she could see, his cruddy backhand hardly gave him any reason to feel the need to be chivalrous. She remembered the promise she made to Shai after the dinner last night and prepared to give him the least lady-like taste of tennis possible.

"Practice serves?" he asked.

"I'll take a few."

Emma Jean tossed a ball high in the air and swung through with the full reach of her height. The ball slammed hard into the net. Her second ball followed the same path, but the third, fourth, and fifth bounced sharply into the court with Wes weakly tapping only one of the offerings. He took a step and a half back and managed to block the sixth practice serve back across the net.

She tossed up another ball, and he set himself again for a rocketing serve. This time the ball came slower, tracing a big curving loop and bouncing sharply to his right from its spin. He barely touched it with the end of his racket.

"I'm ready," Emma Jean said after spinning two more slow serves into the court.

Her first serve of the set came hard and true with a mishit by Wes popping straight up in the air. Two missed first serves by Emma Jean brought tricky spinning second serves to follow. Each time, Wes stretched far to his right, making soft returns that Emma Jean put away with decisive forehand strokes. A blistering service ace gave her the first game at love.

She tossed him the service balls. "Practice?"

"Nah," he said with a wave of his racket.

His first serve came hard and flat to her forehand. She stroked it back to his forehand side and got a weak ball in return. She drove him back behind the end line and then smashed his soft return with a volley at the net.

"Nice shot," he said.

She nodded.

Wes toed the end line and knocked his first serve into the net. Emma Jean took a step forward and bent into ready position.

"Second serve," he said and dinked the ball toward her side of the court.

In ten years of playing tennis, she couldn't remember anyone with such a bad-looking second serve. The ball plunked safely onto the court barely into the service box. She ran forward but barely reached the ball and topped it harmlessly into the net. He missed two more first serves, and after each, she stepped two paces closer to the net and put away both of his second serves for winners. A good first serve on the fourth point finally started a decent rally, and Emma Jean finished the point with a sharp backhand that ticked the side line. She took the next two games with increasingly aggressive shots, while he managed enough good returns to give her a slightly more interesting match.

As she served the fifth game, she thought about the prospect of reporting a 6-0 victory to Shai. Emma Jean hit a hard first serve that Wes blocked back across the net. She stepped in on the short ball and moved to the net behind her sharply struck forehand. He reached for her shot and poked a high lob to the back of the court. Emma Jean retreated with a lumbering gait and hit a twisting backhand before she could get her feet completely set. Her shot dived into the net.

She took the next point, but he followed with two points of his own as he ran down more and more of her shots. He began spraying his soft returns all around the court to keep Emma Jean on the move. They settled into a long deuce game, trading points back and forth. With Wes up a point, Emma Jean slammed her first serve into the net. She wiped the perspiration from around her eyes and spun her second serve—just wide. The set stood at 4-1. There would be no bragging to Shai about a 6-0 match.

Emma Jean broke back immediately to go up 5-1, but Wes surprisingly turned the tables by winning her service game, again. In each successive game, he forced her to cover more court by alternating lobs and dinks and forehands aimed to her wide side of the court. The more she ran, the more power she lost, while he ran with abandon, returning most balls and twice tumbling to the ground in laughter at shots he couldn't quite reach.

Sweat poured off both players as Wes managed to win game after game. An hour and five minutes had disappeared into a single set of tennis, and he had taken the lead in games 6-5. He spanked his first serve into the net. Emma Jean told herself to concentrate as she moved in close for a dink second serve. He tossed the ball and rapped a low hard serve to her backhand. The shot caught her flat footed and bounced by for his first ace of the match.

She scowled and wiped her forehead with the back of her arm. He served and she ripped at the ball with full force. Her shot sailed wide. Down 30-love, she watched him net his first serve then send a hard second serve at her again. Ready this time, she returned a stinging forehand aimed toward the back corner of the court. The ball touched just past the end line.

"Out," he yelled.

"You sure," she barked immediately.

"It looked out."

Emma Jean spun her racket twice in her hand.

"We can play it over if it looked in to you," he said.

"Never mind."

"I'm ahead. Let's play it again."

"That don't mean anything," she fired back. "If it's out, it's out."

"I think it was."

"40-love, then. Your serve."

His first serve carried wide to her forehand side. She stepped in, then back, aware that 40-love was the perfect opportunity for him to chance another hard second serve. With a quick poke, Wes sent a dinky serve on the way. She rumbled forward, caught off guard again. Her lunging shot bounced off the top of the net and sent Wes dashing ahead. Tumbling and laughing for the third time in the set, he lifted his return just over her head. It dropped it safely into the back corner of the court.

"Your set," she said, standing no more than ten feet from where Wes lay on the court. "Nice get."

"Yeah, thanks."

She strode directly to a bench beside the courts and grabbed a towel from her bag. She plopped down in disgust and wiped at the rivulets of perspiration flowing down her face and under her arms.

Wes joined her on the bench. "Good game."

"Yeah," she answered. "My strokes weren't very clean today."

"I suppose it happens."

She didn't think it should happen—losing to some laughing white boy with a dinky-assed second serve.

"I had fun," Wes said. He absent-mindedly reached for Emma Jean's towel.

She stared in surprise as he wiped the towel across his face.

"Oh, I'm sorry," he said, handing it back to her.

"No, it's okay."

She felt an unexpected smile spread across her face. Maybe she had lost to a laughing white boy with a dinky-assed second serve, but no way was he a racist laughing white boy with a dinky-assed second serve.

She smiled again. She wasn't going to be able to tell Shai that she whipped his butt in tennis. She was glad for Shai's sake that she had something better to tell her.

CHAPTER 7

"You like pie?"

Shai giggled at Wes's question. "Everybody likes pie."

They had been shooting baskets for almost half an hour.

"I feel like having a piece," he said. "I was gonna call down to the restaurant and see what's left. You wanna come along if I go?"

"Can't," Shai answered. "Piano lessons at three. Mama's takin' me. Why don't you ask her to go?"

"I meant you and her."

"Good. She usually just sits and waits for me."

"The pie's at the Red Door. My little restaurant."

"I know." Shai shot another one through the hoop. "My lesson's about three blocks from there."

"You know where the Red Door is?" Wes asked.

"We been livin' here three months."

"So your mom likes pie?"

Shai giggled again. "I just said everybody likes pie."

"I don't know what your mom likes. I hardly ever see her."

"Shouldn't have beat her at tennis."

"You think that's it?"

"Prob'ly not." Shai sighed. "Mama's just always busy."

Wes picked up the ball that had rolled near his feet. "I guess that settles it. I'm gonna call Suzie down at the restaurant and see what we've got. Don't let your mom get away."

By the time he finished calling and came back outside, Shai and Emma Jean were both there.

"One piece of black raspberry, two pieces of apple, and one slice of chocolate mayonnaise cake," he said as he approached his two neighbors.

"What?" Emma Jean asked.

"Pie and cake," he answered.

"I didn't tell her yet," Shai said with a sly smile.

"Didn't tell me what, girl?"

"I'm going down to my Red Door Café for a piece of pie," Wes said. "I wanted to ask you and Shai to come along."

"Maybe Shai didn't tell *you* that I have to take *her* to piano lessons."

"I told him, Mama. All you do is sit there and read."

"And I got a lot of readin' to do, girl. Classes start in two days."

"You already know all that stuff, Mama."

"And I still have to review my class notes," Emma Jean said. "You know what I expect of my students, and I don't expect anything less from myself."

"I bet pie is good for energy," Wes said.

"Huh?"

"You know." He made a little muscle. "Energy to get ready for your classes."

Emma Jean's face scrunched halfway to a scowl. Maybe too much sugar was where he got all the energy to play tennis—running all over the place on his skinny, white legs and then lobbing the ball back when she thought she'd hit a winner. Now he was making muscles with his skinny, white arms.

"Whataya say? I already asked Suzie to put on a fresh pot of coffee."

Emma Jean suppressed her thoughts about tennis. "Who's Suzie?"

"She works for me. Or maybe me for her. It's hard to tell. She pretty much runs the Red Door."

"And what's this red door?"

"It's my other restaurant, the one where I started. I'd love to have you see it."

"The thing is," Emma Jean said, "I really do—"

"Come on, Mama," Shai stretched up to kiss her mother on the cheek. "I can show you where it is on the way to lessons. We go right by it. You know you ain't gonna make no pie for yourself."

"How do you know what I'm gonna make for myself?"

Shai covered up the smile that formed on her lips as she thought of her mother in the kitchen trying to make a pie.

"Maybe I'll go," Emma Jean said, "if you'll work on speaking better English. 'Ain't gonna make no pie.' Talking like that with your mother in the English department at the University of Iowa."

"Okay, Mama. Let's go." Shai grabbed her mother's hand.

"See you there in fifteen minutes?" Wes asked.

"If she doesn't pull my arm off," Emma Jean answered. "You slow yourself down, girl."

After his neighbors left, Wes made the familiar drive to the Red Door Café, suddenly aware of the signs of an ebbing summer. Emma Jean's remark about preparing for classes provided this year's unwelcome wakeup call, one that came in some form every August. Growing up in Iowa, Wes loved spring and the prospect of summer ahead. In fact, he loved it almost more than summer itself. The translucent green of trees leafing out in May, rhubarb plants sprouting up full and thick, lilac bushes covered in shawls of purple flowers-they all spoke of a season of promise that lay ahead.

By the end of August, Iowa was full of different signs. A host of garden plants had yielded their produce and begun to die away. Spring blossoms were a distant memory, and already the hues of autumn had started to take over in flower beds. All the way to the Red

Door, Wes noticed the trees. The peak lush green had passed, and a careful eye could see the brittle and broken edges of leaves beginning to lose the suppleness of summer. The changes brought his thoughts back to his neighbors as he pulled behind the restaurant to park. Shai seemed as bright and alive with promise as the best spring day. He and Emma Jean were two Whitcombs with their lives already well into summer.

"How was it today, Sooz?" He asked as he walked in the back door of the café.

Suzie looked up from the stainless steel countertop she had been wiping. "Busy. I'm sorry I gave you the day off."

"So you do need me around here?" Wes joked.

"When there's work to be done, but your timing's perfect as usual. I just finished cleaning up."

"You know what they say. Timing is everything in business."

"I thought it was location. So how come you're locatin' yourself in here on a Saturday afternoon? Don't bosses only come in when they want?"

"I did want to. You know. The pie. I called."

"Obviously you called. I just talked to you."

"So you made the coffee?"

"Yeah, yeah," Suzie answered. "There's a full pot on the burner. I made it right after I hung up."

"Thanks," he said. "I was shooting hoops with Shai, so I asked her if she wanted some pie."

"The little girl?"

"Yeah, except she's not little. She's starting eighth grade."

"I thought you said you were coming with the mother—the famous one."

"I wanted to ask them both, but Shai has piano lessons."

"And you ended up with the mom, who, by the way, isn't with you."

"Right on both counts. I better get up front. Is the door locked?"

"Of course it is. We closed twenty minutes ago," Suzie followed him out of the kitchen. "Seems like something's got you in a fog, lately."

"Geez, I'm sorry, Sooz. You can go home."

"I'm going to. You know how to wash a coffee pot."

"Thanks to your excellent training."

"Right," she said. "It'll probably be full of stale coffee when I come in on Monday. You wouldn't want to wash dishes in front of somebody so famous."

"Famous and looking in the window," Wes said. "Come on."

They walked together to the front door where Suzie flipped the deadbolt.

"Welcome," Wes said to Emma Jean. "There's someone here I'd like you to meet. This is Suzie Bosch."

"It's very nice to meet you," Emma Jean said formally.

"Same here." Suzie reached out her hand. "Wes here has been telling me all about his new neighbors. Especially your daughter. Seems like those two spend a lot of time shooting baskets. It's like we got two kids playing together."

Emma Jean smiled as she grasped Suzie's hand. The tough, wiry grip of the slight woman with salt and pepper hair surprised her. She wondered from the worn feel of hands that sliced, stirred, wiped, and washed all day if Suzie actually was old enough to be Wes's mother.

Either way, Emma Jean definitely was Shai's mother, and she didn't like hearing about basketball again. It was all right that Shai had made friends with a neighbor, and Lord knew that there weren't any other kids at The Manor, but *she* knew how easily basketball could become a pitfall for Shai. No way people weren't going to compare her to her daddy, and in Iowa City, to her Aunt Lu, as well. Shai didn't need all that mess—never being able to measure up. It had happened to Emma Jean with her own work, having everything compared to *The Black Hologram* and nothing ever being as good again. Shai didn't need that with basketball. Emma Jean wanted Shai doing something that wasn't full of stupid comparisons.

Wes's voice broke into her thoughts. "What'll you have? We've got apple, black raspberry, and one piece of chocolate cake."

"Uh, apple," she said.

"How about you, Sooz?" he asked. "You gonna join us?"

"No thanks. I'm gonna head home and put my feet up."

"I'm having apple like Emma Jean. You take the raspberry home with you," he said. The single piece of black raspberry looked good to him, but he knew it was Suzie's second favorite next to rhubarb.

"Talked me into it," Suzie said. "Goodbye, Professor Whitcomb. Nice to meet you."

Somehow the respectful way the older woman called her professor left Emma Jean slightly taken aback. "Likewise."

Suzie moved to the end of the counter and reached underneath for a carryout box. She left the empty plate in the kitchen for Wes to wash with the coffee pot and slipped out the back door.

"Have a seat." Wes gestured toward the tables along the wall. "Coffee?"

"Please."

"Cream or sugar?"

"Both," Emma Jean answered.

He slid open the glass door on a small refrigerated case and picked up a green bowl with individual servings of half-and-half sealed in tiny, fluted plastic containers.

Emma Jean watched as he ferried things across the room. It seemed like he enjoyed running back and forth in his restaurant as much as he did on a tennis court.

"Sugar's on the table," he said, placing a brown coffee mug in front of Emma Jean as he set his own cup across from her.

She emptied two paper packets of sugar and two containers of half-and-half into her coffee and stirred while Wes retreated to the counter.

He glanced back in her direction and smiled.

"Good coffee," she murmured with her lips pressed lightly against the cup.

"Good. How about some ice cream with that pie?"

"Oh, I don't know."

"That's what makes it best."

"And what makes it that many more calories," she said.

"Well, we don't do this every day." He pulled out an ice cream scoop from under the counter.

"You're going to have some?" she asked.

"Thinkin' pretty strong about it."

"I will if you will," Emma Jean said.

"Deal." He dished generous scoops of ice cream to put on the two slices of "Always Apple Pie" and delivered the dessert to the table.

"Thanks."

"No problem." He nodded and sat down. "You know, I haven't asked Shai anything about school, yet. How's she like it?"

"She says it's good. I think possibly she likes the school more than I do. It's different here."

"Yeah, I guess Washington's a lot bigger." He watched Emma Jean take her first bite.

"Mm, good," she said. "Anyway, about school, I wasn't referring so much to the size of the city, but she's in public school here. I had Shai in a private school out east."

"A boarding school?"

"Oh, no," Emma Jean shook her head. "I want my baby close to me. It was a private school *in* Washington. A girl's school."

"I see."

"No, it's not that," Emma Jean answered immediately. "It's not the boys I'm worried about, but I'm not sure her classes are going to challenge her."

"Well, it's only been a week," Wes said. "They always review at first."

"I'm still not sure," Emma Jean insisted.

"But you *are* sure that it's not the boys?"

"Maybe we should change the subject." She pointed at her plate with the fork. "I'm very sure that this is good pie."

"Glad you like it."

"You make it, or Suzie?" Emma Jean asked.

"Suzie. My recipe."

"Well then, congratulations to both of you."

"It's better with ice cream, isn't it?" He grinned.

"Yes, it is. You're a bad influence on me." She lightly patted her thigh.

"Shai, too?" he asked.

"Pardon?"

"Am I a bad influence on Shai, too, with all this basketball?"

"I don't suppose some basketball on a Saturday afternoon will hurt Shai as much as adding some extra pounds from pie and ice cream would hurt me."

"So you know she's interested in the team?"

"What team?"

"The girls' basketball team," he said. "At her junior high."

"It's not basketball season," Emma Jean blurted.

"I guess she hasn't talked to you."

"Talked to me about what, exactly?"

"About going out for the basketball team."

"Not one word. Did she put you up to this?"

"Up to what?"

"This. The pie. The basketball team. Talkin' to me about goin' out for the team."

"No, no. Not at all."

"I have to wonder," Emma Jean said. "Shai knows how I feel about her and basketball."

"It might be good for her. Something to do with other kids."

"She doesn't need the expectations."

"You mean because of her dad?"

"Has she talked to you about her father, too?"

"Just once." Wes answered. "Not much more than you said now—about expectations."

"But somehow you know enough to think she should play?"

Wes held up his hands. "I'm not trying to butt in. She said she wishes she could try out. Actually, she's pretty good for not having played that much."

"And when other people think she's not as good as the daughter of Marcus Williams should be? What about that?"

"Iowa City could be a little different. People here might surprise you."

Emma Jean thought instantly of the Misses to Mrs. Shop. "And you think it would be a good surprise?"

"I'm pretty sure most people around here care more about kids being able to participate in things than they do about who somebody's father is."

"Is that so? An NBA dad or an aunt who coaches the university women doesn't make any difference?"

"I can't speak for every single person, but no, I don't believe the majority are going to put that many expectations on Shai because her dad played or her aunt coaches."

Emma Jean dropped her fork to the table. "You certainly would know about the majority, wouldn't you?"

"What?"

"What does the *majority* expect because Shai is black?"

"Huh?"

"Black," Emma Jean said. "You don't think white people expect black kids to be good basketball players just because they're black?"

"I don't know. Maybe some. A little."

"A little," Emma Jean snapped. "A little is about how much you know. People always got thoughts."

"I'm not a mind reader," he said.

"You think I'm a mind reader? I don't have to be some mind reader. I can tell you all about being Shai's age and black. You see me?"

"Yeah."

"Well, guess what. When I was Shai's age, I had boobs. Not no little teenage titties. I had a woman's breasts."

Wes quietly put his fork down, too.

"You want to know what my white teachers expected from me, a thirteen-year-old black girl with a woman's body? Here's what. One day in school, I'm in behind a book stack in the library, and I hear my English teacher and my social studies teacher talkin'. My two favorite teachers. Both women. 'Oh, Emma Jean, she's so smart, but it's just a shame.' 'I know, a girl that looks like that in this school.' 'I'll give her two years and she'll be pregnant.' So, you can be tellin' me anything you want about Iowa City, and I'll ask you this. How many whites see black skin and think pregnant teenager or welfare check or basketball player? An' you think this special little town's gonna be all that different?"

"The only thing I *think* is that Shai wants to play."

"And I *know* I'm her mother."

"So, your mother told you not to get pregnant when you were thirteen?"

"My mother taught me plenty."

"Taught you is different than told you," Wes said.

"Taught! Told!" Emma Jean exploded. "This ain't no debatin' society."

"No," Wes said in a soft voice, "it's a restaurant . . . I hope you still like the pie."

Emma Jean looked down at the table. She picked up her fork and squeezed the handle tight. Wes picked his up, too, and took a bite of his dessert. He followed the pie with a quiet sip of coffee. Stillness hung in the room, broken only by the breathing of the black woman and white man sitting on opposite sides of a table.

"I do like the pie," Emma Jean finally said. She took another bite and slowly regained her composure. "I even like that we're neighbors."

"Me, too," he said. "How about if I leave the whole basketball thing alone?"

She sighed. "You just don't want to see your baby hurt."

"She's a good kid."

Emma Jean glanced at her watch. "And probably wondering where I'm at. I lost track of the time."

"I guess you better run."

"Thanks for dessert." Emma Jean rose from her chair. "Next time, I'll buy."

CHAPTER 8

"Just put it over here." Emma Jean stepped aside as a maintenance man wheeled a heavy oak lectern into her classroom.
"Like this, Dr. Whitcomb?"
"That will be fine, Mr. . . ."
"Andrews. Ed Andrews."
"Thank you, Mr. Andrews," Emma Jean said. "It's a pleasure to meet you."
"Same here. You need anything else?"
"No, I believe I'm set."
"Well, if you do, give a holler. I'm always here 'til three-thirty." He nodded and ducked out the door.

Emma Jean gazed at the long, oak seminar table that filled the center of the room. The table, fourteen surrounding chairs, several tall bookcases, and a low credenza all matched in the tastefully coordinated room. It certainly offered a contrast to the nondescript classrooms she had grown accustomed to at Howard. There, she always had a desk and lectern at the front and thirty or forty student chairs with writing arms arranged in straight rows to fill the room.

The classrooms at Howard were always too large for the number of students in a playwriting course. The result was a knot of six or seven students near the front of the room with Emma Jean holding forth at the lectern. During her lectures, she rarely ranged more than an arm's length from the symbol of academic authority that held her notes. When the time came for class discussions and critiques, she took a seat at her desk and presided from there. She preferred the Howard setup to what she saw before her.

The class she was due to meet in twenty minutes was a graduate seminar, but the presumed collegiality of a professor and students gathered around a table annoyed her. She did not know this new batch of students yet, but she did know that some, perhaps even most, would never make it to the table of published playwrights. To Emma Jean, the long seminar table looked more appropriate to a corporate boardroom with the CEO chosen from a group peers sitting in the head chair. She was not a board chair. She was a professor. They were the students. Yesterday, she decided to create some appropriate distance and asked the department secretary to arrange a lectern for the room.

The request must have sent Mr. Andrews on a considerable search. The lectern he found, though made of golden oak, did not match the rest of the room's furniture in any other way. The bulky base and sharp edges of its angular top embodied none of the rounded elegance and curving corners of the table, chairs, or credenza. Emma Jean didn't care if the addition to the room wasn't a match for the decor. What the lectern lacked in harmony, it would make up for in space. It would force some distance.

She quickly ran her outline for the day's class through her mind. After finishing up her opening lecture, she preferred to sit for a discussion period followed by the assignment for the next week. She sized up the seminar table once more. She needed some distance there, as well. The tall bookcases that shelved the department's collection of published plays held the answer. She randomly grabbed a selection of works—Simon, Brecht, Wilder, whatever—and spread the volumes in front of the first chair on each side at the head of the table. Emma Jean silently congratulated herself on the new impediments to any student sitting in either position. *Distance.* Then, she spotted a copy of *The Black Hologram* and added it to the grouping of works on the table. *Nice touch.*

"Dr. Whitcomb?"

Emma Jean looked up to see a slender young woman with sandy, shoulder-length hair standing in the doorway.

"I'm sorry. I didn't mean to interrupt," the young woman said. "I'm Sue Albright. I'm in your class this semester."

"Nice to meet you, Ms. Albright."

"I know I'm early."

"That's not a problem," Emma Jean said. "Come in. Find a seat if you'd like."

The woman entered the seminar room clutching a spiral notebook and a copy of *The Black Hologram.*

"If you will excuse me, Ms. Albright," Emma Jean said, "I have a few things to tend to in my office before class."

Sue Albright simply smiled in Emma Jean's direction and watched as her new professor walked out the door.

Emma Jean made her way down a short hall and around the corner to her office. She picked up a class list of her seminar students, her lecture notes, and a pad of lined paper. Her watch showed seven minutes until class time. She dropped into the chair at her desk to wait. She would make her entrance as the last person into the classroom. Playwrights, she mused, should understand about entrances.

She also thought that somebody at the University of Iowa should understand something about plants. At the very least, somebody in charge should know that they grow. Peering out of her office window, all she could see was the overgrown bush that rubbed against the side of the building. The window offered a perfectly good view of the Iowa River if only someone would trim the damn bush. It seemed like the grounds crew had purposely let the thing become overgrown as if some liberal faculty counterparts had stigmatized pruning so that the shrubs might be spared the pain. Emma Jean couldn't figure out the university and its plants.

She reached into her purse and fished out the grocery list she had written at home. She wasn't much of a cook, but she at least tried to stay organized and keep food in the house for Shai. Emma Jean reviewed the list and decided that nothing more needed to be added. She slipped the piece of paper back into her purse and looked at her watch. The time for class to start had just passed. She could make her entrance.

"Good morning," she said as she strode into the seminar room and placed her notes on the recently imported lectern.

Nine students returned an unsynchronized "Good morning."

"My name is Emma Jean Whitcomb, and this is Playwriting 465. I presume by your presence here that you already know this."

She paused and looked at the faces around the table. *All white.*

"As a small group, we should get to know each other quickly. So, rather than personal introductions, I prefer to use the next few minutes to introduce you to this class and what you can expect."

Emma Jean scanned the cluster of white faces again. She had seen students of color on campus. The lack of a single black student in her class perturbed her. Greg Morris flashed through her mind. He had graduated from the University of Iowa. Couldn't he have had time during a break from *Mission Impossible* to father a son? Where was that kid? She remembered how old Greg Morris must be. *Okay, a grandson.*

"Most of you already know that this is my first year at the University of Iowa," Emma Jean continued. "Prior to coming here, I was on the faculty of Howard University in Washington, D.C. I do not hold a PhD, so you should not call me Dr. Whitcomb. While I do have a master's degree, you can probably understand by looking at me that I do not wish to be called master or hold that term in high regard."

Emma Jean studied the eyes of her students and could not detect a glimmer of recognition at the allusion she had made. Surely, they had noticed she was black. In all honesty, a person could hardly have darker skin than she did. They were all graduate students. Had they never heard of the term *master* in connection with the enslavement of black people? *Sue Albright. Sue Albright and the All-Whites.* The nickname slipped silently into Emma Jean's head and lodged there.

"Like the other professors for the playwriting classes here at the university, my work has been published and produced. That is my chief qualification to stand here before you today."

She paused, in part for effect, and in part because of a truth left as silent by the university as Emma Jean's unspoken nickname for her class. The university wanted her as much in the interests of racial diversity as it did in the interests of talent.

"An easy internet search will produce a list of the plays I have written. From that body of work, *The Black Hologram* is probably best known. The purpose of this class is to help you learn the craft of playwriting. You will not read plays. Given your presence in this department, you should have done enough of that as undergraduates. However, I will turn frequently to the works of contemporary and past playwrights for passages that illustrate those parts of the craft I am trying to teach you. If, for some reason, you do not feel adequately versed in the works of published playwrights, I am handing out a list of plays that I know will come up in my lectures over the semester. Use that list, if necessary, to enhance your knowledge. You will see *The Black Hologram* on this list. If you know nothing about *The Black Hologram*, find a copy."

Emma Jean observed Sue Albright sit up a little straighter at the mention of the play's title.

"I say this not because it is the greatest of the works on the list. It is, however, my best-known piece. I will tell you repeatedly this semester that when you write a play, you want to know your characters, your setting, your time period—know them all as well as possible. As a piece of practical advice, the same goes for knowing a professor when you take a course. So, what is there to know about Professor Whitcomb?"

Emma Jean took a step sideways from the lectern. As if pausing to think, she brought her hands up and lightly fluffed the hair at her temples while she arched her back and stretched to her full height. She had assumed this posture often—a pretense of gathering her thoughts, but also a chance to loom as a formidable presence over a classroom or a colleague. She knew, as well, that the gesture and the five gold bracelets that slid from her wrists over her forearms drew extra attention to the exceptional size of her breasts. In its own way, that also suited Emma Jean fine. So what if her body titillated a couple of white boys or intimidated skinny Sue Albright?

"First, because I know at least some of you are curious, I am six-foot two-inches tall."

She could see the next question forming in the eyes of the women around the table. She had no interest in telling them that she weighed 220 pounds.

"I was born and grew up in Milwaukee. I graduated from Northwestern University. I am black. I'm a playwright. I taught previously at Howard University. I have a thirteen-year-old daughter."

Emma Jean paused again, narrowed her eyes, tightened her jaw, and looked directly at the faces seated around the seminar table. She said nothing of Marcus Williams, nothing to indicate a divorced, devoted, or even dead husband to be the father of this thirteen-year-old girl.

"So, why do I tell you these things about myself?" Emma Jean didn't wait for an answer. "Because *you* want to write plays. To write plays, you must write life. To write life, you must write people. To write people, you must know people."

She eased forward and rested one arm on the side of the lectern.

"You must see life around you. You must see the people around you. But to write plays, the first person you must know is yourself. You may want to write a scene about a meal in an Italian restaurant, but first you must know the taste of your own mother's cooking. Even more than knowing the taste, you must know how it made you feel. The fictions of plays are the settings, the plots, the stories, but the truths of plays are the emotions. You must remember the terror of the first time you dreamed of your own death and know the place that makes you feel like you will live forever; recognize the people who have touched you with grace and bring back the feelings from those who have made you burn with anger. Emotion is as much a part of humanity as intellect. As a playwright, you will never reach the audience's intellect without touching its emotions."

Emma Jean looked down at her notes. She was well into her lecture and considerably past the first page of the sketchy outline that lay face up on the lectern. She didn't bother to turn the page.

"Earlier, I referred to the craft of playwriting, but writing plays is both an art and a craft. I hope you will find that there is much I can teach you about the craft. I cannot teach you the art. Frequently, I will use passages from great plays as a lens for examining the work you produce in this class. This process will put you in the presence of the art, but be assured no one can teach you the art. That you must find in the world around you and, even more, within yourself."

Emma Jean stepped behind the lectern and placed both hands on the solid oak top. Nine serious expressions stared in her direction.

"Some of you, possibly the majority, will look within yourselves and not find the art. You will not become playwrights. However, if you give fully of yourself to this class, as I expect of graduate students, you will write better, you will know yourself better, you will go on to success whether your ultimate career is playwright or piano tuner."

She saw the bodies of her students relax slightly as she closed her folder and stepped to the chair at the head of the table. Somehow, saying the words *piano tuner* always cut the tension of students having to hear that some of them would not become playwrights.

"Okay, time to think about next week's class," Emma Jean said as she settled into her chair. "I said you must write what you know. Let's find out a little of what that is. Who is from the farthest away?"

"Des Moines," a young man with red hair offered. The rest of the class chuckled with him at his answer.

"You, Mr. . . . ." Emma Jean started, pointing to another student.

"Dodson," he said. "Scott Dodson."

"Well, Mr. Dodson, let's see if we can do better."

Conducting a quick survey of the students around the table left the group to speculate whether Sarah Ettinger of Tulsa, Oklahoma, or Paul Shelton of Sandusky, Ohio, came from farthest away. Ohio or Oklahoma? Emma Jean wondered if it made any difference.

She continued to gather information from the group. Two students were only children. One had six siblings. Most had traveled to Europe during or immediately after their undergraduate years. One had worked in a donut shop during high school. Another spent the past summer working for a construction company that just finished a big nursing home. By the time she asked the group about their cars and discovered that Brian Hiller had his family's old Chevrolet Caprice station wagon, Emma Jean had enough information.

"All right," she said, "here goes for next week's class. I want each of you to write a scene or some portion of a play. The assignments are as follows. Mr. Kayser, you of the six siblings, I want your play to be about being an only child. Since you, Ms. Gillingham, are an only child, you can write about being one of seven children. Ms. Ettinger, I would like you to write a scene for a play set in a Chevrolet Caprice station wagon. Mr. Hiller, your play will be about working in a donut shop. I believe, Mr. Dodson, that Des Moines is a French name. You will write about being a French professor."

Emma Jean stopped to take stock of the assignments already made and the students remaining.

"Okay, that's five down and four to go. Ms. Albright, I would like you to write something set in Mr. Shelton's beloved Sandusky, and Mr. Shelton, you write about a trip from . . . uh . . . let's make it Des Moines again to Tulsa. From our nursing home builder, Mr. Pyvich, I want a play about celebrating a 98th birthday. And finally, Mr. Clark you seem to have chosen one of the spots nearest to me at the table. I've told everyone that I am six-foot-two. I would like you to write about a person who is three-foot-one."

Emma Jean paused again, taking in the apprehensive looks of the group. She was pleased that the effect of the assignment on Sue Albright and the All-Whites was not much different than it had been on her students at Howard. Emma Jean pondered whether the close-up view of the faces gathered around the table wasn't better than the Howard setup that put her several feet away behind a desk.

"I don't hear any questions from you, but I suspect you have some. First, this is not a party game that I thought of to get to know each other. This is a serious assignment that demands you give me the best writing you have in you. Consider that no different than any assignment you will receive from me. Second, I have made it a point that good playwrights write what they know. I have obviously assigned you what you don't know. How you resolve this is up to you, but you may not go to your fellow classmates for information. Specifically, Ms. Albright cannot ask Mr. Shelton about Sandusky and so on for each of you. Finally, I do not expect anything resembling a complete play from you. I just want a scene or scenes that serve as enough of a play to see where it's going. Now, you will hear me say repeatedly that every line in a play should move it forward. In that regard, every single line in a play makes some contribution to the sense of where it is going. I want you to heed that advice throughout the semester, but I strongly advise that you bring me more than a single line next week. See you then."

CHAPTER 9

The warm sunshine streaming over the outdoor tennis courts in late October should have been enough to make anybody happy. Emma Jean did not feel happy. *Aggravated* would have been a better word. She had suggested to Wes that they try out the university courts two blocks from her office. Lack of time was her excuse. She said that she needed to take Shai to the doctor for a physical, and time wouldn't allow her to drive out to the country club and back today. It was partly true. Shai did need a physical to play on the girls' basketball team, but the outdoor courts had a greater appeal to Emma Jean than the proximity to her office. Their hard, concrete surface promised to give even more speed to powerful her serve and ground strokes. In the end, it hadn't mattered. Wes beat her again—running around laughing like usual and returning just enough of her shots to win another close match.

"I'll be right there," she shouted to him as he sat at a picnic table outside the fenced-in courts.

"Okay," he answered.

Emma Jean stalled as she fiddled with the racket, sweatbands, and extra balls in her tennis bag. She tried to calm herself, but annoyance came easily in Iowa City. In some ways, the two-block walk from her office to the courts captured the essence of her feelings toward the new place where she had come to work and live. The gingko trees scattered along the route had dropped their pungent fruit. *White folks and their plants.* Who would grow trees with fruit that smelled like a baby's diaper with a full load?

As she stood and walked toward the gate on the opposite side of the court, her thoughts turned to Sue Albright and the All-Whites. The first written work from the aspiring playwrights had come back with Mr. Clark falling for Emma Jean's bait. His assignment to write about a three-feet one-inch-tall person produced a scene featuring a dwarf. It was what Emma Jean wanted. It was the kind of scene she always got at Howard—one that let her pose questions she wanted. "Why a dwarf?" "Why not write about a child?" "Weren't you ever a child, Mr. Clark?" They were the same questions she asked at Howard and led to the point she always tried to make with new students: "Write what you know, Mr. Clark."

She had accomplished her goal, but somehow the scenario aggravated her in Iowa City in a way that had never bothered her at Howard. She felt an agitation new to her as she concluded her class with the final statement she always made, "Write the feelings that are true to you." What feelings were true to this group? What passions burned so deeply within them that they could lose themselves in the creation of a play? When she was no older than her current students, she had spent seventeen months lost in *The Black Hologram*.

"Good game," Wes said as she approached the table.

"Yeah, you got me again."

"I had a couple pretty lucky shots today. You wanna sit?"

"Just for a minute," Emma Jean said. "I have to pick up Shai at the school."

"For the physical?"

"Yeah." Emma Jean frowned. "Basketball practice starts Monday."

"I hope she enjoys it."

"The physical?"

"Basketball," Wes answered quickly.

"I know. I know," she snapped. "Just a little joke."

"You don't sound very amused."

"Maybe that's because I'm not."

"I know you don't like it that much. Her playing basketball."

"You got that right."

"I think maybe you could just relax a little," Wes said.

Emma Jean felt her irritation build again. Shai was going to play basketball. What more did he want?

"That's all I think," he offered when she didn't respond.

"You seem to have a whole lot of thoughts about what Shai and I should do."

"Look, I know I said it before, but I really think it can be different here than what you're worried about."

"You *have* said that before. *Different?* Whadda you know about different? You don't know different. You don't know same." She jabbed with her index finger against the top of the weathered wooden table.

"I'm not trying to argue," Wes said.

Emma Jean drew a deep breath, but her anger continued to grow. "Nobody's arguin'," she said. "I'm tellin'. All I want for you is to listen. Hear me through and listen once."

"All right," he said.

"Shai's black. I'm black. I never know when something will be different or when be things will be the same. And, you sure don't know how bad the same can be." Words welled up from inside her, words she never expected to say to a white person. "Where I grew up, I don't know the first time I heard someone say the word *nigger*. In my neighborhood, you heard black people use that word. Somebody talkin' crude about somethin', like a guy gettin' mixed up with a buncha women. 'That nigga got it goin' on.' Or if there was somebody you knew was trouble. Somebody you should avoid. 'Man, that nigga crazy.' You know what I'm sayin'? People used *motherfucker*. People used *nigger*. I don't know the first time I heard the word."

Wes sat perfectly still, frozen by the fierce look in Emma Jean's eyes.

"I do know the first time I heard a white man say *nigger*. Mama had a friend, Mrs. Buford. She was older, but I think they were in a card club . . . Mama and Mrs. Buford. And then her husband died."

Emma Jean squeezed her hand into a tight fist.

"And Mama was gonna take her some food like we did in the neighborhood. So Mama made a cake—chocolate and chocolate frosting, but we didn't have one of those cake plates with the cover and all. Nobody did. When it was time to go to Mrs. Buford's, Mama had the cake on a regular plate and covered over real careful with tin foil, you know, real careful not to touch the frosting."

"Sure, aluminum foil."

"Just let me tell it," Emma Jean said. "We had to go across the street. It wasn't a big street, but it didn't have many stop signs. So it was the kinda street that cars drove through on. More cars than just from the neighborhood."

She drew an imaginary line on the table with her finger.

"I was maybe not quite four, but I was still pretty big. You know, for my age. Daddy didn't go. I don't think he was home, and Mama and Lu and me we crossed that street and a car came up real fast. We weren't in nobody's way. We were almost all the way across the street. No problem at all, but it was summer and the white man drivin' the car had his windows down. He yelled at us, 'Get your black nigger ass out of the street.' I don't know if I even knew the word *ass*, but he yelled. I remember him yellin', 'Get your black nigger ass out of the street.' I don't remember the car. It was just a plain car. No redneck pickup truck. Nothin' like that. The man was white, that's all I could tell you, but he yelled 'nigger.'"

Wes watched her fists clench tighter.

"Then Mama, she put her hand on my head and pulled me in close with one side of my face and one ear up tight against her dress. And she had her hand over my other ear like coverin' it up could keep me from hearin' what he already yelled or maybe the words were still flyin' around and she could keep me from hearin' 'em again. Mama had one hand over my ear, and Mrs. Buford's cake, the one she didn't want to mess up, that's in the other hand. So Lu heard the same thing, but Mama can't reach over to her. Mama and two little girls and Mrs. Buford's cake . . ."

Emma Jean saw Wes's lips quiver and his eyes rim with tears.

"Don't you fuckin' cry on me," she said. "It's my story. Mama didn't cry, and I ain't cryin'."

Wes drew a deep breath and held in his emotions.

"I'm goin'," Emma Jean said.

She rose without another word and walked the two blocks to her car without a single look back. Emma Jean unlocked the BMW and dropped into the seat. She closed the car door behind her. Then she cried.

CHAPTER 10

The tall black woman walking a few steps ahead of Wes in the hallway of Southeast Junior High School was easy to spot. Not only did her lustrous black hair rise above the cluster of people headed toward the school gymnasium, but she was also the only black person in sight. Wes realized that the last time he saw Emma Jean was also from the back as she walked away from the tennis courts. That was two weeks ago. He knew it could be just the result of his schedule. Still, as Emma Jean disappeared into the gym, he wondered if she had been avoiding him. He scanned the bleachers when he reached the gym door and located her taking a place by herself, eight rows up and near midcourt. He made his way toward her spot.

"Hi."

"Hello, Wes."

"Okay if I sit with you?"

"I don't suppose I can stop you."

"No, uh, if you don't want to . . ."

"Wes, I'm kidding." She took hold of his arm. "Shai said she asked you to come."

"I just thought . . ."

"That I was mad 'cause you're the one that got her thinkin' about this basketball thing."

"Yeah, kinda."

She gave a tug on his arm and he landed on the bleacher beside her. "If the Nike fits, wear it."

His only response came as a startled look of surprise at her strength when she pulled him down.

"What? You think I wouldn't know all about basketball shoes?" Emma Jean said. "Seemed like sometimes Marcus spent more time worrying about shoe contracts and endorsements than he did about the games, 'cept Nike would never touch him."

"I guess this is . . ." Wes started to say *different* but he caught himself. He had already said *different* to Emma Jean one too many times.

"Yeah?"

"You know, just junior high," he said.

"S'pose I need one of those junior high uniforms?" Emma Jean asked.

"Huh?"

"That the other moms are wearin'." She gestured toward several women seated together closer to the floor. "Button-down Oxford shirt, designer blue jeans, sweater. Course, you don't wear the sweater. Just drape it over your back, maybe tie the sleeves around your neck."

Wes smiled as he took in Emma Jean's cream-colored pants suit and floral silk blouse. "You look really nice."

"Why, thank you, Mr. Whitcomb."

"You are welcome, Ms. Whitcomb."

Emma Jean's thoughts flashed back to the nights she spent years ago at Marcus's home games, trying to compete in the fashion category with other, sleeker NBA wives. The simple hoop earrings, understated pants suit, and single gold bracelet she wore today would have fallen woefully short back then.

"You okay?" Wes asked.

"I think I'm goin' for the jeans next time," she answered.

A ripple of applause spread through the bleachers as the Southeast Junior High girls ran into the gym from the home locker room.

"Look, there's Shai." Wes pointed to his young neighbor wearing a maroon and gold basketball jersey with the number 36.

The other side of the gym broke into cheers as the opposing team ran onto the court, but Emma Jean and Wes kept their eyes on Shai. Her team broke into two lines for their layup drill with Shai at the front. She jogged toward the basket, retrieved the shot of a teammate, and threw the ball to the next girl at the head of the layup line. Shai trotted in the direction of their spot in the bleachers as she headed to the back of the line. Wes gave a discreet wave. Shai smiled up at her mom and neighbor. They watched as she received the ball for her first try at a layup. She fumbled the pass, throwing off the rhythm of the drill, and her shot grazed off the side of the hoop.

"I need somethin' to drink," Emma Jean said as she rose from her seat. "You want anything?"

"No, thanks."

"Be right back, then."

From the court, Shai could see her mother making her way down the bleachers. Shai tilted her head and sent a questioning look to Wes. He could only offer a smile and a small shrug of his shoulders.

Emma Jean followed a handmade sign for refreshments into a side hall. A portable Pepsi fountain machine stood next to a folding table covered with an array of candy bars and snack chips. A woman in her thirties drew cups of pop while two junior high girls waited on the customers at the makeshift concession stand. A Snickers bar suddenly looked good to Emma Jean. Maybe it was the gnawing in her stomach or maybe it was just because she liked Snickers. She smoothed her hand along her thigh to remind herself of why she didn't need one. As she stepped toward the table, a little boy with red hair to match the woman at the pop machine scurried across Emma Jean's path.

"Kevin, watch out," the pop lady scolded. "You'll trip somebody."

Emma Jean asked for a Diet Pepsi but barely noticed the girl who handed her the cup of pop. Emma Jean had her mind on Shai . . . and Marcus. She drifted over to a string of empty folding chairs placed along the wall and sat alone with her thoughts.

More than ten years had passed since the last time she attended a basketball game. It was one of Marcus's early season games. Shai was almost four. For three years, Emma Jean held onto the hope that Shai, their beautiful baby, would draw Marcus back as a true partner in their marriage. But as Shai grew, Marcus was just as untrue as ever. Emma Jean realized she didn't want to arrange any more babysitters so that she could spend an evening in a basketball arena full of overamped player introductions, six-dollar cups of beer, and players' wives made up like magazine models. She never went back to another game and never again hoped that she and Marcus could stay together. Now, Shai was playing the game that Emma Jean wanted to have out of her life.

She returned to the gym just as the two teams' starting players were taking their positions on the court. Ten white girls arranged themselves at the center circle for the jump.

Emma Jean slid down on the bleacher next to Wes. "Shai's not starting?"

"It's her first game—ever."

"But you said she's pretty good."

Wes smiled. "Relax, Mom."

The game started with the players quickly sorting themselves into roles. Half a dozen of the most aggressive girls dominated the action: dribbling the ball hard up the court, defending with arms flailing, and diving to the floor for loose balls. Though Wes was an avid basketball fan, he had never been to a junior high girls' game or ever seen a game with so much diving on the floor.

Emma Jean cataloged her own differences between the game in

progress and her memories of Marcus's teams. Most notably, the girls on the bench found reasons to clap their hands almost constantly, but nobody's hand patted anybody else on the butt. *Why did men do that?*

The game settled into a pattern with the biggest girls on each side scoring most of the points by simply shooting over a shorter opponent or rebounding a teammate's miss and putting it back in the basket. Shai didn't enter the game until the first quarter was almost over. Although nearly as tall as the girls leading the scoring, Shai fell into the role of the girls on the periphery of the action. Emma Jean, on the other hand, seemed intent on making up for Shai's lack of assertiveness right from the stands. As a savvy guard in the scarlet uniform of the other team stepped in to steal the ball, Emma Jean lurched to her right. Her movements couldn't turn Shai away from the defender, but they did give Wes a pretty good bump. When Shai grabbed a defensive rebound, applause and shouts came from her teammates, while Wes got a solid nudge in the ribs from Emma Jean's elbow. Shai played only a handful of minutes in the first two quarters, but Wes still reached halftime feeling pretty jostled around.

"She did okay," he said after the teams had gone to their locker rooms.

"Didn't play much."

"Like I said, it's her first game. You can't say the coach is pressuring her. You know, because of her dad."

"I think she's gotta play harder."

"But it still looks like she's having a good time. You can tell that the other kids like her."

"I'm just sayin' she's gotta go after that ball if she wants to play more. I've seen my share of basketball. Prob'ly more 'an my share."

"Okay, Mrs. Williams."

"I beg your pardon." Emma Jean's eyes narrowed. "You an' Marcus on a first-name basis? I didn't know you two ever met. You have dinner with him las' night or somethin'? He in town? I didn't hear nothin' about it."

Wes held up his hands. "Sorry. I didn't mean anything. I guess I crossed the line."

A sudden burst of cheers interrupted their exchange as Shai's team ran back onto the court. Emma Jean and Wes both chose to escape their conversation by standing up with the crowd and clapping. As they watched, Shai took her turn in the layup line with noticeably greater confidence after just one half of junior high basketball.

"You're right," Emma Jean said.

They settled back to their seats. Wes turned toward her, but Emma Jean kept a steady gaze on the court, leaving him no clue as to what he might have been right about. Crossing the line? Shai having fun? Something else altogether? He decided that rather than ask, keeping quiet offered the best chance to survive unscathed and enjoy the second half of basketball.

The game stayed close throughout the third quarter with Shai making another brief appearance. When she returned to the floor in the fourth quarter, her team held a four-point lead. Wes couldn't suppress a smile as Emma Jean tensed up beside him. He prepared for his next pummeling.

Shai took a position about ten feet to the side of the basket as her team prepared to throw the ball in play. Their quick little guard broke toward the sideline, but the girl throwing the ball in looped a surprise pass to Shai. She gathered in the ball, pivoted, and sent a high arcing shot toward the basket. The grace of Shai's movements in her shimmering maroon and gold uniform caught Wes's eye almost as much as the ball dropping cleanly through the hoop.

"She made it!" Emma Jean yelled as she spontaneously pulled Wes into a bear hug. "She made it."

Shai had already begun to run back to the defensive end of the court before Emma Jean realized she still had her arms around Wes.

"Nice shot, Sugar," she shouted, releasing her neighbor and primly straightening her pants suit.

Wes's face broadened into a big smile.

"It was a good shot," Emma Jean said.

"Very good."

Shai's basket was the first of three in a row made by her team, and they stayed comfortably ahead until the game ended with a 33-26 victory.

"I gotta tell Shai to meet me at the front entrance," Emma Jean said after the timekeeper's horn ended the game. "You know, to drive her home."

Several parents, probably on similar missions, had already begun to converge on the court. Emma Jean hesitated as if it would be rude to rush away.

"Go on," Wes said. "Better hurry. You wanna catch her before they head to the locker room. Tell 'er good game."

"Very good," Emma Jean said.

Wes watched her make her way through the crowd toward Shai—the only two black faces and the lone pants suit in a swirl of white skin, maroon and gold uniforms, pullover sweaters, and designer blue jeans.

CHAPTER 11

A chime sounded in Emma Jean and Shai's third-floor apartment at The Manor. Their guest was signaling for the elevator.

"That must be Wes, Sugar. Why don't you buzz him up."

"You're closer," Shai answered her mother.

"And you're the one who asked him," Emma Jean shot back.

"Not really. I just said we should 'cause he's who told us where to git a tree. You asked him."

"Still your idea."

"Honestly, would you two quit bickering," Lu Whitcomb said. "Shai, maybe you think your gramma should answer."

"I don't care if nobody answer," said an elderly woman sitting in an upholstered wing chair. "I ain't never met this man."

"All right, Gramma." Shai sighed and rose from her cross-legged position on the thick oriental carpet. She walked the length of the spacious living room past her grandmother, aunt, and mother before disappearing into the hall just as the chime rang again.

Emma Jean turned her eyes from the doorway to the Christmas tree in the far corner of her living room. The large Scotch pine stood bare except for five strings of lights. When Emma Jean and Shai lived in Washington, the afternoon they decorated the tree became a little family tradition all their own. Emma Jean would buy fancy cookies from her favorite pastry shop near DuPont Circle, and two Sundays before Christmas, the tree went up.

This year, they had a bigger family circle. Iowa City had been Lu's home for eighteen years. Two years ago, their mother turned eighty and moved to Iowa City to be close to at least one of her daughters. With Emma Jean and Shai's arrival, the whole family was in one town. Emma Jean had wanted trimming the Christmas tree to remain within the family, but Shai wouldn't give up on inviting Wes.

Shai was probably right. Emma Jean realized just how much she had relied on Wes to get to know the town. Where can I get my oil changed? Ask Wes. How long does it take to get to the airport? Call Wes. Where can we buy a Christmas tree? Wes will know. Plus, he had already been to all six of Shai's basketball games, and he did live right next door in the carriage house. Shai reemerged from the hall with Wes a step behind just as the antique clock on the mahogany side table rang two o'clock.

"You're right on time," Emma Jean said to him.

"Not a very long trip."

"Wes, I'd like you to meet my sister Lu Ann. Lu, this is Wes Whitcomb. He owns City Streets."

Lu stood up from the small loveseat where she was sitting.

"Nice to meet you," he said.

"The pleasure is mine. Doubly so since I've had the pleasure of eating at City Streets more than once. Your food is terrific."

"Thanks."

"And this is my mother, Anna Whitcomb," Emma Jean said as she ushered Wes across the room to her mother's chair.

"Nice to meet you, Mrs. Whitcomb."

"Well, it's nice that yer here. I thought maybe we jes' had an ol' hen party."

Wes chuckled at the old woman's joke.

"Course, yuh might wanna leave again, nows yuh know yer outnumbered," Mrs. Whitcomb added.

"One guy and four beautiful women. I don't mind those odds."

"I'm sorry my friend Sylvia couldn't make it five to one," Lu said.

"I wouldn't say nothin' 'bout no odds. Shai's too young. I'm too old. And Lu ain't gonna do yuh no good. Sylvia neither if'n she was here."

"Mama!" Lu exclaimed.

"That pretty much leaves yuh with the mean one."

"Mama!" Emma Jean exclaimed.

"I guess she ain't mean," Mrs. Whitcomb amended. "Jes' mad half the time."

The last comment took Wes up short. He was used to some pretty lively—even risqué—comments from Suzie down at the Red Door, but what could he say to Mrs. Whitcomb? Emma Jean was mad a lot.

Mrs. Whitcomb gave a wave of her hand. "Here, come sit down on this couch where's I can talk to yuh. I already heard everything them other ones got to say."

Wes sent a questioning look toward Emma Jean.

She shrugged. "Go ahead. I've gotta get the Christmas ornaments."

"Want help?" Lu asked.

"Sure."

"What can I do, Mama?" Shai asked.

"Why don't you come with us and put some cookies on a plate."

Wes had settled into the corner of the couch nearest to the chair where Mrs. Whitcomb sat. He tucked a small paper bag he was carrying up against the skirt of the heavily brocaded sofa. He thought he saw Emma Jean shake her head as she, Lu, and Shai left the room.

Once in the hall, Emma Jean leaned over to Shai. "I've got two tins of special butter cookies on the kitchen table. Get our Christmas plates out of the hutch in the dining room and arrange the cookies real nice."

"You trust her in there with him?" Lu asked as Emma Jean straightened up.

"Mama's gonna say what Mama's gonna say," she answered. "If we go get the ornaments, least we don't have to hear it all."

"True."

"That why Sylvia's not here?" Emma Jean asked. "Mama sayin' stuff about not likin' men?"

"Where's the ornaments?"

"In the spare bedroom. No answer?"

"Huh?"

"I asked you about Sylvia," Emma Jean said.

Lu didn't respond as the two women walked down a long, formal hall completely furnished with antiques.

"So?" Emma Jean prodded as they entered the guest room.

"Look, I'm pretty sure Syl is more comfortable with the things Mama says about lesbians than the way you feel about white people."

"Sylvia's welcome here."

"And she's still white," Lu said. "Welcome and comfortable are two different things. Anyway, it's not like she's never been here."

"Wes is white. Case you didn't notice."

"And you don't go to bed with him."

"So maybe I got more sense than you," Emma Jean snapped.

"You know, Mama was right. You are the mean one."

"Maybe Mama also knows you're a pain in the ass."

"I wouldn't think you'd notice," Lu said, "not with that big bubble-butt of yours."

"Yeah, and you still got legs like a giraffe."

"A pretty giraffe?" Lu asked.

"Yes, a pretty giraffe," Emma Jean said. "Here, pretty giraffe, reach that box down off the top shelf."

While Lu and Emma Jean worked in the bedroom closest, Wes was on his own with Mrs. Whitcomb in the living room.

"I'm surprised them two let me alone with you," she said to him. "I know how them girls think jes' as good as they do. Prob'ly think you ain't safe."

"I'm a pretty fast runner."

"Who says yer worth chasin'?"

"I suppose you got a point."

"That runnin', that how yuh beat Emma Jean at tennis?"

"She told you about that?"

"Jes' once. She was visitin' an' I ask where she been. She says tennis, an' I ask how she done."

"We play a couple times a month."

"You beat her most the time?"

"Yeah."

"Most the time or all the time?"

"So far, all the time."

Mrs. Whitcomb let loose a gravely laugh. "I bet she don't like that."

"Probably not."

"Don't be telling me that prob'ly stuff. I know my daughter," Mrs. Whitcomb said. "I thought she s'posed to be good. All them tennis lessons."

"She is good."

"But you still beat her, an' she's bigger'n you. You some kinda star?"

Wes laughed this time. "No."

"Then how come you beat her every time."

"She hits harder. I run faster," Wes said. "That's mostly it."

"You full of prob'lys and mostlys."

"Maybe, sometimes, Emma Jean's too aggressive. She hits hard every time. I aim it around a little more."

"She'da never got nowhere in life 'cept by doin' everything hard."

103

"A little more strategy and she'd beat me," Wes said.

"How many black friends you got?" Mrs. Whitcomb asked abruptly.

"Uh." Wes hesitated. "Two, I guess."

"Countin' Emma Jean and Shai or not countin'?"

"They're the two."

"Thought so." Mrs. Whitcomb smiled.

"So how many white friends do you have?"

"Emma Jean tell you I live at the old folks home, Crestview?" Mrs. Whitcomb asked. "I got lotsa friends and ain't but one other black face in that whole mess."

"Okay, how many white friends in Milwaukee?" Wes teased.

"Z—ro!" Mrs. Whitcomb answered. "Didn't need none."

"So, I guess I'm ahead. Two beats zero."

"Who beats what?" Emma Jean had entered the room with a big box marked X-mas in her arms.

"We was jes' doin' our numbers." Mrs. Whitcomb laughed loudly. "Two beats zero. I like this here boy. He's a smart one."

Emma Jean and Lu both gave their mother perplexed looks. And both decided better than to ask anything more. They carried their boxes across the room and put them down next to the tree.

"Look at them two," Mrs. Whitcomb said. "Don't have to worry none 'bout reachin' them tall branches in this house. They was big even as babies. I should still be sore, poppin' them two out."

"Mama, I don't think Wes cares anything about that," Emma Jean said.

"No, he prob'ly cares more 'bout them cookies my grandbaby got on that plate," Mrs. Whitcomb said as Shai returned from the kitchen.

"That looks good, Sugar," Emma Jean said. "Come set those down on the end table where your gramma can reach 'em—even if she don't deserve it."

Shai delivered the cookies as her mother asked.

"Come help us put the ornaments on," Emma Jean said to Wes.

"You go ahead," he answered. "You've probably all got favorite ones you like to hang."

"That's all right," Emma Jean persisted. "Come on and join us."

"No, I'll sit awhile and keep your mom company."

Mrs. Whitcomb smiled again. "See, he wants to keep me company. You ain't the only pebble on the beach."

Wes looked over at the feisty old woman seated to his right. Her eyes showed deep laugh lines, but the rest of her face was remarkably unwrinkled for a woman in her eighties. With only streaks of gray in her thick black hair, she easily could have passed for a woman ten or even fifteen years younger. Still, her loose-fitting dress couldn't hide an ample build closer to Emma Jean than Lu. It was the rich brown tone of her skin that linked her to Lu. Emma Jean's deep, ebony black skin matched neither her mother nor sister.

"They's good daughters," Mrs. Whitcomb leaned over and whispered. "Didn't have 'em 'til late. Didn't meet their daddy 'til I was thirty-eight."

Wes nodded and listened intently.

"We went and had Louisa Ann right away. An' I said to myself, 'That's enough.' Then Emma Jean, she come along when I'm forty-five. Forty-five! She an oopsie, sure enough."

"But you ended up with a granddaughter," Wes said softly.

"I did fo' sure. A beautiful grandbaby. An' now we all in Ioway. I tell people I was born in Ioway, but I wasn't. You ever hear of Buxton?"

"Nope."

"Well, you should. A little bitty coal minin' town—all black. Black folks in Buxton an' white folks in the next town down. I was born in Milwaukee, but I was made right there in Buxton, Ioway."

"Your family moved?"

"My daddy died. When the mines closed, buncha them Buxton

folks goes to Des Moines and some others to Milwaukee. My daddy, he stayed. Tearin' down things for the company. Had a big ol' loada timbers fall offa wagon. Kilt' him right there."

"I'm sorry."

"Ain't no sense you bein' sorry. That was a long time 'fore you was born. 'Fore I was born, too. My mama always said it kilt' him right away, he didn't suffer. But she moved to Milwaukee, right with them Buxton folks. They always helped. Sit me when my mama was workin'. Didn't let us go hungry. Them Buxton folks was my heart."

Mrs. Whitcomb's voice had grown louder as she talked.

"Mama, you tellin' Buxton stories again?" Emma Jean asked.

"I heard you, Mama," Lu said. "Them Buxton folks was my heart."

"An' it's true," Mrs. Whitcomb answered.

"You told Wes enough stories," Emma Jean said. "You send him over here 'cuz all we got left are the silver balls. He ain't gettin' no cookies if he don't help out a little."

"You mean he isn't getting any cookies?" Shai teased.

"Oh shush, it's Christmas."

"I don't think that's an excuse," Shai said.

"Wes, get over here before Shai scolds me again."

He joined the trio at the tree, and Emma Jean handed him a small styrofoam ball wrapped in shimmering silver satin.

"We got a couple dozen of these," Emma Jean said.

Shai hung one of the ornaments on a branch. "We spread 'em out real even on the whole tree."

Wes picked out a spot, but Shai took hold of his hand.

"Move it up a little," she said.

"Okay."

She guided his hand with the silver ball to a higher branch. "See how the light shines on it there."

"That is nicer," Wes said.

"You gettin' bossy like your mama," Mrs. Whitcomb said from her chair.

"Gramma, I was just helpin'," Shai said. "'Sides, I know who taught Mama to be bossy."

"Well now, ain't you a sassy one." Mrs. Whitcomb waved a cookie with mock indignity.

"Here's a spot," Emma Jean said, hanging a ball high on the tree.

Four pairs of hands—three black, one white—carefully found places for the remaining shiny decorations.

"Last one," Lu said, filling a niche next to a fuzzy knitted snowflake.

"That does look nice," Emma Jean said. "Maybe our best tree ever."

Wes moved back to the sofa and picked up the small paper bag he had left on the floor. "Here's somethin' to put underneath." He reached into the bag and handed Emma Jean two rectangular packages wrapped in red and green Santa Claus paper.

"What's this?" she asked.

"One for you and one for Shai. For under the tree."

"You didn't need to," Emma Jean said.

"I know."

"Still . . ."

"Oh quit yer fussin'," Mrs. Whitcomb interrupted. "Why don't you jes' open 'em'?"

"Mama, Wes said they're for under the tree," Emma Jean said.

"How's I gonna see what's in 'em under the tree?"

"You'll be here at Christmas."

"Well, yer big sister won't. She got some basketball someplace. Where you goin'?"

"San Diego."

"See, San Diego," Mrs. Whitcomb said. "Not that it makes no sense. Gone at Christmas."

"It's a *holiday* tournament, Mama," Lu said.

"Still ain't gonna be here to see 'em." Mrs. Whitcomb pointed to the packages. "Hand that one over to Shai."

Emma Jean followed her mother's orders.

"Now shake it."

Shai followed her grandmother's orders.

"Hear anything?" Mrs. Whitcomb asked.

"Nope," Shai answered.

"I say that settles it right there. Didn't find nothin' out by shakin'. Not even a little bitty clue. Jes' as well open 'em."

"Mama, you're impossible," Emma Jean said.

"I'm old. S'posed to be impossible. Why don't you ask Wes? I ain't heard him complainin'."

Emma Jean turned to Wes with an imploring look.

"It's okay with me. They're not much."

"See," Mrs. Whitcomb said.

Emma Jean did see. She saw that she didn't get the answer she wanted from Wes. She also saw that she was going to lose another argument with her mother.

"Okay," Emma Jean said. "Come on, Shai. You go first."

Everyone found a place to sit, and Shai carefully began to open her package. She slid a slender finger under the paper and popped loose the tape. She pulled back the Christmas wrapping to reveal a book bound with a fabric print of swirling orange and brown autumn leaves.

"It's a blank book," Wes said. "To write in. If you want."

Lu and Emma Jean's eyes met as Shai thanked Wes. The thoughts of each sister flashed back to a gift that passed between them years ago. Emma Jean saw the question forming in Lu's eyes and discreetly shook her head no. Emma Jean was sure she had never mentioned to Wes the journal Lu had given her as a child.

"Your turn, Mama," Shai said.

Emma Jean distractedly tore the paper from her package. She

opened the lid on a white gift box, and her eyes fell on the present inside. She pulled out a silk scarf in variegated tones of cream and dusty rose.

"It's beautiful," Emma Jean murmured. "I've got a blouse it'll go with perfectly."

"I thought so," Wes said.

Emma Jean silently looked over at Wes, her tennis foe and Shai's basketball fan. She had switched from her pants suit and silk blouse to an Oxford shirt and blue jeans after Shai's first game, but Wes had remembered.

"Your presents are so nice," Emma Jean said.

"Not as nice as the afternoon," Wes said.

"If you two gonna git all mushy, I wish I'da kept my mouth shut. Ain't nobody gonna feed an ol' woman some cookies?"

"Oh Mama, they're right next to you." Lu pointed.

"Mama's right." Emma Jean stood from her chair. "I'll make some tea."

"Sounds good," Wes said, settling back comfortably in the company of three generations of Whitcombs.

CHAPTER 12

The black BMW accelerated smoothly as Emma Jean started up the I-380 on-ramp in downtown Cedar Rapids. A stinging, twenty-five-point loss by Shai's basketball team made Emma Jean's foot a little heavier on the gas pedal. The force of the engine as the car accelerated to highway speed pushed Wes back into the leather passenger seat. Emma Jean shifted through the gears and darted onto the highway as if maneuvering the crowded beltway around Washington rather than entering the sparse traffic of Cedar Rapids during an early evening in January.

"Gonna put this town behind you in a hurry?" Wes asked as the sleek sedan cut through a light skiff of snow.

"Prob'ly should after a whuppin' like that."

"I still don't think it was very good sportsmanship." He repeated the thought he had already expressed three times since they left the junior high gym. He didn't know a lot about girls' basketball, but apparently Cedar Rapids was developing a powerhouse program with summer leagues, booster clubs, and aggressive coaching all the way down to the elementary school. The results already showed with the junior high girls. They had completely overwhelmed Shai's team. Shai had played badly, though no worse than her teammates.

"Our coach didn't help much," Emma Jean said. "He shoulda pressed 'em back."

The full-court press used by Cedar Rapids had accounted for much of the lopsided score.

"That other coach could have taken his starters out way earlier," Wes said.

"And our coach coulda pressed."

"Listen to us. Shai said the kids get to stop at Dairy Queen on the way home. They'll forget the game and be eating sundaes while we're still talking about coaches."

"So quit talkin' about 'em," Emma Jean teased.

"Well, that would be easier if you would've taken *me* to Dairy Queen."

"Poor Wes."

A black and white highway sign marked the beginning of the sixty-five-mile-an- hour speed limit on the outskirts of town. Convenience stores and fast food restaurants gave way to low metal buildings housing service companies and self-storage units. Past the last lighted sign on the building for Mid-State Welders, the highway carried Emma Jean and Wes into the blackness of empty cornfields on both sides.

"Might get a little slick," he said.

"I don't think there's that much snow," Emma Jean said as she followed the red and yellow running lights of two semitrailer trucks in the distance.

Wes shifted uneasily in his seat as she closed on the trucks.

"It'll be good if—shit!" The car had started to fish tail. Emma Jean turned the steering wheel left into the direction of the skid, but the back of the car continued to twist as it slid into the passing lane. Her foot tapped the brake as she gave the wheel more pressure to the left. In an instant, the car overcompensated. "Wes!"

"Hold on."

The car gave a violent jerk and spun in a complete circle. Emma Jean jammed on the brakes as it continued across the passing lane and into the median, kicking up loose gravel and weeds before coming to a stop facing north in the dead grass beside the southbound lanes.

"My God," Emma Jean said, trying to refill her lungs with air as she let herself breathe again.

"Better put on your blinkers," was all Wes could say in return.

"Yeah, I should." Her voice was shaky.

Wes could barely make out her face in the darkened car. "At least you've got good brakes. It could've been worse if they'd locked."

"I don't know what happened. It's hardly snowing."

"It's the road," he said. "Built up like this, it's open to all the wind."

"That wasn't no wind blowin' us off the road."

"No, but there's no protection. The road's up higher than everything else. Any traffic melts the snow and the wind freezes it just like that." Wes snapped his fingers.

"With this amount of snow?"

"It's a prairie thing. Sometimes, a little bit of snow is the worst. They call it black ice." Wes hesitated. "They don't mean anything by it. Just that you can't see it."

"I don't care what they call it. Black ice, white ice. They can call it fuckin' mulatto ice if they want to."

The tension in Emma Jean's voice kept Wes from laughing at the thought of mulatto ice.

"Now what?" she asked.

"You want me to drive?"

"Would you?"

"Sure."

They opened their doors and crossed by each other in front of the car. Wes scuffed the bottom of his shoe on the asphalt to check the slipperiness. Emma Jean picked a clump of old weeds off the front bumper.

He got in and moved the seat up a little closer to the steering wheel. "It doesn't seem too bad. I'll just take it real easy."

"I appreciate this."

Wes feathered the gas and coaxed the car out of the grass. He turned back in the right direction on the almost empty highway and eased up to thirty-five miles an hour. A lone set of headlights in the rearview mirror gradually closed on them from behind.

Suddenly, Emma Jean stiffened in her seat. "What about Shai?"

"I'm sure they're still eating," Wes said.

"But what about after? This crap is treacherous."

"The salt trucks are probably already headed out. It's not that cold. Some salt'll take care of it pretty fast."

"Are you sure? Maybe we should go back."

"Emma Jean, we don't even know where she is. Her bus driver will know what he's doing. Anyway, the salt will work. She's gonna be fine."

"I don't like this."

"They're not gonna do anything dangerous with those kids." He reached over and squeezed her hand before resuming his cautious ten-and-two grip on the steering wheel. "Why don't you put some music in."

"Okay."

She opened the console between them and slipped a Wynton Marsalis CD into the player. She reached for the lever on the side of seat and tilted it back as the music flowed through her. Even though she trusted Wes, she wanted the ride to be over. She wanted to hear Shai's voice on the telephone asking to be picked at the school.

"Shai's gonna be fine," Wes said without Emma Jean uttering a word.

She closed her eyes and wondered how he got to be so sweet.

It seemed like that was the way with these skinny Iowans. Her thoughts flashed to Sue Albright and the short play she wrote for her final project. In the story, a forgetful young woman kept losing things that ended helping the lives of other people: a tax accountant's business card led a woman who had been adopted as a child to her birth mother; a teenage boy used two quarters lost by the young woman to call his girlfriend and make up after a fight; a bag of kitty litter helped an old man who had his car stuck in a snowdrift. The play was sweet and lyrical and, in Emma Jean's mind, fifty years past its time. Now, it felt like Wes could have starred in the play like some good guy in an old movie. They rode on with the hum of tires and the soothing sound of jazz infusing the air. Eventually, she felt the car slow.

"Just about home," he said as he slowed further for the off-ramp.

"I'm ready."

It only took five minutes to reach The Manor and park in the garage.

"The streets in town aren't slick at all," he said. "You want me to wait with you 'til Shai calls?"

"I'd like that."

"Good."

They walked to the elevator. As it started toward the third floor, Wes gave the same faint smile Shai always did. Emma Jean wondered if there was a little bit of her daughter in him, or vice versa.

"You want some coffee?" she asked as the elevator door opened.

"That would be good."

He followed her into the spacious kitchen with its new cabinets and built-in ceramic top range. The large, butcher-block work table in the center of the room looked barely used.

She filled a red tea kettle and placed it on the stove. "All I have is instant."

"That's okay."

He watched as she opened a cabinet. A small clutch of metal spice boxes held pepper, cinnamon, oregano, and a handful of other herbs. A box of chocolate pudding, one of raisins, and a container of oatmeal shared a shelf with a can of pineapple, two cans of green beans, and a tin of tuna. Only a box of rice and a bag of noodles occupied the top shelf. He marveled at a kitchen cabinet so sparsely filled that he could almost inventory its contents with a single glance.

"Regular or decaf?" she asked.

Wes spotted a red and white box with packets of instant cocoa. "How about some of that hot chocolate?"

Just like Shai, Emma Jean thought. "Comin' right up."

She busied herself getting out two mugs and teaspoons—putting a spoonful of decaf in one mug, emptying the contents of a hot chocolate packet in the other.

"The stove takes a little while," she said. "I hope Shai calls soon."

"I wouldn't worry. They were already working on the roads before we got home. The last few miles weren't bad at all."

The uneasy silence of a worried mother hung in the air until the teakettle began to whistle. Emma Jean moved back to the stove and poured steaming hot water into the mugs. They each took one and sat at the round oak table in the breakfast nook. Wes started to take a sip, but she touched his arm.

"Not yet," she said. "You don't want to burn your tongue."

Wes cupped his hands around the warm mug. "Yes, ma'am."

"Are you makin' fun of me, Wesley Whitcomb? Mama had a friend once who burned her esophagus drinkin' hot coffee. Wasn't *nothin'* funny about that, so you just listen up."

"You always do what your Mama told you to?"

Emma Jean reached over and playfully tugged at his earlobe. "Had to, or she'd take a holda me like this and tell me what for."

"Guess I better mind. I'll blow on it."

"Well, all right then."

Wes lifted his mug and elaborately blew across the hot chocolate before taking a sip. "Tastes good."

Emma Jean didn't touch her coffee.

"Still nervous about Shai aren't you?" he said. "I think she's having a lot of fun on the team."

"I know." Emma Jean just stared into the cup.

"Actually, I was thinking it would be fun sometime if we were a team."

"What?"

"A team," he said.

"Sorry, this is the one non-basketball-playing member of the Whitcombs . . . well, me and Mama."

"I wasn't thinking about basketball. Tennis. Wouldn't it be fun to play mixed doubles? Maybe find somebody to play against at your club. We could be a team."

"You gettin' tired of beatin' me?"

"You've won a couple."

Emma Jean was quiet.

"I'm sorry," Wes said. "I didn't mean to invite myself. It's just that we always play against each other."

"No," she said, "I like the idea. I just don't know if I can find somebody for us to play. I mean, I should be able to. It's a whole club. I like mixed doubles."

"That would be—"

Emma Jean straightened up immediately at the sound of her phone ringing.

"Hello . . . Hi, Sugar . . . You made it . . . It was slick for us . . . Yeah, I'll be right there. I'll tell you then."

"You want me to go with you?" Wes asked.

"You said the streets are fine?"

"Yeah."

"You don't have to bother," she said. "I can manage."

They set their coffee mugs in the sink, took their coats, and rode the elevator to the first floor.

Emma Jean paused at the front door. "I'll see what I can do about that tennis."

CHAPTER 13

"Damn it!"

"What's going on in there?" Suzie peeked her head in the kitchen door of the Red Door Café and saw Wes kneeling on the floor.

"I was mixing the mayonnaise cake and dropped the damn bowl."

"On the floor?"

"That's what's down here," he said.

"Boy, you did make a mess. Good thing there's nobody out front. No customers to hear you swearin' at the top of your lungs."

"I said *damn*."

"Twice."

"Okay, twice," he said. "And what's good about not having any customers?"

Suzie tapped her watch. "We can close on time. It's ten minutes to two."

"Always got an answer."

"And I know you appreciate it. So, d'you break anything?"

Wes looked up from one knee. "It's a stainless steel bowl, Suzie."

"Okay, no broken glass, no bits of china." She touched her hand to his shoulder. "We could just scrape it back into the bowl and put it in the fridge overnight. I can run a special tomorrow."

"Floor pudding," they said in unison.

"Or," Suzie said, "I could clean it up while you go off and play your tennis."

"Not playing today."

"Why not? I thought you two were on a winning streak?"

"Emma Jean's in Chicago. She's speaking at a conference."

"So, no salt-and-pepper doubles today."

"Mixed doubles, okay? Mixed doubles."

"Well, aren't we touchy, Mr. My-Girlfriend-Stood-Me-Up."

"Friend, Suzie. Just friends, and she didn't stand me up. I knew she was going."

"Here." She gave him a handful of paper towels and retrieved the large, gray, plastic garbage can that stood at the end of the work counter.

"Thanks."

"Just friends, huh?"

"That's what I said."

Suzie moved over to the sink to wash her hands. "Wes, who knows you better than me? You work here almost every day. Then it's City Streets almost every night. Once in a while on a Sunday you drive up to Princeton to visit your folks. In between that, you play tennis with *Emma Jean*. You help *Emma Jean* move a piece of furniture over to her office. You and *Emma Jean* go to Miss Shai's basketball games."

"Basketball's over," he said.

She went back to the counter. "You get my point, Mr. Basketball's-Over."

"There's no point to get." He reached under the sink for a bucket and sponge.

"That's why her book's in your car?"

"So now you're searching my car?"

"For God's sake, Wes, you park right out back every day. The book's on the front seat with Emma Jean Whitcomb in big letters."

"It's a play, not a book."

"Yeah, I know," she said, "*The Black Hologram*."

He filled the bucket with water while she instinctively reached for another mixing bowl. As he rinsed the floor, Suzie measured out cocoa, flour, sugar, and baking soda and sifted them together.

"So, the play? Is it as bad as they say?" She stirred in water and mayonnaise.

"It's good—the story is," he said. "But it's raw. It shakes you up."

"So, what is the story?"

"It's about a black woman. She's an opera singer. And she's a . . . I don't know, like a phenom." Wes wiped the floor with his sponge.

"A diva?"

"I suppose, but she's young. Real young and she's made it big in this major opera company."

"Okay."

"Anyway, she and this black radical, they become lovers. That's where the language and the story get pretty rough. You know, it's pretty graphic."

"Sex?"

"Some, but more violence, or actually talking about violence. See the guy who's the radical goes around the country giving speeches about what if blacks started doing to whites what had been done to them. It's the way he talks, that's the most graphic part—lynchings, beatings, rapes. It's pretty hard to take."

"And how does an opera singer figure in?" Suzie buttered and floured two cake pans.

"Well, like I said, she's a star in a major opera, so they've got lots of big corporate sponsors and rich white donors. The opera wants her to dump her lover."

"I'm thinking she doesn't."

"No, and that's how the play ends. The black woman tells the opera company where to go. That's pretty intense, too."

"But her writing all this violence stuff, that doesn't bother you?"

"The end of the story is more about prejudice today than violence, you know, past or present."

"That's not what I asked you." She poured the batter into the pans.

"I don't think I'd really want to see the play. I also wonder if she's let Shai see it. Or even read it."

"You can count me out for sure."

He stood. "Still, she had to have a lot of courage to write it. Getting so deep into something that terrible, and while you're writing you know it's all true."

"So, we're back to where I started. I hear more than 'just friends' in there."

"Suzie, think about it. She's famous, she's rich, and I don't think she's looking for a white guy." He walked to the floor sink in the corner and emptied the bucket of dirty water.

"Well, Mr. White-Guy, maybe it wouldn't be so bad if you found out for sure. You're not seeing anybody. I think even the art department has pretty much given up on you."

"Very funny."

"Who's kidding? For a while there, I thought the girls in art just passed you along each year like one of their studios. Maybe you're gettin' a little old for 'em."

He came back to the counter. "You know, if you cooked half as well as you exaggerate, I'd be a rich man."

"Is that so? How many of those art students *did* you go out with?"

"Three."

"Four," Suzie said.

"Three. Julie and Sarah and then Allison just a couple of times one year."

"Plus, that redhead. The one who wore the pink pedal pushers."

"Kendra. We had coffee once, and they weren't pedal pushers. Pedal pushers are from when you were a kid."

"Well, they were pink and went halfway up her calves, and they sure didn't do anything for her. A redhead in pink!"

"Showed off her behind," Wes said.

"Which wasn't anything to write home about, either."

"It was one date, if you can call it that."

"One date, ten dates," Suzie said. "You're still gettin' a little old to be passed around between art students."

"For chrissakes, they were grad students!"

"All I know is, when Ruth went to college, I told her she couldn't be an art major. I figured you'd end up dating her."

"Ruth is nineteen years old."

"That's my point."

"All right. All right."

"Listen, Mr. All-Right-All-Right, I'm serious. You like the mom. You like the daughter. You know what I would have given for someone like that when I was raising Ruth all by myself?"

"Okay then, I'll be serious. We have fun together. I like Shai, too. But I've read the play. You read it and you'll know what I mean about her not looking for a white guy."

"And what are you lookin' for?"

"I'm looking for this cake to get baked."

"Want to lick the bowl?" Suzie asked as she ran water over the spoon. "It's chocolate."

"Suzie!"

"What?"

"You know what."

"Okay, I'll stop talkin' so much if you'll start thinkin' a little."

CHAPTER 14

"Red Door?" Wes asked Emma Jean as he leaned against the chain-link fence around the tennis courts.

On tennis days, Wes always made sure to have an extra pitcher of iced tea left in the refrigerator at the restaurant. An hour or so after Suzie closed, he and Emma Jean would arrive at the front door. Wes would unlock, and for a few minutes, the salt-and-pepper doubles team would drink tea, scrounge for leftover desserts, and relive their just-completed tennis match. Today, they had another victory to celebrate.

"Man, those two had us goin' for a while," Emma Jean said. "I could almost use a beer."

At the end of tennis, her face and arms always glistened with sweat, but Wes noticed that both he and Emma Jean were perspiring a little harder today.

"A beer does sound good," he said. "You wanna stop somewhere?"

"I got some at home," she answered, "if you don't mind Coors."

Coors, in fact, was not a favorite with Wes, but he answered, "Suits me fine."

"Prob'ly less calories than a piece of your cake or pie." Emma Jean smiled as she patted her unquestionably round hips.

"I'll have to get you to drink two beers. I don't want you going all virtuous on me."

"Skinny people are so wicked," she said as they headed toward their cars.

"Restaurant owners just don't like to hear the word *calories*," he said.

He followed Emma Jean's familiar BMW along the route back to The Manor. The translucent green of leaves in May filled the tree-lined streets of Iowa City. He thought back over the winter months not that far past. He didn't even know that Emma Jean drank beer. Twice, she and Shai had been his guests for dinner at City Streets. Both times Emma Jean demurely sipped a glass of wine.

A changing traffic light on the way back home separated their cars. By the time Wes arrived, Emma Jean stood waiting for him by the mailboxes in the entry hall.

"You're popular," he said looking at the stack of mail in her hand.

"Mostly bills."

"You must pay them."

"That's pretty much the deal with bills," she said as they started walking to the elevator.

"Well then, I'd still say you're popular—at least with the people you owe money." He waited to let Emma Jean enter first when the elevator door slid open.

"As a comedian, I'd say you make a better restaurant owner," she said.

They reached the top floor and walked to her kitchen.

"Want a glass?" she asked.

"Nah, beer tastes better out of a can."

"You're talkin' like one of the brothers back home." She pushed in the tab on the aluminum can which made the familiar kpsh sound.

"'Course, I should be handin' you a malt liquor."

"Never tried it."

"So you're not 'Wes from the 'hood,'" she said. "Let's go sit down."

He followed her into the living room and they each took one of the armchairs on either side of an antique end table. Wes had been in Emma Jean's apartment often enough to feel comfortable, but the beauty of the furnishings impressed him every time. "You know, when I met you, I wouldn't have thought you were an antique person."

"Don't like antiques?" she said.

"No, they're okay. My parents buy antiques. I just didn't figure that . . ."

"Because I'm black?"

"Not exactly."

"Well, speaking *exactly*, that *is* why I collect. Because I'm black. I started in Washington. My things are all from Virginia and North Carolina."

"Mom's stuff is Midwest, nothing fancy. Not as old as yours, either."

"I collected things from slave times. A lot from the 1790s but some up to the 1830s," Emma Jean said. "That far back, the best Southern cabinetmakers all had slaves in their shops. I figured if black hands did the work, a black person should own some of the pieces."

"I guess so." Wes brought his beer to his lips.

Emma Jean wasn't sure what she heard in his voice. "That bother you?"

"No, it seems like you." He paused. "*I will sing with the power of my soul, but I will not desert the soul of my people. I will bring forth every measure of beauty in my music, but I will not hide all that is ugly in race. I will stand real and solid as a black person blessed with opportunity, but I will not be your black hologram.*"

"You read the play," she said.

"Yeah."

"Memorized it?"

"Just that part."
"But you read it all?"
"Yeah."
"It made a lot of people mad. Did it bother you?"
"Not now. It might have if we never met." he said. "Now, I can hear your voice in it, the way you would say the words. Especially that part. I don't know how to . . . I mean, it sounds corny . . . I admire you."

Without saying a word, Emma Jean rose from her chair. She took the beer from his hand and put it on the end table next to him. She bent slowly and kissed him, gently at first, but stronger and deeper as she felt him respond. Her tongue parted his lips and the passion in their embrace grew. She slipped her hands down to his waist and slid them up under his white tennis shirt. He gradually raised his arms as he felt her hands travel up each side of his body.

Emma Jean pulled back and lifted the polo shirt up over his head, dropping it on the floor. She stayed transfixed for a moment by the sight of her ebony fingers running down the pale, white skin of his chest.

"Here," she said, taking his hand and leading him out of the living room. "I hate to tell you something. You gotta come up with another voice in your head for *The Black Hologram*. I'll never be an opera star. I can't sing a lick. Can't dance neither."

"Same here," he said.

Emma Jean laughed and guided him into her bedroom.

"What about Shai?" he asked.

"Home late today. She's practicing her piano solo for the school recital. Gonna call me to pick her up."

They closed in another tight embrace and rolled onto the king size bed with Emma Jean coming to rest on Wes's chest. He felt the air push out of his lungs and squirmed a little to his right. He wondered if a woman had ever felt the same way under him. Emma Jean lifted up slightly on her elbows. Her face looked younger and softer than he had ever seen it as she smiled down at him.

"Mama, you here?"

"What the heck?" Wes said as he heard Shai's voice down the hall.

Emma Jean jerked up to her knees and hurriedly reached behind her back to straighten her tennis dress. "It's Shai."

"Mama?"

"Just a minute, Sugar."

"Jeez," was all Wes could say.

"Take a shower."

"What?"

"Take a shower," Emma Jean whispered. "I'll tell Shai you're stayin' for supper."

"Huh?"

"Just do it. I'll cover with her somehow. I don't know what I'll cook."

Wes remembered the state of her kitchen cabinets. "Do you have anything?"

"Pork chops in the freezer."

"Thaw 'em in the microwave."

"Okay, just git in the shower."

Emma Jean exited from the bedroom and quickly closed the door behind her. "Hi, Sugar. I thought you were stayin' late."

"Mrs. Belger was sick today. I got a ride home from Samantha's mom."

"Oh."

"What's that noise?" Shai asked as the shower started in the bath off the master bedroom.

"It's the shower."

"How come you're not in it?"

Emma Jean veered into the living room and made a beeline for the two beer cans. "It's Wes. He's stayin' for supper."

"What are you talkin' about?"

Emma Jean kicked Wes's tennis shirt under the skirt of the sofa as Shai strolled into the room. "We played tennis and Wes came up for a beer. I just asked him to stay for supper."

"So why's he in the shower?"

"It's tennis. We git sweaty."

"He just lives next door."

"And this was just easier."

"You're cookin' dinner?" Shai said. "What you makin'?"

"Pork chops."

"Mama, your pork chops are kinda dry."

"Wes is gonna help. He's a cook, remember?"

"Whatever."

"If you got any homework, Sugar, you better get started."

"Mama, I just got home. Besides, I don't have very much."

"What if Wes stays after supper? I told him maybe we could rent a video. Now you know you're gonna wanna watch."

"But Mama—"

"I don't need no buts from you or no whinin' later, girl."

"Okay." Shai trudged off to her room with her maroon backpack slung over one shoulder.

Emma Jean hurried to the kitchen and poured two nearly full beers down the sink. She turned immediately back to the living room and grabbed Wes's shirt from under the sofa. Her walk usually announced her approach, but she moved as quietly as possible down the hall and into her bedroom. She heard the sounds of water still running in the shower, and she opened the bathroom door.

"I got your shirt."

"Huh?"

"Not too loud," Emma Jean said. "I got your shirt."

"Right, thanks."

"You have to stay and watch a video after supper."

"What?"

"I told her we decided to rent one. Can you stay?"

"I guess. I'll have to call work. It's Thursday night. Should be okay."

"I better get outta here," Emma Jean said, taking a sideways glance at the blur of the slender white body outlined on the milky glass of the shower door.

She made her way quietly back to the kitchen and opened a package of six pork chops from the freezer. She placed them in a clear glass baking dish and set the microwave to defrost as Wes had asked. The timer dinged just as he entered the kitchen, his hair glistening from the shower.

"I see you started," he said. "I know something really easy."

"'Bout now I could use that."

"Got ketchup?"

Emma Jean nodded.

"And I know you've got cinnamon. How about a broiler pan?"

She grabbed the ketchup out of the refrigerator, retrieved the cinnamon from its cabinet, and produced a broiler pan from a cabinet under the kitchen counter.

"I could use some cooking spray," he said. "You know, no stick."

"Sorry."

"Don't really need it," he said. "Just makes the pan a little more challenging to clean up."

Emma Jean smiled and shrugged. "You wanna cook and I'll clean?"

"Deal." He opened the freezer compartment of her refrigerator. "Those broccoli spears will be good and the tater tots will work."

"I got regular potatoes," she said.

"Better. Let's start those first."

Emma Jean washed the potatoes while Wes turned on the oven and set it at 350 degrees. He took the three potatoes, jabbed them a few times with a fork, and placed them on the bottom rack.

"Come on and I'll show you." He nodded toward the pork chops.

"This is good. You might wanna take notes."

She moved to the counter and peered over his shoulder. He put his arm around her waist and pulled her closer.

Emma Jean laughed softly and swatted his arm away. "Wes, remember Shai?"

He placed the pork chops on the broiler pan and squeezed ketchup on each one. He smoothed it evenly with a knife and then sprinkled cinnamon generously over the top. "We'll let the potatoes go about ten more minutes, then put these in."

"That's it? That's what I'm s'posed to be takin' notes on?"

"I was kidding. These are really simple and really good."

"You cookin' dinner?" Shai's voice from the doorway startled them.

"With your mom's help."

"Got your homework done, Sugar?"

"Almost. I'll go back."

"No, that's all right. Go ahead and finish later," Emma Jean said. "Maybe you and Wes could go for the video. Is there time, Wes?"

"This takes about an hour. Yeah, that would work."

"Mama, don't you wanna go?"

"No, I gotta clean myself up yet."

Wes opened the oven door and put the pan of pork chops on the top rack. "Tell you what. I've got just the thing for this meal. A bottle of sparkling apple cider. I'll run home and get it and change quick."

"And the movie?" Emma Jean asked.

"Shai and I can still go. If we're not back by a quarter to six, you go ahead and start the broccoli. Shai, I'll see you downstairs in about five minutes?"

"Whatever."

CHAPTER 15

Wes had been waiting all night to hold Emma Jean's hand. Standing in the lobby of the student union while Emma Jean was in the ladies' room, the right time still hadn't come. It certainly wasn't right when he picked her up at the apartment. Shai stood there in the hallway as they left, giving them her best grin—the one she usually wore when teasing people.

Shai was the reason for tonight's "Traditional" date. After she nearly walked in on them two weeks ago, Emma Jean insisted to Wes that they cool it. They both agreed to slow down and try a regular date. Nothing seemed more traditional for dating than dinner and movie, even if the movie was part of the university's Fifties Film Fest.

Unfortunately, dinner at Armond's didn't lend itself to hand-holding, either. The heavy drapes, white linen tablecloths, Rococo silverware, and tuxedo-clad waiters all made hand-holding seem too teenage. Wes imagined that the only hand-holding that ever took place in Armond's elegant restaurant involved an engagement ring.

The dignified manner of Roland Armond, himself, also might have restrained Wes's behavior. When City Streets opened, Iowa City finally had a second restaurant that could match gourmet meals, if not opulent décor, with Armond's. Yet Roland, though forty years older, always treated Wes like a respected colleague rather than an upstart competitor. Tonight, the early June evening proved unseasonably warm, but for dinner at Armond's, Wes wore a sport coat and white turtleneck. That was as close to dressing up as he ever came, except for the dark suit he saved for weddings and funerals. As expected, Armond's food was worthy of the elegant surroundings. Wes ordered a superb coq au vin, and Emma Jean's beef stroganoff looked even better.

Emma Jean chose the movie, a showing of Jimmy Stewart at his disarming best in *Harvey*. Moving to her territory on campus for the film fest produced enough greetings of "Hello, Professor Whitcomb" to continue inhibiting Wes's hand-holding impulses. On a positive note, Emma Jean's fascination with the movie as an example of "stage play aesthetics translated into film" prompted her to lean close to him and offer hushed commentary at several points. While remarks such as "action off camera" or "blocked like a stage scene" didn't necessarily fill him with excitement, the feel of her warm breath against his neck while she whispered in his ear did send a tingle down his spine. Nonetheless, he waited now with only his own hands clasped together as he watched Emma Jean return.

"Ready?" he asked as she got close.

"All set."

He reached to open the door with his right hand and lightly touched her back with his left as he escorted her out into the June evening.

"So, you liked it," she said.

"Yeah, I really did."

"It holds up pretty well even after fifty years."

"It's funny."

"It's always been one of my favorites," she said.

"That kinda surprises me."

"I identify with the rabbit."

"The invisible part or the six feet part?"

"Now *you're* trying to be funny." Emma Jean reached out and took his hand. "I'm glad you hadn't seen it before. I thought maybe with cable and everything."

"I've got City Streets. I don't watch much TV. You know, all the night work."

"I suppose I shoulda figured that," she said. "In my position, I feel I should know what's on TV, even if it isn't very good. Which it usually isn't."

"But you still think you should watch?"

"It's full of plays. Movies, sitcoms, cop shows—they're all cousins to a play. If I have students who eventually make it as writers, a lot of them will do it writing screenplays."

"Students must like you," he said. "You can tell by all the 'hellos.'"

"Perhaps," she answered. "Perhaps not. I don't teach to be liked. Frankly, I had recommended to my students that they see this film as one faithful to the stage version. I imagine that accounted for most of the greetings. They wanted to be sure I noticed their presence."

They lapsed into silence as they strolled the sidewalk along the Iowa River back in the direction of his car. The feel of their fingers finally entwined was all the communication they needed in the quiet of the evening.

They walked nearly to his car before Wes finally spoke. "You want some dessert?"

"Dessert!" Emma Jean burst into laughter. "Weren't you sittin' across the table from me at dinner? Don't tell me you didn't see how rich that stroganoff was. I shouldn't be eatin' dessert for a week."

"Good, huh?"

"Incredible. And those noodles. I could eat those all by theirself."

"Yeah, they were like a dumpling noodle. Almost a spaetzle."

"Whadaya mean a spatula?" Emma Jean teased.

"Spaetzle, spaetzle. It's a Swiss noodle."

"I thought stroganoff was Russian. Now you're talkin' Swiss. Russian, Swiss, I can't keep all you white folks straight."

"And now you're just givin' me a hard time. Besides which you never really answered me about dessert."

She stopped and turned to face Wes, taking both of his hands in hers. "I'm having a really good time, but I should go home. Marcus comes day after tomorrow to pick up Shai. Seems like I always put off the packing."

"We'll make it quick," Wes answered. He pointed across the parking lot at the end of the sidewalk. "See the lights on that field over there? It's a kickball league."

"Kickball?"

"Yep, sounds like something for kids, but Iowa City has adult kickball leagues. Somebody I know used to play. There's always a guy there with an ice cream cart."

"You're a bad man, Wesley Whitcomb."

"Is that a yes?"

"Yes, that's a yes. If we're quick."

The noise that floated toward them as they approached the field came mostly from the players. Emma Jean wondered how much ice cream could be sold to the handful of spectators standing along the sidelines of each field.

An angular old man with a white smock, a white paper hat, and a two-day growth of stubble greeted them eagerly. "Ice cream?"

"What'll you have?" Wes asked Emma Jean.

She studied the colored pictures of ice cream bars and popsicles plastered on the side of the cart. "I guess just an ice cream bar."

"Give me a drumstick," Wes said as the old man pulled open the lid.

"Can I change?" Emma Jean asked.

"Whatever you'd like," the ice cream man answered.

"A drumstick," she said. "I'm gonna copy."

Wes reached into his wallet and handed the old man four worn one-dollar bills.

"There's a bench over there," Wes said to Emma Jean.

They sat and tore the red, white, and blue wrappers off their ice cream.

"That's good," she said after her first bite.

He nodded. "Only thing is, half the peanuts always fall off. Somebody ought to invent one of these where the peanuts stick better."

"You're the food guy."

"I guess I am." Wes paused and crumpled the wrapper from his ice cream. "Is it hard? When Shai leaves?"

"It's always hard," Emma Jean answered without hesitating. "More this year. New York didn't seem so far away when I lived in Washington."

"You worry about her in the city?"

"Marcus lives in Westchester County. Bedford. A rich suburb."

"He doesn't seem like a suburb guy, you know, when I see him on TV. More like a Hollywood guy."

"The network executives are in New York. And the sports departments. Marcus knows where the power is."

"Makes sense."

"He used to have a place in L.A., when he was tryin' to act."

"I didn't know he did that."

"It didn't work out. He had a few small parts, but Marcus is a better actor in person. I guess he couldn't fool a camera. Anyway, he moved back east." Emma Jean looked at her watch.

"We better go, huh?" Wes popped the last bite of ice cream cone into his mouth.

"Yeah," she sighed.

They walked across the asphalt parking lot without speaking. In the silence, new fluorescent blue lines painted to mark the parking spaces suddenly jumped out at him. Weren't parking lots always lined in yellow, or maybe white? He had never seen bright blue, but here it was, and at a university obsessed with using the gold and black school colors on everything possible.

"Here we are." He unlocked the doors on his silver Thunderbird. "You're quiet."

"Thinkin' about Shai."

"And Marcus?"

"Him, too. He's a good daddy. He spoils her, really, but he didn't forget her. Plenty of fathers do. Marcus and I got our history, but he doesn't forget Shai."

"Shai never says much about it," Wes said. "Has he been here before?"

"Not yet. Wintertime's all basketball. That's why he takes her two months in the summer. Basketball season, he's callin' a game in this city, callin' a game in that city. Always on the move. That's Marcus."

Wes heard the edge hardening in Emma Jean's voice, but he still asked, "You must've moved a lot, too. When he was traded. I would think that's gotta be hard."

"We moved. I didn't mind where he was workin'." She stared straight ahead through the windshield. "I minded where he was sleepin'."

"Oh," Wes said.

Another silence filled the car for the rest of the drive back to The Manor. Wes parked and they stepped into the still warm air of the evening. He leaned against the roof of the car and looked across at Emma Jean.

"That was fun," he said.

"I had a really good time."

"You wanna come in?" he asked.

"Not tonight."

"I understand."

They exchanged a polite kiss, and he turned toward the carriage house. Emma Jean started in the direction of the main house, certain that there was much about her that Wes wouldn't understand. Inside the building, she paused in front of a golden oak, Eastlake-style settee. She had never seen anyone sit on the furniture in the downstairs hallway. She sat anyway. The squared off arms and rectangular back panels, covered in thinly-padded green upholstery, made the settee as uncomfortable as it looked. It didn't matter. Emma Jean wasn't ready yet to go upstairs.

She shouldn't have said so much about Marcus to Wes. It wasn't his business. He hadn't asked. They were just talking about Shai. Shai was the one thing that went right between her and Marcus, maybe the only true thing between them.

Emma Jean thought about the nights with Marcus, the nights he slept at home, the nights he slept with her. She made love fiercely. Her passion was bigger than love, stronger than lust. In their marriage, she felt an intensity greater than the intimate moments between two people. Her passion grew not only from her feelings for Marcus, but also from her hopes for black people. She saw their union as that of two strong, intelligent, committed black people. The children of that union would be children born of strength, guided by intelligence, nurtured to embrace commitment.

That was the extra fire Emma Jean brought to making love with Marcus. When she first touched the taut muscles of his chest and saw him grow hard and larger than any man she had known before, it only added to her passion. She didn't care if his body fit a stereotype that she knew to be untrue from her experience with previous boyfriends. She didn't care about the occasional discomfort when they started to make love. With Marcus, she would bear special children. Black children smart enough, strong enough, even intimidating enough that they could not be forced into second-class status by a white world.

And then, Shai was born. Just a baby. A baby with the softest brown eyes and the sweetest smile Emma Jean had ever seen. Suddenly, Emma Jean didn't care about producing little soldiers to become warriors in a social crusade against racism. She just wanted Shai, her baby, to be kept safe and soft and sweet.

Shai's birth didn't strip away Emma Jean's convictions, blunt her outrage against racism, or change her heart, but in some undefinable way, it changed her passion with Marcus. When they were in bed at night, just the two of them, something was different. She wasn't sure if Marcus could tell, but later she would be certain that Marcus had already strayed—strayed many times—well before Shai was born. Still, she wondered how the change she brought to their bed had changed the rest of their marriage. She wondered then, and fourteen years later, she continued to wonder as she sat alone in Iowa City on an uncomfortable antique settee.

CHAPTER 16

His ringing telephone roused Wes out of the sports page in the Sunday paper. He dropped it onto the large upholstered footstool that matched his swivel rocker and reached for the receiver. "Hello."

"Hi, Wes. It's Shai."

"Hi! I didn't know if you'd left already."

"That's why I called. Daddy's here to pick me up. Mama said it's all right to ask you to meet him."

"Your dad?"

"Yeah, we're just about to leave."

Wes paused to let the information sink in. "Yeah, sure, it's good. I wanted to see you, anyway. We ought to say goodbye."

"Daddy's takin' my stuff down right now. We'll be outside in a minute."

Outside. The word settled into Wes with a sudden swirl of realization. In a year's time, neither Shai nor Emma Jean had set foot in his apartment. *Apartment.* That word seemed too grand for the space Wes had lived in for eight years. It was really more of a studio, although his tiny bedroom was partitioned off in the area that jutted out over the portico of the old carriage house.

He had fixed the place up nice enough. A large oriental rug dominated the living area with a design in deep blue and beige on a field of burnt orange. He was always good with color and managed to harmonize the upholstered swivel rocker, a sofa, and his curtains with the rug. A small walnut, drop-leaf table to eat at, a cherry rocker, and the short, pine chest-of-drawers that held his phone provided accents in soft wood tones. The stove, sink, and refrigerator stood discreetly in the short hall that led to the stairs. Even so, no amount of tasteful decorating could disguise the fact that the apartment was small—barely larger than a typical grad student's quarters. He knew that from the art students he'd dated.

He wondered if his apartment fit the same pattern of arrested development that Suzie had complained about in his dating habits. He had to admit that the place didn't match the image of a successful business owner in his midthirties. In fact, it was so poorly suited to entertaining that he had never considered inviting Emma Jean and Shai for dinner or dessert or even to exchange Christmas presents.

He looked out the window to see Shai emerging from the front door of the house. He ran a comb through his hair, bounded down his apartment stairs, and stepped out into the sunlight with a big wave.

"Lots of stuff." He said as he got closer to Shai and two big suitcases beside a Cadillac Escalade with a rental car sticker.

"I'm gonna be there two months," she said with the smile she gave him whenever he was being clueless.

A tall black man closed the back of the luxury SUV and stepped around toward Wes.

"Wes, this is my dad."

"Marcus Williams," the man said, extending his hand.

"Nice to meet you. I'm Wes Whitcomb." He reached out and felt his fingers engulfed in the largest hand he had ever seen. No wonder Marcus Williams had been able to wave a basketball in the air with one hand as he spun or soared for the acrobatic dunks that basketball purists always called showboating.

"So, you're the man who got my daughter playing basketball," Marcus said.

The comment caught Wes off-guard. "I think it was mostly that she wanted to."

"She seems to think you helped." Marcus flashed a car salesman's smile. "Says you went to all her games."

"That was fun . . ." Wes's voice trailed off. He couldn't help wondering if his words made Marcus feel he had missed something precious as a father.

"It's great you could go." Marcus gripped Wes's shoulder with a glad-handing squeeze. "Seems like anytime I talk to Shai, there's always something good to say about Wes."

"I'll bet you're gonna have a great summer." Wes wasn't sure if he was directing the comment to Marcus, to Shai, or to his own desire to change the subject. "A lot more to do in New York City than itty, bitty Iowa City."

Shai giggled and nestled up close to her father. "I told you he talks funny sometimes."

"That's not a nice thing to say, young lady." Emma Jean's voice came from behind the car. None of them had seen her come out the front door of The Manor.

"Mama, I was only kidding."

"I know you were, Sugar. I just came down for one more hug. Say bye to Wes."

As Shai and Wes exchanged goodbyes, he realized that her eye level had almost reached his own. She must have grown three inches in the last few months. Shai was another tall one, even if she had a ways to go to catch her mother.

"Marcus, you'll call and let me know when you get there?" Emma Jean asked.

"Absolutely."

Wes took a few steps back and observed the family tableau from the sidewalk along the drive. Shai turned to her mother and gave her a last, long hug while Marcus leaned against the open door on the passenger side of the car. Shai let loose of her mother's embrace and slipped into the front seat. Her father closed the door behind her.

Emma Jean motioned for Shai to lower her window. "Have a good time, Sugar. Write me some postcards, and I'll call every Sunday night."

"Bye, Mama."

Emma Jean waved vigorously, never once taking her eyes off Shai as Marcus Williams pulled away with their daughter. Wes watched Emma Jean's arm drop to her side when the car drove out of sight down the curving hillside driveway.

"Wow," Wes said.

"Marcus?" Emma Jean asked without moving.

"No," Wes answered. "That it's this hard . . . I mean . . . even for me."

Emma Jean turned and took his hand.

Wes squeezed.

"Walk with me," she said, starting across the lawn.

"No dew."

"What?"

"In the grass," he answered. "It didn't get that cool last night, so no dew. Maybe a hot summer coming."

"Who notices no dew?"

"People."

"Iowa people."

"Or playwrights. Aren't playwrights supposed to notice everything?"

"No banter today, Wes. I don't have the strength."

"Sorry."

Emma Jean's steps guided them to a small concrete bench by a bed of daylilies at the edge of the property. From there, the hillside dropped off sharply to a limestone bluff overlooking the Iowa River in the valley below.

"You okay?" Wes asked.

"It's good for her."

"That's not what I asked."

"I will be." Emma Jean looked away. "I'm never okay right when she leaves."

"I don't know what to say."

"There's nothing anybody can say. She'll be back. She'll have a good time. When she comes home, she'll try not to say too much about his current live-in."

"He's living with someone?"

"Marcus is always livin' with someone. This one's named Chiniqua," Emma Jean said. "Sounds black. The last two were white."

"Is that right for Shai? A bunch of different women?"

Emma Jean gave a barely audible laugh, looked down and slowly shook her head. "Sweet, sweet Wes."

He started to speak, but she touched a finger to his lips.

"I talked to Marcus about Shai's visits a long time ago. He knows the rules. Funny thing is I can tell he's changed. Now that he's not married, he's just one woman at a time."

"Still."

"Wes, do you think I'm a good mother?"

"You're a great mother."

"Okay, then listen. Marcus loves Shai. Everything at his house will be dignified and respectable. If it wasn't, I could tell in a second just by the sound of Shai's voice."

"And I'm sticking my nose in," Wes said.

"Yeah, and if I didn't know it's 'cuz you care, you'd be hearin' about it. You know what the sad part is? I think Marcus has got to the point where he thinks each new one is gonna be *the* one."

"Not?" Wes asked.

"Not. And also not worth talkin' about any more. I've got to start thinkin' about Milwaukee."

"Leaving tomorrow?"

"This afternoon. I speak tomorrow. It's a three-day conference, but I asked to be on the program tomorrow."

"So you can speak at the first day of the conference?"

"No, so I can be gone the first night, here. When Shai leaves, the first night is the worst. I can drive to Milwaukee, or I can go sit in her room and cry."

Wes took her hand and squeezed again.

"Wes, come with me to Milwaukee," she said abruptly.

"This afternoon?"

"Yeah, this afternoon. I told you I'm drivin'. No plane tickets to worry about."

"I don't know."

"What's to know?"

"Two restaurants, just for starters."

"Talk to the owner. I hear he's really nice."

"That's not what the people who work for him are gonna say if the tells 'em he's disappearing for three days."

"Two, if you don't count today. The conference is three days, but I'm only stayin' two."

"I don't know."

"If it's too hard—"

"No, I didn't say that," he said, "but let me get this straight. For our first date we go to a movie, and then for our second we go away together for three days."

Emma Jean moved in back of the bench and bent down to wrap her arms around his neck.

"You were the one who just said I'm a playwright," she whispered in his ear. "Think of it as a plot twist."

"And if I want to find out how the play ends, I have to go?"

"Exactly."

"I've got a lot to do, then. I have to make some calls, and I gotta go into the office."

"So go. Who's holdin' you back?"

"Right now, you're holding me."

She rose to her feet and pulled him up with her.

"Go do what you gotta do." She kissed him on the cheek. "Call me as soon as you get home. We can leave whenever you're ready."

CHAPTER 17

Emma Jean finished writing *Emma Jean and Wesley Whitcomb* on the registration slip for the elegant historic hotel in downtown Milwaukee. Wes stood a step behind and admired the old-style beauty of the lobby. Wood-paneled walls, polished marble columns, crystal light fixtures, damask-covered chairs, and a carpet of rich autumn colors blended into understated but unmistakable luxury.

"Have you stayed with us before, Mr. and Mrs. Whitcomb?" The desk clerk, attired in an impeccably tailored forest green blazer, looked up and peered over his glasses at Wes and Emma Jean.

She arched an eyebrow and answered with an enigmatic smile, "I've been here several times."

"We're pleased you've chosen to join us again. As you may remember, the concierge is to the right at the end of the lobby. Our restaurant is reached through the door next to the concierge desk. It opens for breakfast at seven. It is well known in the city for both lunch and dinner. This card is your room key. Your room number is written on the envelope. This key opens the mini-refrigerator in your room which is fully stocked with snacks and beverages."

Emma Jean nodded and accepted the keys.

"If there is anything we can do to assist you during your stay, please let us know." The clerk raised his arm and summoned a bellman.

"He was looking at us," Wes whispered to Emma Jean as they walked behind the bellman to the elevator. "What I mean is, you black and me white."

"I told you during Shai's basketball people were watching us. Sittin' together every game."

"I didn't see it before."

"Of course not," Emma Jean said.

They entered the elevator with the bellman and fell into the silence that elevators invariably invoke. When the doors opened at the fourth floor, they followed the bellman to room 421. Wes watched each precise move as the bellman managed to unlock the door, swing it open, and still stand off to the side with their bags so that Emma Jean and Wes could enter first. A carefully choreographed routine delivered baggage to the suite's bedroom, pointed out amenities in the sitting room, and switched on the bathroom light. "Will there be anything else?" the man asked.

"No, thank you," Emma Jean said.

Wes reached into his pocket and discreetly handed the man a five-dollar tip.

"Thank you, sir. Enjoy your stay."

Wes surveyed the suite more closely. A large mahogany armoire opposite a cream-colored loveseat dominated the sitting room. The doors of the armoire swung open to reveal a twenty-seven-inch television set. An identical piece of furniture with an identical television was positioned in the bedroom to be viewed from the high, four-poster bed.

"This is nice." He peeked into the bathroom. "There's even a little TV in here."

Emma Jean chuckled at the surprise in his voice and walked over to take his hand.

"The clerk thought we were together," he said.

"We are together." Emma Jean chuckled again.

"You know what I mean. Same name. Married."

"Well, I don't suppose he'd take us for brother and sister." She raised her arm and lifted up their tightly entwined black and white fingers for emphasis.

He started to draw her into an embrace, but she pulled away. He watched as she picked up the key for the mini-fridge from the mahogany writing table where she had left it. She bent down to open the refrigerator and peered inside.

"Ever had Leinenkugel's?" she asked as she looked at the selection of beers.

"Of course."

"Of course?"

"I own a restaurant, remember? You sample plenty of beers at restaurant conventions."

"Want one?" She reached for two bottles without waiting for his answer.

"Sure. It's good beer. Made in Wisconsin. An old brewery in a little town called Chippewa Falls."

Emma Jean twisted the cap off each bottle. "Ever been there?"

"No, but Miller owns the Leinenkugel's brand now, so I can get it in Iowa City. I've been thinking about adding it at City Streets."

She handed him a bottle, and they each took a long swig.

"I was hoping to find Coors Light," she said in a low, breathy whisper.

"Is that your sexy beer commercial voice?"

She took the bottle from his hand and placed it next to hers on an end table. "I thought you'd remember the Coors Light from my apartment. That, and where we left off."

She slowly ran her hands down his chest to his waist. He could feel her touch through the soft cotton of his short-sleeved pullover. She tugged the shirt out of his pants and lifted it up over his head as she had done two weeks earlier. This time the bedroom was only a few steps away.

Standing next to the elegant bed with its pure white comforter, Emma Jean unbuttoned her blouse and dropped it to the floor. She twisted and reached behind her back to unhook the heavy black support bra she wore. As the bra loosened, Wes could see a line pressed into her flesh where the wide band of elastic wrapped around her ribcage. She turned to face him and her breasts hung heavy and low on her chest.

He had known only the light lacy bras and perky little nipples of the art students who had shared his bed. Sadness flowed through him as he thought of Emma Jean being continually bound up in a heavy support bra. He slipped his arms around her and buried his face against the smooth black skin of her neck as he gently caressed her back. She murmured in a low voice that came to him more as a tremor against his cheek than a sound.

"My sweet, sweet Wes."

She stroked his smooth straight hair then gently tilted his head back. Their lips met in a slow, deep kiss. Emma Jean reached down and opened the button on his jeans. She guided his hand to the hook in the waistband of her pants. They stayed lost in a kiss while an urgent quest guided their hands. They loosened each other's clothing and tugged awkwardly at their own, finally managing to pull down their pants and step out of their underwear.

Emma Jean pulled back the comforter and rolled onto the bed. Wes drew a quick breath at the sight of her thickly muscled ebony legs meeting in a broad triangle of coarse black pubic hair. She smiled up at his fully excited body. He lay down beside her and their lips met again. They searched for each new bit of excitement, touching, caressing, slowly finding the spots to give the other the most pleasure.

Emma Jean drew back from their kiss and rolled to her back, pulling Wes atop her. The tenderness on his face startled her, and as he entered her body, she understood that she had never truly been in love before. Tears began to roll down her cheeks.

"Did I hurt you?"

Her tears turned to a shaky smile.

"Did I?"

"You ain't that dangerous," she said with her whole face transforming into a broad grin.

"Huh?"

"No, it's okay. You didn't hurt me." She felt the tautness in his body soften.

"That's a funny way to say it."

"I didn't mean anything," she said.

"'Didn't mean anything' sounds like you *did* mean something."

"Wes, come on."

"Come on, what?"

"Just come on."

"Look, if I don't measure up—"

"Oh, for God's sake. Get off of me."

"So now *you're* mad." He dropped onto the bedsheets beside her.

"Mad? We're s'posed to be makin' love. What the hell's anybody bein' mad about?"

"I didn't say I was mad. It just sounded like maybe you were comparing or something."

"Whattya mean comparing? I didn't hear nobody say the word *comparing*. Ain't nobody in this bed comparin' nothin' unless you're comparin' my great big booty to some skinny-assed white girl you know."

Wes didn't say a word.

"So, you are comparing."

"Maybe a little," he said. "Sorry."

"You should be." She rolled over immediately.

He saw the smile return to her face.

"It just slipped out," she said.

"Slipped out?"

"Yeah, you slipped in and the words slipped out. I wasn't measurin' nothin'."

"It's okay."

"It's better than okay," she said. "Truth is, Wesley Whitcomb, you ain't got nothin' to be ashamed of in that department."

"You don't have to say that."

"I ever say somethin' to you I didn't want to? I can say it 'cuz it's true, so you can stop all that fool talk about it."

"Just one thing."

"An' I thought I said stop," she scolded with the smile still on her face.

"No, I'm serious," he said softly. "You cried."

Emma Jean hesitated. Finally, she reached over and touched his cheek. "I cried because I love you."

"I love you, too," he said.

Stillness enveloped their elegant suite. Then Wes whispered in Emma Jean's ear, "Make love to me."

CHAPTER 18

"This isn't too hard to find. Go back down Locust Street the way we came in toward campus." Emma Jean handed Wes the directions she had written on a sheet of hotel stationery. "When you come to the interstate, keep on going past it. Turn right on the first diagonal street you come to. That's Fond du Lac. Then look for the number I gave you. I've never been to her building. She moves all the time."

"I'll find it," Wes said.

"It's a main street."

"No problem."

"Yeah, well, I've known Brenda since high school . . ." Emma Jean didn't finish her thought. She leaned in the car window instead and kissed him on the cheek. He looked good sitting behind the wheel of her BMW.

He glanced up. "That's a nice goodbye."

"I really appreciate you doing this," she said. "And Wes, don't give her any money."

"I'll be back in time for your talk. Two o'clock, right?"

"That's right. I'll be looking for you. Brenda said all she needs to do is run a couple of errands, but you remember what I told you." She patted the car door. "No money."

Wes pulled out and turned left at the next street. He had been amazed when Emma Jean told him that the University of Wisconsin—Milwaukee and the University of Iowa had almost the same number of students. Most of the Milwaukee campus squeezed into a four-square-block area crowded with brick buildings in the plain, rectangular style that architects seemed to favor for colleges in the 1960s. It had none of the feel of the sprawling Iowa campus, bisected by the Iowa River and distinguished by the classical-style stone buildings that formed the university's main quadrangle. Only the two- and three-story clapboard houses converted into student apartments along the adjacent streets in Milwaukee reminded Wes of Iowa City at all.

As he headed to pick up Emma Jean's friend Brenda, the university area gave way in a few blocks to a neighborhood on Milwaukee's near north side that Emma Jean said was poor and mostly black. By the time he turned on Fond du Lac as directed, torn or missing window screens, peeling paint, broken steps, or some other sign of disrepair marked nearly every house. He counted three storefront churches and an equal number of bars—the bars in better condition—before he came to any building displaying a street address. It was a small neighborhood store with all its windows boarded over by white plywood. Blocky hand-drawn lettering all across the plywood in red and blue paint announced to the world: meat, produce, cigs, food stamps accepted, bus passes, liquor, and a half-a-dozen other messages about the business. On the white door frame in crude black numbers he made out 2735. Brenda Gordon's building, 2828, had to be a block up on the opposite side of the street.

He found a place to park in the next block across from a cream-colored, three-story brick apartment building. If Wes had gained nothing else from dating art students off and on for almost a decade, at least he had a pretty good sense of building styles and architecture. Decorative tile at the cornice, an arched entry portico flanked by small fluted columns, and the designs in the building's concrete lintels all spoke of 1920s Spanish revival. It was an attractive building, though one not helped in any way by a broken newspaper box in front, empty potato chip bags and discarded cigarette butts littering the sidewalk, or windows that obviously had not been washed in years.

He locked the car and crossed the street to the apartment building. He saw a pad of doorbells and pushed the number 3 that Emma Jean had written in her directions.

The door opened almost immediately. A chunky, black teenage girl in cutoffs and a T-shirt with the name of a band Wes didn't know stepped out. Her perplexed expression seemed to indicate that she didn't expect to find him, or probably any white guy, standing at the front door of the apartment building.

"That bell don't work," she said.

"I was supposed to meet Brenda Gordon."

"She lives across the hall from me, in number 3."

"Uh, you suppose you could tell her I'm here or something." Wes pointed to the entry door that had closed behind the girl.

"It don't matter." The girl stepped aside. "Lock don't work, neither. Just push."

"Thanks." He pushed the door open.

The dingy hallway inside showed none of the charm of the exterior. A single bare lightbulb burned in the center of the hall. The varnished woodwork and apartment doors had darkened and crackled with age. A broad scatter of cracks, dents, and chips marred the pistachio green walls. Several splatters on the floor and baseboards left stains that Wes didn't want to identify. He stopped in front of Brenda Gordon's apartment and knocked.

He waited, but no one answered. He could hear a television playing inside. After a louder knock, he heard footsteps coming in his direction. Locks clicked and the door swung open to reveal a short, thin woman with close-cropped hair and mocha-colored skin.

"Yeah?"

"I'm Wes, Wes Whitcomb. Emma Jean's friend."

"You E.J.'s friend?"

"Yeah, am I early?"

"No, no honey. I been 'spectin' ya. Here, let me turn that TV off," Brenda said as she left Wes standing in the hall.

"Emma Jean said you needed a ride," he shouted after her.

Brenda returned with a small, red clutch purse in her hand.

"I didn't mean to surprise you," Wes said. "The buzzer doesn't work."

"Ain't nothin' works around here. I just got my phone turned back on two days ago. Couldn't pay last month 'cuz they was doggin' me 'bout the electric, and I know that meter don't work right. It's prob'ly old as this whole building."

She slammed the apartment door shut, turned her key in the lock, and started quickly down the hall with Wes trailing behind her.

"Where's your car, baby?" she asked when they got outside.

"Across the street."

"That black one?"

"Yeah, it's Emma Jean's."

"So that's E.J.'s car. Ain't that fine," Brenda cooed.

Wes unlocked the car and they settled into their seats.

"Emma Jean says you need to go downtown."

"No, that appointment got *all* messed up. It's for my baby, Rondell. He's six. Rondell gets a check 'cuz of his ear. Disability."

"So, you don't need a ride downtown?"

"Nah, I gotta git a different appointment. Rondell don't hear in one ear. Had a fever when he was two, and the doctors didn't do him right. He's s'posed to get eight hundred a month *federal* disability, but now they only sendin' seven-fifty."

Wes looked at Brenda and nodded.

"See, Rondell's my youngest, but I got two other babies. How'm I s'posed ta git by on seven hundred fifty a month? You know what I'm sayin'?"

"But you don't have an appointment?"

"Nah, but his check come yesterday, so I still gotta git that cashed even if they did short me. Les' jus' head on out. I'll tell ya where to go."

"Okay."

Wes put on his turn signal, looked over his shoulder, and pulled away from the curb.

"So you E.J.'s friend."

"Yeah."

"She never told me you was white." Brenda laughed.

"Oh."

"You think she was messin' with me?"

"Uh—"

"I think she was messin' with me."

"Maybe."

"E.J. and a white guy," Brenda mused.

Wes hit the brakes as a rusty green Pontiac came out from an alley into the street.

"These niggers in this town can't drive," Brenda said, bracing her hands on the dashboard. "Jus' turn up at that next street."

"Which way?"

"Right, baby. Jus' turn right. Then see if there's a place to park."

He followed her instructions, but the block was parked full.

"Make another right, baby."

He turned onto a side street and found a spot just around the corner. He looked in the rearview mirror and saw a blue building with a bright yellow and red plastic sign across the façade. He managed to decipher the tall red letters reversed in his mirror: Check Cashing.

He followed in Brenda's wake as she hurried over to the check-cashing place. With the amount of personality she stuffed into a small package, he guessed he wasn't the first person to follow around behind her.

Once inside the building, they joined a line behind four young women. The line led to a service counter topped by an inch-thick partition of scratched and fogged Plexiglas that separated the clerk, and the cash, from the customers. Behind the counter stood a middle-aged, black man in a blue polyester shirt with the fabric pilling from wear. Each time he spoke, he revealed a gap caused by a missing right front tooth.

"This won't take long," Brenda said, acknowledging the line.

The front door opened and another couple entered. The woman got in line while the young man slid off to the side and leaned up against a window frame. The clerk handled checks quickly, counting out money in return, and the front door continued to open with a steady flow of people in and out until Brenda received her cash, and she and Wes were the ones to use the door. During the whole time, his was the only white face in the building.

"They charge a fee for that?" Wes asked as he and Brenda settled back into Emma Jean's car.

"Oh yeah, baby, you live in the city, they got all kinda ways to git your money. You ain't never been in one of these places before?"

"Nope."

"There's a first time for everything."

"I wonder how many white guys they've seen in there before."

"Give 'em somethin' to talk about, baby. That clerk can go home and say, 'No way you gonna guess what I saw at the check-cashin' place today.'"

"He was the only one who didn't seem to pay much attention to me."

"Prob'ly jus' think you an undercover cop."

"Not much of a disguise," Wes said.

Brenda laughed then waved with the back of her hand for him to pull away from the curb.

"Come on," she said, "we gotta get goin'."

"Goin' where?"

"Shoes," she said. "I gotta git me a job, but I ain't got no decent shoes. Make a U-turn and then go right at the corner."

"I'll just go around the block."

"Ain't no traffic cops around here, baby. Cops ain't gonna stop no white man anyway, 'less he's goin' like a hundred or somethin'. Jus' get us turned around so I can go git me some shoes. What you see on my feet is all I got." She lifted one foot and wiggled a torn, light blue canvas sneaker. "You can't go on no job interview in shoes like this."

Wes made the U-turn and followed Brenda's directions to the main street.

"We gotta git to the interstate," she said. "I know a good place for shoes that ain't gonna rob me. You know what I'm sayin'?"

"I'll just go where you tell me."

"Now, I like *that* in a man." She nodded her head. "And you E.J.'s man."

"Right now, we're just friends."

"Friends travelin' together?"

"I just meant—"

"Here, baby," Brenda interrupted. "Take the interstate south. It don't make no difference to me, baby. I'm jus' glad E.J.'s got a man somehow, whatever kinda friends you are."

Wes returned Brenda's smile as he guided the car from the on-ramp into the first lane of the highway. Traffic seemed light for the middle of the day in a city.

"So, you a professor like E.J.?"

"Nope, I own a restaurant."

"A restaurant! What kind?"

"Well, two really. One's a little diner. That's where I started, but my main place is called City Streets. It's, you know . . ."

"More expensive."

"Yeah."

"Two restaurants. Man, you got it goin' on, Mr. Wes."

He just shrugged.

"So, you *rich* like E.J.?"

He patted the steering wheel. "I drive a Ford."

"I say you *do* got it goin' on." Brenda shook her head. "Two restaurants and a rich girlfriend. You after E.J.'s car?"

"You call Emma Jean E.J.?"

"That's what I always called her from 'bout two days after I met her. That was her name all through high school."

"She said you met in high school."

"Then I guess she don't remember too good. Eighth grade. That's when I gave her the name E.J. She was callin' herself Emma, then."

"Not Emma Jean?"

"She didn't like Emma Jean, but she didn't know Emma wasn't no better. That girl was *all* messed up."

"Like how?"

"Like calls herself *Emma*. And she didn't know nothin' 'bout how to dress, neither. I don't mean no offense, but she already had that big ol' butt, and her mama didn't know nothin' 'bout clothes. Her mama was old when E.J. was born. Then by eighth grade, she wasn't thinkin' 'bout E.J. anyway, not when E.J.'s daddy jus' died of the cancer."

Brenda's last words startled him. Emma Jean had never told him how her father died. He sat quietly, embarrassed that he didn't know and hadn't asked.

"Yeah, E.J.'s mama was old. Course, mine was too young. Turned seventeen and popped me right out. We got the same birthday. I didn't have no daddy. Anyway, 'bout E.J., I said, 'I gotta help that girl.' So, I told her, 'I'm callin' you E.J.' Then I showed her how to shop, too, and I said, 'We're gonna work on that nappy hair of yours.' I told my best friend Diane, I said 'This our new friend, E.J.'"

"How far do we go?" Wes asked as they approached the huge interchange for downtown Milwaukee.

"Keep on goin' south, baby. Ain't no bargains 'less you git a little ways outta town. We got E.J.'s new car. We can go where we need to go."

"You mentioned Diane," Wes said.

"Diane Fuller."

"Emma Jean's goin' out with you and Diane tonight."

"That's right. Jus' like always when E.J. comes to town. She don't forget. Me and E.J. and Diane. They're my girls. We're goin' to Corny's jazz club."

"Corny's?"

"That's the guy who owns it," she said. "Don't know why but everybody calls 'im Corny."

"Maybe his name is Cornelius."

"I ain't ever heard of no black man named Cornelius, and it sure ain't got nothin' to do with no cornrows. He's too damn old for cornrows."

"Okay."

"You oughta come tonight."

"I don't know."

"Corny's has white folks there, least wise it would if you showed up." Brenda laughed.

"I kinda got the impression that this is the girls' night out."

"So, she brought you all the way to Milwaukee to sit in some ol' hotel room?"

"We didn't exactly plan this out."

"I hear that. I didn't plan on no government check shortin' me fifty dollars, and I gotta get some shoes."

Brenda saw Wes glance up at the sign for the exit to Milwaukee's airport.

"Not much farther, baby," she said. "Three more exits."

"It's a ways out here."

"Like I said, ain't no bargains in town where it's easy for black folks ta git to 'em."

Wes pondered Brenda's words as they drove without speaking into stretches of less developed land south of the city.

"Here, baby." She pointed to the exit ramp right next to the car. "It's that big sign up there. Bargain Ben's. Head for that."

Wes hit the brakes and swerved onto the ramp, thankful that Emma Jean had a great-handling car. He turned right at the stop sign and made an almost immediate left into the parking lot for Bargain Ben's Shoe Bin. The place looked didn't look like a "bin" at all but rather an abandoned truck stop. Brenda led the way into the store and to a high open space that must have once been the truck service garage. Worn brown carpeting covered the floor and gray steel shelving stacked with shoeboxes filled most of the room.

"You can sit there." She nodded toward a row of flat wooden benches at the front of the room.

He sat down and let his mind drift back over the things Brenda had told him. He tried to imagine the eighth-grade Emma Jean, the girl with the wrong clothes who had just lost her father, the girl with the nappy hair. He wasn't really sure what nappy hair meant.

Brenda flitted from aisle to aisle while Wes took an occasional glance at his watch. Finally, she emerged with an open shoe box in her hand. He saw a pair of black flats with narrow strips of silver and gold on each side reaching from the pointed toe to the ball of the foot. They looked like anything but "sensible shoes" for a job interview.

"Man," she said, "This place ain't got the bargains it used to."

"No?"

"I guess without no car, I ain't been out here in a while."

"Prices go up."

"It's still better'n downtown, but with the government shortin' me," she stared down at the box, "I guess I better do *my* job huntin' in these ol' tennis shoes."

"How much do you need?" Wes asked.

"I sure could use the fifty I got shorted."

He reached into his wallet and pulled out a ten and two twenties. Without moving from the bench, he handed her the money. She bent down and hugged him around the neck.

"That E.J.'s a lucky one," she whispered in his ear.

Her rambling discourse on a black woman hunting for a job in Milwaukee filled most of the ride back to her northside neighborhood. She had thanked him for the shoes for a third time when she asked him to pull into the parking lot of a new chain drugstore just a few blocks from her apartment.

"We finally got one decent store around here," she said as they got out of the car. "I only gotta git one thing quick."

Wes looked again at his watch.

Brenda went immediately to the cosmetics display near the front cash register and picked up a bottle of nail polish. "I gotta have my color, case I git any job interviews."

Wes nodded as they got in line at the register behind a heavy set, young black woman with a little boy hugging one of her legs and a little girl pressed up against the other. A teenage girl at the cash register was taking items out of the young woman's bag and scanning them to check the prices again.

"That won't be enough," the girl said. "If you get rid of the Band-Aids and the can of soup, you're still thirty-five cents short."

As the young woman stared back helplessly, two black men about her age joined the line behind Wes and Brenda.

"And then," one man said to the other, "she put a great big motherfuckin' dent in the door. That bitch don't know how to drive. How you put a motherfuckin' dent in a motherfuckin' door?"

"I don't know, man. She's your girlfriend," the other said.

"And now look at this," the first man started again. "She ain't got no motherfuckin' money up there."

Wes shifted uncomfortably. He hated the word *motherfucking*.

"Some motherfuckin' day," the man continued. "Some bitch always fuckin' somethin' up."

Wes turned toward the two men without Brenda noticing and said in a low voice, "You don't have to say that."

"Say what?" the first man answered without lowering his voice.

Brenda turned toward them.

"She's got two little kids," Wes said. "They don't need to hear that."

"Whatta you, some kinda motherfuckin' do-gooder?"

Brenda stepped in closer to Wes as the second man spoke, "Naw, man he's right. You jus' mad 'cuz Janelle put a dent in your car."

"Well, he's got his girlfriend's car," Brenda said, playfully slapping Wes's chest. "Wes, tell this brother you'll make it even and put a dent in E.J.'s car."

The two men looked at Brenda and started to smile.

"Naw, that's cool. It ain't gonna fix the dent in mine. That Janelle just can't drive."

"Good thing you said that." Brenda poked Wes this time. "His girlfriend's bigger'n he is. She'da prob'ly whupped his ass."

"No shit?" Janelle's boyfriend said.

"No shit," Wes answered quietly. He turned back to the cash register where the young woman was still trying to decide which of her items to leave behind. He took a five-dollar bill from his pocket and handed it the clerk. "This should take care of it."

The clerk rang up the total and took twenty-two cents out of the cash drawer. She looked at the young woman and her two children and then at Wes. He nodded toward the woman and her children, and the clerk handed her the change.

"Thank you, sir," the young woman said.

"No problem," Wes said.

Brenda put the nail polish on the counter and grabbed a candy bar, too. "You gonna help another sister out?"

He took out another five and handed it Brenda.

"Thanks, baby."

"I better hurry," he said. "I'm already late for Emma Jean's talk, and she will whip my ass if I'm not there to pick her up when it's over."

"I hear that." Brenda pocketed the change. "Let's go."

CHAPTER 19

Wes couldn't remember Emma Jean ever wearing such heavy eye shadow, and he was sure he had never seen the iridescent, deep-blue top or tight black slacks she wore as she stood in front of him holding out two twenty-dollar bills and a ten.

"Take it," she said.

"Emma Jean, I'm not poor."

"I know that, but she's *my* friend."

"And you told me not to give her any money."

"And I knew Brenda would get some anyway."

He brushed her outstretched arm to the side and placed his hands on her waist. "You can make it up to me later," he said. "You look pretty sexy tonight."

"Maybe some other guy will think the same thing."

"So, that why you're leaving me here?"

Emma Jean reached up and lightly caressed his cheek. She started to speak, but he touched a finger to her lips.

"It's okay," he said. "They're your friends and you already had this night planned."

"You're sure it's all right?"

"Better than all right. As soon as you're gone, I'm gonna spend the night ordering pay-for-view movies and raiding the minifridge. Run up your bill," he said, ushering her to the door.

With a quick kiss, she was on her way. Although she left Wes behind, her thoughts did not. Riding the elevator down to the parking garage, tooling out into the streets of downtown Milwaukee, and heading toward the north side, she kept thinking of him and the thrill of their bodies locked together the night before. She *would* make it up to him later.

Only as she drove into her old neighborhood did Emma Jean's mind turn to an evening of jazz at Corny's Elite with Brenda and Diane. The familiar surroundings prompted a flood of memories that temporarily swept Wes from her mind. The whole area seemed to exist in some kind of suspended animation so that even where things had changed, they somehow still looked the same. The five-and-dime store she loved as a kid was gone, replaced by a local charity's secondhand store, but the slatted bars covering the building's dirty windows were no different. The number of barbeque shacks and beauty shops seemed the same even if the locations had changed. Buildings appeared as weathered and worn as ever, although some of them must have been painted or patched up since she was a girl.

Corny's Elite, a brown concrete-block building surrounded on three sides by an asphalt parking lot, still looked better suited for housing a machine shop or a commercial laundry than a jazz club. It might even have been built for some such use, but it had been Corny's for as long as Emma Jean could remember. The sinking June sun still left a slit of color on the horizon, but the red neon sign mounted on the roof glowed bright in the dwindling dusk. She opened the front door and entered a world far apart from Wesley Whitcomb.

As the door closed behind her, Emma Jean stood motionless in the entryway to let her eyes adjust to the dimly lit interior. Gradually, shadowy outlines began to fill in with the faces of African American brothers and sisters all dressed for a night out. Even on a Monday, most of the tables were taken. The deep maroon color of the tablecloths barely registered in the soft glow cast by candle lamps on the tables and strings of tiny white lights hung from the ceiling. Her eyes scanned the clientele of Corny's and finally came to rest on Brenda and Diane across the room near the dance floor. Brenda's arm shot up with a big wave, and Emma made her way toward her two friends.

"Well, look at you, girl," Brenda said, "just as big and black as ever."

"And look at you. Skinny as ever and still runnin' your mouth like always," Emma Jean said with a smile.

"Can't you ever say somethin' nice first thing?" Diane said to Brenda. "How long's it been since we seen E.J.?"

Emma Jean laid her hand on Diane's shoulder. "Thank you, sweetie."

From the beginning of their friendship, Diane had seemed like a buffer between Brenda and Emma Jean. At five-foot-six with rich brown skin, even Diane's physical appearance found the middle ground among the three friends. Of the trio, Diane always had been the prettiest, though at any given time ten or fifteen pounds of extra weight partially hid that beauty. It had been more than a year since Emma Jean had seen Diane, and it appeared that Diane's waistline had grown a little more. Wearing a tight pullover top that contoured to the roll around her middle, she looked softer and rounder than ever. Most times, Diane's personality reflected that softness, but Brenda always had the capacity to rile her up. Somehow, their frequent bickering only strengthened the friendship the two had shared for almost thirty years. Throughout high school, Emma Jean had taken a place in the inner circle of three but never quite reached the closeness that united Brenda and Diane.

"You gotta sit down, E.J.," Brenda said. "You way too tall to be standin' while we're sittin'. What you wanna do, break my neck lookin' up at your tall ol' self?"

Emma Jean settled into the third chair at the small round table and nodded at the drinks in front of Brenda and Diane. "See you got started without me. Rusty nail?"

"Same as always," Diane said. "The three of us go out, we gotta start with a rusty nail."

Brenda put one hand on Emma Jean's arm and waved her other hand at the waitress. "I'm gonna order you one, girl. We got us a tab goin'."

Emma Jean had no doubt who would pick up Brenda's tab at the end of the night.

"I been tellin' Di all about your new man," Brenda cackled. "I told her 'E.J.'s got herself a white boy.' I says, 'Good lookin' one, too.'"

"Slow down, girlfriend," Emma Jean said. "Let that stuff wait. I haven't been back in town in a year. I wanna know what's up with you two."

"Since when you the one decides what we talk about," Brenda said. "Ain't nothin' happens in this backward town. Jus' the same ol' same ol'. We wanna hear what you got goin' on with your Mr. Wes."

Emma Jean felt a smile spread across her face at the mention of Wes's name.

"I been thinkin' you shoulda give *him* to me, girl," Brenda said. "You bigger'n he is, anyway."

"Why you always gotta say that stuff?" Diane said. "All the way back to high school, there you are sayin' somethin' about some boy I liked, somethin' about somebody E.J. liked."

"Yeah, you gotta leave our men alone," Emma Jean said with a laugh.

"Who says I didn't?" Brenda wagged a finger. "Shoot, I remember your own self tellin' me how Marcus was built like a stallion, and I *still* left him alone. Maybe I *shoulda* tried me some of that."

"I'm surprised he didn't offer," Emma Jean said.

"I ain't sayin' he did, ain't sayin' he didn't. Jus' sayin' I left him alone." Brenda cackled again and poked Diane in the arm.

"Maybe you coulda taken that one," Diane said, looking at Brenda. "E.J.'s better off without him, never knowin' where he was stickin' that big thing."

Suddenly the table jiggled, and Brenda's nearly full drink sloshed over the side of its glass as a tall black man backed into her shoulder. Emma Jean gave silent thanks for the interruption of talk about facts from her marriage that she wished she had never told Brenda or Diane.

"Sorry, baby," the slightly inebriated man said.

"I guess you should be," Brenda answered.

"So let me make it up to you, pretty lady. I'll buy you another one, or maybe a dance later. Let you see I ain't so bad."

"I already *been* seein' ya," Brenda said, "and I'd rather see ya than be ya. So, *see ya*."

Diane smirked at the words of her friend who always had an answer. Her face blossomed into a full-blown smile as the man uttered, "Chill," and wandered away from the table.

"We need E.J.'s Mr. Wes here to protect us," Brenda said.

"This many brothers around, 'specially one that big. I wouldn't be lookin' to Wes for protection." Emma Jean laughed.

"He did all right this afternoon," Brenda said.

"This afternoon?" Emma Jean said.

"He didn't tell you?"

"Tell me what?"

"'Bout the drugstore," Brenda answered. "How he told two fools to watch their mouth."

"Say what?"

"Yeah, girl. I'm buyin' me some nail polish, and we're waitin' in line to pay, waitin' with these two fools sayin' motherfuckin' this and motherfuckin' that. So, Wes, he tells 'em somethin' 'bout watch their language."

Emma Jean felt her face flush hot. Wes had told her about the long drive to the shoe store, the fifty dollars he gave Brenda, and even a stop at a check-cashing store, a place she figured Brenda had no business taking him, but this episode was news to her.

"So, these were two brothers?" Emma Jean asked.

"Black as you, almost. 'Bout nineteen or twenty."

"Brenda, you can be crazy as you want, but you ain't got no business drivin' him around bein' crazy with you."

"Uh, oh," Diane mumbled as she saw anger rise in Emma Jean's face.

"He the one that said it," Brenda offered weakly.

"And you the one runnin' him 'round this town where he don't belong. Otherwise maybe he wouldn'ta said nothin' or had nobody to say it to. You oughta have 'nough sense not to be draggin' him all over this neighborhood, and he oughta have 'nough sense to keep his mouth shut and maybe be a little scared of someplace where he ain't from."

"He don't seem scareda too much." Brenda regained some of her spunk. "Might not even be scareda you, E.J."

Diane blurted out a laugh, then covered her mouth with her hand.

"Well, he's gonna be bein' scared when I git back to that room tonight." Some of Emma Jean's anger began to dissolve in the sound of Diane's laughter. "It's a good thing we're leavin' tomorrow, or I'da had to send his ass home, anyway."

"Girl, if you don't want him, you jus' send him on over to me," Brenda said.

"What I tell you before," Diane said to Brenda. "Now you after her man, again."

"I ain't *sayin'* I'm after nobody, but least I'd know how to treat him if I had him."

"And who says I ain't treatin' him right?" Emma Jean answered.

"Girl, you raggin' 'bout him right now. You better go back to that room tonight and do him right or maybe I will take him on."

"What I'll be doin', you won't be knowin'," Emma Jean said.

"I still wouldn't mind takin' him on," Brenda said with a wide smile. "'Sides, I heard white boys will lick ya jus' about anyplace."

"I'm surprised you ever hear anything the way you always flappin' your gums." Emma Jean's quick answer didn't stop her face from growing hot as she remembered Wes in bed the night before.

"I'm lookin' at you right now," Brenda said, "Thinkin' maybe what I heard 'bout that lickin' is true. Maybe I *should* go find me a white boy."

"You don't need to be findin' nobody," Diane said to Brenda. "You already had three babies with three different daddies. Ain't one of 'em ever lived with you, neither."

"I'd say it ain't your business how many babies I had."

"And I'm sayin' you don't need you another one with cream in the coffee," Diane shot back.

Suddenly, Emma Jean found herself on the outside of an argument about her own boyfriend.

"I know what you're sayin'," Brenda said, "so you should know *I* ain't listenin'."

"Then how come I gotta be listenin' to you carryin' on 'bout 'white boy this' and 'white boy that,'" Diane said. "All's I know is, some white boy come up on me, I'll keep my legs crossed."

"Girl, you don't have to worry none 'bout keepin' your legs crossed," Brenda said. "You gettin' so fat, ain't nobody gonna be able to get in between your legs."

"I ain't heard Gerald complain none. And *he* been with *me* fifteen years, not like your babies' daddies."

Emma Jean had listened to the words between Brenda and Diane grow harsher and harsher like a building thunderstorm, and then just as suddenly as a summer storm, it was over.

"That's 'cuz you married to the bestest man in the world," Brenda said. "Workin' down at that post office, bringin' home all that money and then lettin' you go out with your girlfriends and spend it."

"That's right," Emma Jean said. "How'd you get so lucky?"

"Maybe it's not jus' luck. Maybe Gerald did all right for hisself, too."

"I think he did, sweetie." Brenda leaned over and kissed Diane on the cheek. "You my girl."

Diane smiled, then all three women turned quickly toward the sound of three sharp notes from a trumpet. On stage they saw a gaunt black man with a thin mustache standing at the microphone. A satiny red shirt hung over his slightly hunched frame and reflected sparkling pinpricks from the stage lights above.

"I'm Earl Harris," the man said, "and since there's three of us up here, this must be the Earl Harris Trio. That's Ray Eldrick at the keyboard, Art Cole on the bass, and I'm gonna play this little ol' horn."

Emma Jean looked at her watch. She had been in Corny's Elite for twenty minutes. The talk had barely strayed from the new man in her life, but it had only made her friendship with Brenda and Diane seem more real than her relationship with Wes. Alone on a quiet summer evening, she would have wondered how that could be, but as Earl Harris said, "Here we go," and raised his horn to his lips, the smooth jazz sounds saved her from all the wondering she didn't want to do.

172

CHAPTER 20

Rolling along Iowa Highway 67, Milwaukee felt more than four hours back in the rearview mirror to Emma Jean. Record rainfall for the beginning of June had transformed the low-lying land along the Wapsipinicon River north of Princeton into a literal backwater. Skinny trees stood with water encircling their trunks like city workers up to their knees fixing a broken water main. A handful of rusting RVs and campers occupied small knolls just above the river's reach but were completely surrounded by water. Muddy pickup trucks along the road and the huge hole gashed into the earth two miles north for a gravel quarry created a landscape totally foreign to Emma Jean Whitcomb.

"Is this redneck country?" she asked.

"I don't know. Maybe a little," Wes answered.

"A little?"

"Prob'ly more poor than redneck. I mean, not real poor. Along here, a place big enough to park a broken-down camper is pretty cheap. Guys come out here to fish. Spend weekends."

"You mean like a getaway?"

"Yeah," he said. "I know they don't look like much."

"You got that right."

Wes shrugged. "You can't see it, but the Mississippi is just beyond those trees. This is actually the Wapsi delta. I guess it feels a little backwoodsy."

And maybe a little redneck, Emma Jean shuddered to herself.

Detouring through Princeton was probably her fault. The drive back from Milwaukee had been full of Emma Jean's stories about the city and Wes's questions about her friends. When they reached the Wisconsin border and crossed into Iowa at Dubuque, he mentioned that his grandfather had been born there. It seemed only natural to Emma Jean to ask a few questions, but Wes didn't know much about his grandfather's early life. He picked up the story after his grandfather moved to Princeton and took a job in the railroad repair shops at Clinton. On the spur of the moment, Wes suggested they detour south to Princeton instead of continuing straight to Iowa City.

"This is it," he said as they passed a green highway sign that read *Princeton—806*.

He turned left off the highway and immediately crossed a set of bumpy railroad tracks. The car coasted half a block down a short incline, and he turned right at a stop sign. Business buildings, mostly empty or converted to residences, lined one side of Princeton's main street with the Mississippi River on the other. Clusters of small docks for outboard motorboats stretched into the water. Wes pointed to a narrow, single-story building with dingy white siding and a Miller Lite beer sign in the window. "That's where I learned to cook."

Emma Jean couldn't help but wonder when the last time was that a black person had ventured into the place for a hamburger or a beer.

He turned the car back toward the highway and bumped over another railroad crossing. "I wanna show you my house."

"Are you sure your parents aren't home?"

"Like I said, they're in Des Moines. My niece's twelfth birthday."

"How do you know they went?"

"Since my dad retired, let's just say they don't waste their freedom. They're out antiquing or down in Des Moines anytime they want. They went."

Emma Jean started to speak, but Wes interrupted her. "This is the church where my mom's the secretary."

Emma Jean studied the white frame building and wondered about the last time a black person had set foot in Princeton's Methodist church.

"This is it." Wes stopped in front of a small bungalow with a dormer on the second floor peering out over the roof of a porch that ran across the front of the house.

This time, Emma Jean didn't wonder. She felt certain there had never been a first or last time a black person had been in the house.

"Looks like nobody's home," she said.

"My gosh, would it be so bad to meet my folks? I've met your mom."

"That was before."

"Before what?"

"Don't be givin' me that. You know exactly before what."

"Okay, okay," he said, "you're right. Still . . ."

"Still?"

"You know. Being together . . . like we are now. It's all the more reason to meet them pretty soon."

"How about one step at a time?" she said. "It's good to see your town, but let's head home."

Was seeing Wes's hometown really good? She couldn't say it made her feel good. She was surprised at how small Wes's house was, but several nearby houses were smaller or only as big by virtue of some ungainly addition. Whoever lived in them might not have had much more money than people in the neighborhood where Emma Jean grew up. Did they work in the factories back up the road in Clinton? Did they handle rancid chemicals like her father had in the tannery in Milwaukee? Did they clean greasy machinery with toxic solvents like her father? Did they die of cancer at the age of fifty-three as he had? Or was that "nigger work" even in Clinton?

"Home it is," Wes said. "You okay?"

"I've got a headache," Emma Jean lied. "I think I'll just close my eyes."

She pulled the lever beside her seat and reclined back as far as it would go. She could feel the car pick up speed as they left Princeton. After ten minutes in Wes's hometown, it was Diane's voice from the night before that filled Emma Jean's head. *Some white boy come up on me, I'll keep my legs crossed.* Why was it Diane who had the better sense? Emma Jean, not Diane, was the one who had been to college. She, not Diane, was the one whose history courses taught about black families broken up by slave auctions, black people hunted down with dogs if they tried to escape, black women forced to lie beneath white men who owned slaves and used their "property" for pleasure if they chose. Emma Jean's face contorted and she let out a low groan. Her whole body flinched when Wes reached over to lightly caress her arm.

He pulled back his hand. "Is it that bad?"

She reached again for the seat lever and brought herself upright. "Maybe we've been cooped up in this car too long."

"I think you're right. I've got an idea."

She sat quietly as Wes drove through another small town. On the outskirts, he passed the interstate highway entrance for Iowa City and chose to go east back across the Mississippi. Over the bridge, he exited and headed south. Within a couple of miles, he turned into a gravel parking lot next to the navigational dam that stretched across the river.

"How about a little walk?" He opened his door and circled in front of the car.

Emma Jean stepped out on her side but leaned back in for her purse when Wes reached for her hand.

He pointed to the dam. "We can walk part way out."

She nodded and they walked without touching or speaking onto the gravel-covered earthen wing dam. They passed two black men with fishing lines cast into the river and didn't stop until they reached a fence that prevented entry to the massive roller dam that regulated the water.

Wes patted a concrete abutment anchoring one end of the chain-link fence and said, "Wait here. I'll be right back."

She sat and watched as he jogged back to the car. She studied the two fishermen. They sat at least a hundred feet apart on upended white plastic buckets like the ones for bulk foods at the Red Door Café. The men didn't seem to be together. It made her feel good to be in a place where black people obviously felt comfortable enough to come alone.

She glanced back over at Wes who was closing the trunk of her car. As he walked back, he veered down the bank of the wing dam to the edge of the water. He spoke to one of the men who pulled a bottle out of his cooler. Wes reached into his pocket, but the man shook his head "no."

Wes quickly covered the ground back to Emma Jean's spot by the dam.

"We're in luck," he said. "The guy had a bottle of water."

"You didn't need to bother him."

"You'll need it for these." He handed her a red packet of Tylenol. "I had them in my bag."

"It's not that bad," she said. "I don't think I need them."

"Can't hurt anything."

She realized his words were probably true, even if her claim of a headache wasn't. Two Tylenol taken for no reason probably wouldn't do her any real harm. She opened the package and washed down the two pills with a swallow of the bottled water.

"Thanks," she said.

He moved behind her and brought his hands up to her temples. His fingers lightly touched her skin and began to move in slow, small circles.

"My mom used to do this," he said.

"My mama did, too."

She drew in a deep breath, then exhaled slowly as if to expel all her thoughts of black and white. She let her eyelids droop almost shut, so all that was left to see were the blurred, rolling gray waters of the Mississippi River.

CHAPTER 21

Emma Jean reached out and lightly brushed Wes's hair. She closed her eyes and wondered if Iowa City played some sort of mystical role in their relationship—a kind of neutral ground where anything was possible between them. It had been less than two weeks since their trip to Milwaukee, and they had found their way into bed together for the fourth time. Now, as they lay quietly spent from making love, thoughts of white Princeton or black Milwaukee, rednecks or crossed legs seemed far less important to her than the soft, reassuring sound of Wes's breathing or the warm touch of his skin.

Emma Jean lazily pondered a quick trip to the living room to retrieve the Sunday paper that Wes had brought over to share almost two hours ago. Just as she lay back and decided that the news could wait for a few more minutes, the telephone rang. Wes lifted up on one elbow and looked at her as she took the cordless phone from her nightstand.

"Hello."

"Hi, Mama," came Shai's voice from the other end of the line.

"Hi, Sugar. Everything okay?"

"Uh huh. I just wanted to call."

"I was gonna call you tonight like always." Emma Jean turned toward Wes and silently mouthed Shai's name.

"I know, Mama, but Daddy and I are gonna be gone."

"Where to?"

"Into the city," Shai answered. "He's takin' me to a jazz festival this afternoon. Then we're havin' dinner."

"Some place good, I hope."

"Prob'ly expensive. You know Daddy. It'll be good."

"Maybe as good as Wes's."

Wes looked at Emma Jean and scrunched his eyebrows into a silent question.

"You wanna talk to Wes?" Emma Jean asked. "He's right here."

She held out the phone. He took it from her hand as he clenched the bed sheet tighter against himself. Suddenly, he wished he had some clothes on.

"Hi, Shai."

"Hi, Wes."

"Couldn't wait for your mom to call tonight?" he said in a weak attempt at kidding.

"I'm gonna be gone. Daddy's takin' me to a jazz festival."

"Sounds like fun. Your mom went to a jazz club in Milwaukee a couple of weeks ago."

"I know. She tell you about that, too?"

"Uh . . . yeah." Wes hesitated as he realized Shai didn't know he also made the trip to Milwaukee. "I've been seeing a lot of your mom lately."

Emma Jean, listening to one side of the phone conversation, pulled down the bed sheet to uncover her ample breasts as she smiled and stuck her tongue out.

"What you guys doin'?" Shai asked.

"Uh . . . I brought the Sunday paper over to read."

"That must be pretty exciting." Shai giggled.

"I know she doesn't get it on Sunday . . . the paper," Wes stammered. "How about if I give you back to her?"

"Okay. Bye."

"Bye."

"Who you gonna hear at the festival?" Emma Jean said into phone as she took it back.

"I don't know. It's gonna be in Central Park. Daddy says it's supposed to be a pretty big deal."

Wes slipped out of the bed and put on his boxers and a T-shirt.

"I hope you have a good time, Sugar," Emma Jean said. "Why don't I call you back tomorrow, and you can tell me all about it."

"Okay, Mama. Bye."

"Bye, Sugar. I love you."

Emma Jean put down the phone just as Wes started across the bedroom.

"Where you goin'?" she asked.

"I thought I'd get a drink of water."

"I've got juice in the fridge."

"That sounds good."

"Will you bring me a glass, too?" Emma Jean smiled. "And the paper?"

"Okay."

She watched as he moved toward the bedroom door. The boxers spoiled a perfectly good view of his cute, white butt.

"I'm glad Shai called," Emma Jean said when Wes returned. "I'da wondered where she was tonight."

He placed her glass of orange juice on the nightstand, and she picked up a section of the newspaper that he had plopped onto the bed beside her.

"She sure is good at surprising us in bed," he said.

"Why, Wesley Whitcomb, I believe you're embarrassed." Emma Jean laughed. "She's a thousand miles away."

"Even so," he said. "Handing me the phone. Flashing me. Me without any clothes on."

"I like you that way." She ran a finger under the elastic of his underwear.

"You're gonna make me spill this juice," he said.

"Depending on where you spill it, maybe I could lick it off."

"I hate to be a disappointment, but I think I'm getting too old to spend absolutely all day in bed with you."

"You're a year younger than I am," she said.

"Well, then, you're old enough to stop leading me astray."

"All right, you lead. What you wanna do?"

"I don't know," he answered. "Get some lunch? Take a ride?"

Emma Jean rolled to the edge of her king size bed and stood up. Wes watched her step away and open the door to a huge walk-in closet. She reached a fluffy, purple bathrobe off a brass hook on the back of the door. She slipped her arms through the sleeves and turned toward him with her body still fully exposed before cinching the robe closed with its fuzzy belt.

"Let's pass on the ride." She sat down on the edge of the bed with one leg tucked underneath her and the other dangling to the floor.

"Not interested in the beautiful Iowa countryside?" he asked.

"I think I'm gonna see plenty of cornfields next week."

"Going someplace?"

"Thursday, Lu and I are taking Mama to Buxton."

"Really?"

"She's never been, and she wants to go."

"But that's where she's from."

"Her parents were from there. She was born in Milwaukee," Emma Jean reminded him.

"That's right, I remember. 'Born in Milwaukee, made in Buxton.'"

"You do remember." Emma Jean shook her head. "I guess Mama always makes an impression."

"But she's never actually been there?"

"I don't think there's really anything left of the town. I got a book out of the library. It was all archaeology. So, the town's gone, but Mama wants to go, anyway."

"Nothing left?"

"Just a cemetery."

"That's good. Your mom can at least see that."

"I hope so." Emma Jean put down the paper she had been holding. "I'm kind of interested, myself. I've been thinking I want to learn some family history. Both sides."

"You mean your father, too."

Emma Jean looked away. "He's the one I know less about. His younger brother, my Uncle Hank, he's still alive, but we never see him."

"Some reason?"

"Distance, I guess. He moved away years ago. Got a job in San Diego. He's been retired for who knows how long."

"You could still call him."

Emma Jean turned back toward Wes and gently kissed his forehead.

"What was that for?"

"For telling me to call Uncle Hank. I should," she said. "You know, I should also call my friend Gates Crawford at Howard."

"Who's that?"

"He's a history professor. We used to play doubles sometimes."

"Seeing's how you seem to carry on with your tennis partners, I'm not so sure I want you calling *him*."

"He's done a lot of black genealogy," she said. "Besides, we used to play opposite each other."

"Different teams?"

"Yes, different teams."

"Not partners?"

"Not partners."

"Well, I guess that's okay."

"I don't think I heard me askin' nobody's permission to call Gates." She leaned over and gently twisted his ear. "I'd say you're a lucky man that I'm headin' off to the shower, or I mighta hadta put you in your place."

"But we didn't decide what we're gonna do."

"After my shower," Emma Jean said with a smile and a quick peck on Wes's cheek.

CHAPTER 22

A backyard with an apricot tree surprised Wes. He didn't think apricots would produce very well in Iowa. Maybe this house had the tree more to be stylish than to yield fruit. Stylish was a good word for the whole place. The rough stone used to construct the house seemed to grow out of one of the gentle hillsides defining Iowa City's most exclusive neighborhood. The ground had been evened out to create a spacious yard that harmonized with the lines of the home's low-slope roof. A cedar privacy fence, weathered to a tasteful gray hue, shielded the area from the eyes of neighbors, but Wes could look back into the house through the floor-to-ceiling plate glass windows that formed one wall of the kitchen. Inside, he saw Emma Jean still talking to the realtor who had organized the open house. The woman's tailored red suit contrasted sharply with the muted tones of the stone building. At short intervals, she nodded her head and gave enthusiastic smiles, apparently in response to questions from Emma Jean.

He had escaped from the house about the time the realtor launched into a glowing description of the home's "polished aggregate floors" and "unique in-floor heating system." He had enjoyed looking at the sprawling, four-bedroom house, but all the real-estate speak from the agent finally got to him. What impressed him most about the polished aggregate floors was the certainty that a glass dropped in the kitchen would shatter into a thousand pieces. Wes had slipped out the back door thinking he, a renter his entire adult life, would be of little help if Emma Jean was seriously considering buying a house. He really didn't know why she had invited him along, except for the fact that they had found little time to spend together during the past week.

Wes watched as Emma Jean opened the sliding glass door to the patio and walked toward him. Even in loose, white summer slacks and a light blue, short-sleeve pullover, she had an imposing presence—almost like royalty.

"Whataya think of the place?" she asked as she joined him next to the apricot tree.

"It's interesting."

"Interesting? That the best you can do?"

"No, it's nice. It seems pretty big for you and Shai. Four bedrooms and a den. Three fireplaces."

"I need one room for a study."

"So, you're serious about this place?"

"I'm not sure, but I know I'm serious about someplace. Shai's starting high school in a month. Four more years, and she'll be gone to college. I want us to have a house."

"Your apartment's bigger than some houses."

"Still an apartment. It's time for a real home. This place is close to The Manor, so that means Shai would still go to high school on this side of town. She'd be with the same kids from her junior high—"

Wes completed Emma Jean's thought, "so she wouldn't have to make new friends again."

"Exactly."

"That part makes sense."

"What part doesn't?" she asked.

"Huh?"

"About the rest of it."

"The rest of what?"

"The house." Emma Jean pointed in its direction.

"I don't know. I've never owned a house."

"So you don't know nothin' about houses? An' here I thought you grew up livin' in a house. I was sure that was a house you showed me when you was draggin' me around white folks' town."

Wes turned his head sharply. "What kind of a crack was that?"

"A frustrated crack, if you can't figure it out. I want to know what you think of this house. Is that a hard concept?"

"Do you think I'm a house expert?"

"Well, what about the kitchen? Last I knew, out of the two of us, you're the only one who can cook."

"The kitchen's fine," he said. "It's big. I'm not sure about the sink and countertop as a center island, but I suppose that's because the big windows eat up the outside wall. All that glass for a breakfast area is really nice."

"So the kitchen's okay," she said.

"Better than okay, really. I mean, it's got everything, two ovens, plenty of cabinet space, the works."

"The rest of the house?"

"I don't know . . . it's . . . pretty unique."

"But?"

"I don't know if there is a but."

"Then how come I'm hearin' one?"

"Okay, it seems like you're really getting into history. Especially since you went to Buxton. This place isn't that old or historic."

"Buxton's family history. Having an old house in Iowa City wouldn't have the same meaning."

"Guess you're right."

"I saw the driveway has a basketball hoop," Emma Jean said.

"When did you become a basketball fan?"

She put her hands on her hips. "I have accepted the fact that you and Shai like to shoot baskets."

"Speaking of Shai—"

"You want to know if I've asked her about the party," Emma Jean interrupted.

"I'm not trying to push. It's just what I said before. We could have a few people over to City Streets—Lu and Sylvia, your mom, maybe a couple of Shai's friends—just a little welcome back."

"I haven't mentioned it to her yet."

Wes pursed his lips in the barely perceptible expression Emma Jean had learned to recognize when something was bothering him. She didn't know how he could be so cute and so clueless at the same time. She didn't bring him here to talk about parties.

"Are you going to?" Wes put his foot on a bench under the tree.

"Sit." Emma Jean said as she took a spot on the bench, too. "Lately, when I call Shai, she's been kind of moody. It hasn't been as easy to talk to her."

"You don't think you can ask her about a party? If we're gonna invite any of her friends, it's only two weeks 'til she comes back."

"I think I know better than you when Shai's coming home."

"I didn't mean it that way," he said.

"I know. The thing is . . . I don't know how to say this. It's like it's partly you."

"Huh?"

"Ever since I told Shai that you and I were developing a relationship, she's seemed a little distant."

A smirk crossed his face. "You actually said 'developing a relationship'?"

"Wes, you're thirty-five. I'm thirty-six. What was I supposed to say? Going steady? Anyway, who cares how I said it? I'm serious. Something seems different."

"You really are serious."

188

"I've been tryin' to be serious this whole time. 'Bout this house. 'Bout your opinion. And, yes, I'm serious about Shai."

"I don't know," he said. "Shai and I get along."

"You two more than get along. Shai thinks you're special."

"That should make it better that we're dating."

"That's what I thought." Emma Jean held back her real thoughts. Was Shai jealous? Was she old enough that some part of her saw Emma Jean as a rival for Wes's attention? The idea turned the warm summer air cold on Emma Jean's arms.

"Maybe it's something out there," Wes said.

"I don't know."

"It's just the way you say Marcus lives. Maybe it's not so easy if her dad has a new live-in every year she goes out there."

"I don't know if I like the word *live-in*."

"Jesus, Emma Jean, it's the word you use."

"An' Marcus is *my* ex-husband, not yours."

"You don't have to be so defensive. You're the one who said Shai's upset."

"I said 'a little distant.' I'm sayin' distant an' you're sayin' upset. I'm sayin' it might be *us*, an' you're attackin' her daddy."

"I'm not attacking anybody, but you just said us. So, *us* includes me. And me, I wonder if it's something out at Marcus's place. When he played basketball, he always had a reputation for doing anything he wanted, and from what you've told me—"

"To hell with what I've told you!" Emma Jean bolted up from the bench. "To hell with reputation! You're talkin' white man's reputation. White men he worked for. White men who couldn't make Marcus Williams a boy. He's a man who stood up for himself, and he's Shai's daddy. He ain't gonna die tearin' down buildings like my mama's daddy did. Tearin' down buildings so some white company can make every last penny off some little coal mining town where black folks did all the work. An' Marcus ain't gonna die like my daddy did, either, breathin' in some goddamned white man's chemicals every day. You got nothin' to say about Marcus Williams."

Wes sprang up. "You done?"

"I'm done when I feel like bein' done! I'll say when I'm done!"

"Well maybe I got somethin' to say, too! Maybe I got somethin' to say about being a white man! Maybe I'm sick of some of the stuff you say! Maybe I'm not responsible for everything every white man ever did! Maybe—"

Wes stopped in midsentence as he glanced over Emma Jean's shoulder to see a middle-aged couple—two other open-house visitors—retreating back into the house. Emma Jean glared down at him with a mixture of anger and surprise still flashing in her eyes.

"I think we better tone it down." He nodded toward the house.

Emma Jean turned to see the couple standing next to the glass wall of the kitchen talking to the realtor. The agent reached into the beige purse that perfectly accented her red suit and pulled out a cellphone. As her eyes met Emma Jean's, the realtor covered the phone and turned away.

"Who do you think she's calling?" Chagrin replaced the anger in Emma Jean's voice. "The cops?"

"Prob'ly her boss. If somebody gets rowdy at City Streets, I'm the first person the staff looks for."

"You have rowdy customers at City Streets?"

"Never mind. I think we should get out of here."

"There's a side gate by the driveway."

Neither said another word as they made their way across the lawn and out of the gate. Within half a minute, they were seated in Emma Jean's car. She started the engine, put the car in gear, and drove two blocks before turning right onto another street. She eased off the gas and pulled over to the curb.

"I'm sorry," she said.

"Me, too."

After a quiet moment, Emma Jean shook her head. "Oops."

"I know. I think you better get another realtor." Wes let a laugh slip out.

Emma Jean's eyes scrunched and her mouth turned up at the corners. She burst out laughing with a snort. Wes joined in just as hard. The laughter shook the car and filled their eyes with tears.

CHAPTER 23

Suzie poured her boss a cup of coffee then plopped down across from Wes in a booth at the Red Door Café.

"You look bushed, Suzie," he said. He was glad, himself, that they had just closed for the day.

"I was thinking the same thing about you."

"You suppose we're getting' older?"

Suzie ran her hands through her graying hair. "I can get away with groaning about my age, but you're way too young for that line."

"Maybe it was just a busy day."

"It was a great day," she said. "We haven't had this much on the register in a month."

"Things always pick up in September with the university back."

Suzie watched Wes absent-mindedly trace the handle of his cup with his index finger then rock the cup ever so slightly without bothering to take a drink. He sloshed the coffee to the rim of the cup but managed keep any from spilling over on the table.

"Somebody's got something on his mind," she said.

He settled his cup on the table and let out a shallow sigh.

"Don't want to talk about it?" she asked.

"I don't know if there *is* anything to talk about."

"Well, Mr. Fidget-With-Your-Coffee-Cup, I've known you long enough to tell when there's something botherin' you."

"It's kind of Shai, I guess."

"Kind of Shai?"

"Mostly the party . . ."

"You're leavin' me hanging here," Suzie said. "What party?"

"Actually, there isn't one. Shai got home and I was gonna have a party to welcome her back."

"And?"

"Emma Jean said Shai didn't want one."

"Did you talk to Shai?"

"No." Wes picked up his coffee cup and took a slow sip.

"But you think it's strange the girl doesn't want a welcome-home party from a trip she takes every year because her parents are divorced."

"I suppose you've got something there."

"Duh."

"Still, it's not just that. Emma Jean says Shai has been really moody lately."

"Emma Jean says so."

"Yeah, I haven't noticed, but I haven't seen much of Shai since she got back."

"Wes, it's called a *teenage girl*."

"You think?"

"I'd show you an example first hand, but lucky for me, Ruth just turned twenty."

"Well, at least that explains Shai."

"Okay, I'll bite," Suzie said. "What big mystery doesn't it explain?"

"Emma Jean," he said. "She's been pretty moody herself the last month or so. Like, she wants to buy a house, and I've gone with her to look at a couple. But yesterday, she wants me to go, and I couldn't get away. So, she gets all annoyed with me. Not *mad* mad, but I can tell she's aggravated."

"Because you wouldn't look at this house?"

"Right, sometimes she acts like I've got nothing to do. We had that big banquet over at City Streets last night. You know, I told you about it. I mean, I had to be there."

Suzie smiled and nodded.

"Emma Jean seems to think 'cuz I own City Streets, I can just come and go as I please. It's like I've got no real work to do."

"Oh, you mean like here," Suzie said.

"Very funny." Wes wadded up his napkin and tossed it at her.

"Okay, okay, I know how hard you work."

"I just wish Emma Jean could realize that. I don't get it."

A smile spread across Suzie's face. "You know, you're making this way too easy."

"What?"

"Giving you advice. First, you need to be told that teenage girls are moody. Now, you wonder why your girlfriend wants you to go house hunting with her."

"So you think I'm a house expert, too?"

Suzie shook her head. "Let's review. First, you and Emma Jean play some tennis. Then, you play every week. Then, you're in here together eatin' pie and drinkin' coffee. Next thing you know, you're dating. Then, you go off to Milwaukee together, and now she wants you to go house shopping. You don't see a pattern here?"

Wes put his hands flat on the table and stared into his coffee cup. Slowly, he looked up. "Are you serious?"

"Look Mr. Are-You-Serious, you and I have worked together for nine years. I've never seen you act this way with anybody. Do I think Emma Jean feels the same way about you? Yes, I do."

"She never said anything."

"Some things aren't easy for a woman to say," Suzie answered.

"You don't know Emma Jean. Nothing's ever stopped her from saying anything else."

"This is different. A woman . . . any woman, even a rich and famous one, she wants to feel that a man wants her."

"If I said something like that to Emma Jean, she'd jump down my throat."

"You're not supposed to say it. You're supposed to act on it. Maybe really look at houses with her like you might be living there, too." Suzie said. "Maybe be smart enough to think she wants that to happen. Be smart enough to know she wants you to say, 'Will you marry me?'"

"Geez, Suzie."

"Geez what? You're both thirty-five, you dote on her daughter, she knows you're not after her money, and you two must have something goin' on in the bedroom. How much better is she gonna do than that?"

Wes felt his ears warm as he thought of the bedroom.

"Oh, and I forgot," Suzie added, "you're not that bad looking, either."

"Even if you're right . . ."

"If I'm right? You know I'm right."

"Maybe, but . . ."

"But she's black and you're white," Suzie said.

"That's got to be part of it. At least for her."

"Let her figure her part out. You do your own part. It looks to me like she's pretty interested."

"Even so, we've only been dating four months."

"Like I already said, you're both thirty-five—"

"Actually, she's thirty-six."

"That's not the point, Mr. I-Want-to-Play-Accountant. Just

because you don't understand a thing about teenage daughters doesn't mean you couldn't learn. Maybe even have one of your own someday. Or a son."

"I could think of Shai as a daughter."

"I believe you could, Wes." Suzie reached across the table and placed her hand on top of his. "All I'm saying is don't let your time go by."

CHAPTER 24

Bullwinkle Moose dipped and bobbed on the TV screen in his slow progress down the windy streets of New York. Shai looked out the window to the backyard of her new home and saw bare branches also dancing in the wind. She turned her attention back to the television and tried to pick out landmarks from her trip to the city last summer. She knew the Thanksgiving Day parade went right down the middle of Manhattan, but nothing looked familiar.

"You think it's windier here or there?" she asked.

"I don't know," Wes answered. "Those big balloons are shaking pretty good, but coming over it was bad here, too."

"I'm glad you wanna watch the parade. Nobody in my family cares about it."

"I always liked it when I was a kid," Wes said.

"The only thing I don't like is all the fake singing and dumb interviews."

"They didn't have very much of that back then."

"I think they should just show the parade."

"Me, too, but it's still part of what makes Thanksgiving. Macy's parade, turkey, football."

"You can have the football," Shai said.

"But not your turkey?" Wes kidded.

"No way. I'm goin' for the drumstick."

"There's two drumsticks."

"Gramma always gits the other one."

Wes held up his hands. "No way I'm messin' with her."

"You got that right."

"I'm surprised your mom doesn't have you out in the kitchen helping her cook."

Shai giggled. "Mama can't cook. Aunt Lu's doin' the cookin' and *she* can cook."

"Smells good already."

"Mm, hmm," Shai murmured as she settled back into a corner of the soft, brown leather sofa that dominated the TV room. Emma Jean had purchased the house a month ago. Both Shai and Wes grew quiet in the comfort of plush furniture and a friendship that didn't require constant conversation.

Wes missed seeing Emma Jean and Shai at The Manor, but he knew he was missing something more imagined than real. During the previous year, the times he actually had run into Emma Jean or Shai in his comings and goings around The Manor were few. He and Emma Jean still met at the courts for tennis, just as they had before the move. Emma Jean and Shai had begun to stop every Saturday at the Red Door for a snack after piano lessons, and he had been over to the new house much more than he had ever visited their apartment.

The house was the sixth one he and Emma Jean had seen together. They both agreed immediately that it was perfect. The neighborhood was close to Shai's high school, and the half-timbered, Tudor Revival house had a substance and elegance that Wes thought mirrored its new owner. The asymmetrical floor plan also provided a wonderfully private study for Emma Jean's work. A broad, stone fireplace highlighted the living room while each bedroom window upstairs looked out into an oak canopy that created its own neighborhood of birds and squirrels.

In the warm surroundings of Emma Jean's new place, Wes could have remained peacefully immersed in a Thanksgiving world of huge balloons and marching bands, but a barrage of commercials aimed at Christmas shoppers interrupted the parade coverage. He wondered how many times he had already seen the same ads pushing video games, fast-food gift certificates, and power tools "for dad."

"Looks like the parade's almost over," he said. "Maybe I should go out in the living room with the other old folks."

"You're not old."

"See, Shai, that's what I like about you. I gotta teach your mom to say more things like that."

"Good luck."

"Well, anyway, I should go out and talk to your grandma and Sylvia for a while. You coming?"

"Nope. I got a book I'm reading."

"Good?"

"It's called *The Golden Compass*. I like the writer a lot."

"Sounds interesting."

"It's all about this special country kinda like medieval times except that they have airships and armored bears—"

"Bears?"

"It's a fantasy. All the characters have animals as helpers, but the animals can talk. The main character is this girl who discovers a plot . . ." Shai looked at Wes and started to giggle. "It's too complicated to explain. You should read it."

"Maybe I should get a talking animal to read it to me."

"You can make fun, but lots of adults read fantasy."

"You finish it and I'll give it a try."

"Really?"

"Yeah. Right now, I better make my appearance in the living room."

Wes wended his way to the living room expecting to see only Mrs. Whitcomb and Lu's partner, Sylvia. Instead, Emma Jean and Lu had managed to break away from their kitchen duties, and all four women were clustered together in a grouping of chairs near Shai's piano. Lu and Emma Jean flanked their mother, who had a large photograph album open on her lap. Sylvia perched on the edge of a round ottoman near Lu's side.

Sylvia's chosen spot captured something in her personality or maybe in her relationship with Lu that Wes couldn't quite describe. When Sylvia was with Lu, she was always near but never touching—at the side, on the edge, or a half step behind. She'd fleetingly enter a conversation in ways that showed she'd been listening and then quickly exit, leaving the impression that her thoughts must be elsewhere. Thin and pale with her brown hair pulled back tight, Sylvia had a presence next to her statuesque, dark-skinned partner that was neither shadow nor mist but held traces of both. So thin that she probably had heard many times she might disappear altogether if she turned sideways, there was something about Sylvia that seemed like she purposely held herself a little sideways to the world. It was the sideways posture that allowed her eyes to meet Wes's first when he entered the room.

"You four look busy," he said.

Emma Jean glanced up. "Parade over?"

"Just about. I thought you were supposed to be hard at work in the kitchen."

"Everything's under control. I wanted Mama to go over these pictures with us."

"Family album?" Wes asked.

"An old one," Emma Jean said. "I gotta get ready for our trip to Wisconsin."

"I don't git all this family history mess," Mrs. Whitcomb said with a scowl toward Wes.

He smiled. "Don't look at me. I'm just going along for the ride."

"Mama, you know you enjoyed the trip down to Buxton," Lu said.

"Wasn't nothin' there."

"You know you enjoyed it," Lu repeated.

"Jes' what I had to do to git my two daughters to take me for a ride in the country."

"Well, then, you got your ride," Emma Jean said.

"Didn't know I was gonna have to pay by spendin' my Thanksgivin' lookin' at a bunch of faces I can't mostly remember no more."

"Mama, you've identified a lot of 'em," Emma Jean said. "Besides, I only wanted to know more before I go to Madison."

"Why you goin' there, anyway?" Mrs. Whitcomb asked. "I thought you already been to that historical society here in Iowa City."

"All I worked on was your family because they were in Iowa. I'm gonna start on Daddy's family, and they came from Kansas."

"What Kansas got to do with Wesconsin?"

"The historical society in Wisconsin's got a bigger library than here. They've got census records for the whole country."

"Bigger. You an' your sister is jes' alike. Always after somethin' bigger, as if you two ain't big enough already."

"Oh, Mama, quit pickin' on Emma Jean."

"I put you in it, too," Mrs. Whitcomb answered Lu.

Wes had taken a seat in a wingback chair opposite the four women. He smiled at how Mrs. Whitcomb always had an answer for her two famous daughters.

Emma Jean looked his way. "What you grinnin' at?"

"I'm staying out of this," he answered.

"I'm thinkin' you should do a little family history, your ownself," Emma Jean said.

"Yeah, I hear you're going to Madison, too." Lu said.

"Just tagging along. I'll leave the research alone. Sunday we're gonna stop and see my folks on the way back."

"'Bout time you met his parents," Mrs. Whitcomb said to Emma Jean.

"Mama, don't start."

"You the one goin' on 'bout family."

"Oh, Mama, I want to know about your family *and* Daddy's. What's wrong with that?"

"Didn't say nothin' was wrong with it. Don't mean you should be tellin' someone else what to do."

"How would hurt it Wes to know more about his family?"

"I know some things," Wes said. "For instance, I'm named after my grandfather."

"He a Wesley, too?" Mrs. Whitcomb asked.

"Yeah, I think it's a family name. When I was young, he'd tell me, 'There's always been a Wesley Whitcomb.' Like I should grow up and have a son with that name. Of course, he named his own son John—you know, my dad."

Emma Jean and Lu looked at Wes and laughed in unison.

"Never mind," he said.

"My mother named me after a TV newswoman," Sylvia said. "She thought it sounded sophisticated. The whole time I was growing up, there was never another Sylvia in school."

"Ain't nothin' wrong with Sylvia as a name," Mrs. Whitcomb said. "Louisa Ann, neither, but somebody got to go by Lu."

"Oh, Mama, it's shorter," Lu said. "It's just a nickname."

"Ain't nothin' wrong with a longer name," Mrs. Whitcomb said. "Louisa Ann sounds nice. It's like the name Winslow. Winslow Whitcomb—sounds good."

"I just got that name!" Emma Jean said.

"You done what?" Mrs. Whitcomb asked.

"I found that name in my research."

"Your daddy's granddaddy," Mrs. Whitcomb said.

"Did you know him, Mama?"

"Died before your daddy an' I met. Where you git aholt uh his name?"

"Uncle Hank told me."

"When you talk to Hank? I ain't seen him in years."

"I wrote him," Emma Jean said. "He's still in San Diego."

"I know, I know. I'm old, but I ain't done gone senile. I know where Hank is."

"I didn't say you were senile."

"Ain't nobody can forget Hank," Mrs. Whitcomb added. "He was the blackest man I ever knew."

"Mama!"

"I didn't say there was nothin' wrong with it. All them Whitcombs was black. Your daddy, too."

"Not like Uncle Hank," Lu said.

"Now that's the pure truth. Louisa Ann, you take after my side of the family, but Emma Jean, you's a Whitcomb. Just like Hank, coal black and hairy."

"Mama!"

"Ain't no need to git upset. You got a man here who mus' like it."

"Oh, for God's sake!" Emma Jean blurted. "I'm goin' to the kitchen. I just might be eatin' in there, too, if you can't be better company."

Lu saw Emma Jean holding back tears and jumped up from her chair. "I'm gonna go help, too."

"She ain't hurt none," Mrs. Whitcomb said.

"I'm on her side," Lu answered, looking back over her shoulder on the way to the kitchen.

"S'pose I went and done it now," Mrs. Whitcomb said to Wes. "I jes' figured you already seen everything there was to see with Emma Jean."

"What we see when we're with somebody, we see through our own eyes," Sylvia said. "I think that's private."

"Can't say that ain't true. What with you and Wes, I guess I know my two girls got pretty lucky," Mrs. Whitcomb said. She gripped the arms of her chair and struggled slowly to her feet. "They ain't jes' lucky, neither. They's good girls, too. I guess I better go fix it up so's we all eatin' turkey dinner at the same table."

CHAPTER 25

Emma Jean bent in and squinted at the splotchy image projected by the ancient microfilm reader. The thing had to be from the 1960s. Wes had better appreciate all this effort. She had told everyone that the sole purpose of her trip to the State Historical Society of Wisconsin was to work on genealogy for her daddy's side of the family, but Thanksgiving Day gave her a second mission. When Wes said there had always been a Wesley Whitcomb, Emma Jean decided to track down the all Wesley Whitcombs that preceded him on his family tree. This branch of his family history would be part of her Christmas present to him.

She reached out and patted the soft, black leather briefcase that held her research on genealogy. If she was going to get to her daddy's family today, she needed to make quick work of the Wesley Whitcombs, and the beat-up microfilm reader wasn't helping. Had she known that all the good readers would be taken by eight-thirty on a Saturday morning, she would have stuck to her original plan to be there when the building opened. The problem was, it felt so good to have Wes lying next to her that forcing herself out of bed wasn't all that easy.

Emma Jean regathered her thoughts and rolled steadily through the film copy of the 1920 federal census for Iowa. The index said that page 189 of the Dubuque County census had a Wesley Whitcomb. Just the name made her smile. Her Wes was probably in the shower by now getting ready for his day. Lu had used her athletic department connections to score Wes a good ticket to the Wisconsin football game. It seemed ridiculous for a college football game to start at eleven in the morning, but Wes said something about the game being on TV. She knew from Marcus's work that sports teams would do anything for television. Right now, she would do anything for a better microfilm reader.

A tug at the workings of the reader brought the top of the film page down to the bottom of the screen. She could just make out page number 179. She rolled the film slowly as numbers in the 180s scrolled before her eyes—186, 187, 188, 189. She centered the film and scanned down the page to see an entry for Charles Whitcomb. She read across the line with his name: age 51, white, born in Iowa. On the lines below were his wife, Helen, 44; daughter, May, 18; son, Wesley, 16. Emma Jean did some quick math. The numbers seemed right. The son had to be Wes's grandfather. But who was the Wesley Whitcomb on the next line? The columns of information indicated father, 84, born in Missouri. The old man must have lived with his son Charles's family. That made three generations in the same house—Wes's grandfather, great-grandfather, and great-great-grandfather.

Three generations! Emma Jean smiled at her good luck. It almost made up for the lousy microfilm reader. She pushed away from the machine and walked to the census index list posted on the wall. It showed no index for Iowa from 1880 through 1910. Searching those films line-by-line would take forever, and she still had her family to trace. She took the 1870 Iowa index from its shelf and hoped for the best. Her luck held. The index listed a Wesley Whitcomb in Dubuque, page 64. Emma Jean moved with even greater anticipation, quickly grabbing a roll of film and cranking through it to page

64. Thank god the census taker had good handwriting. Maybe everybody practiced penmanship in the 1800s.

Wesley Whitcomb appeared on the seventh line of the page. Age 34, born in Missouri. It had to be him. Listed below were his wife, Sarah, 30; son, John, 6; daughter Margaret, 5; son, Charles, 1. Working backwards, the age fit perfectly. This Wesley Whitcomb had to be Wes's great-great-grandfather. She filled out a genealogy form for him, ending with the occupation listed in the census—mining. Dubuque was nowhere near her mama's coal mining town of Buxton. She wondered if Dubuque had coal mines, too. She got up from the reader and headed toward the main reference desk.

"Excuse me," Emma Jean said to the red-haired man at the desk.

"Can I help you?"

"I'm not sure. My question is really about Iowa."

The librarian smiled. "That's okay. We've been known to keep an eye on Iowans from time to time."

"I should have said it's about Iowa history."

"Which is good because we're the historical society."

Emma Jean returned the man's smile.

"And what's your question, ma'am?"

"It's about the census. I found an entry, and it says the person's occupation was mining. I'm wondering if it could have been coal mining."

"What part of Iowa?"

"Oh, I'm sorry," Emma Jean said. "Dubuque, Dubuque County."

"I think that would be lead mining."

"Lead? Would that make sense in connection with Missouri, too?"

"A lot of sense," the librarian answered. "We had a number of lead miners come to Wisconsin from Missouri in the nineteenth century. This was all down in the southwest corner of the state quite near Dubuque."

"Do you know where in Missouri?"

The librarian swiveled in his chair, stood, and walked briskly to a row of shelves holding oversize books. Emma Jean followed behind him, taking advantage of her long legs to keep pace with the energetic man. He pulled a large volume from a shelf and laid it open on a library table.

"This is an atlas of natural resources in the United States," he said as he turned through the pages. "The maps showing mineral deposits are about in the middle."

Emma Jean watched intently over his shoulder.

"Here we are." The man pointed to a cluster of dots on a map that included the state of Missouri. "These represent lead."

"I see."

The librarian immediately pulled another book from the shelves. "This shows the counties in Missouri. Just comparing the location of the dots, I would say Washington and Jefferson Counties would be your best bets. Also, Franklin."

"Thank you."

"You're very welcome."

A check of the 1860 census index for Missouri revealed a Wesley Whitcomb in Washington County, and Emma Jean hastily plucked a roll of film from the bottom drawer of a gray metal cabinet with Missouri records. She loaded her machine and hurriedly cranked past the entries for Warren County before slowing at a page marked Washington County.

She looked for a number at the top of the page, but couldn't find one. As she scanned down, something was wrong. The entries looked different. Only a few lines had names. Most had only sex and age—Female 11; Male 6; Male 54; Female 23. Emma Jean scanned back up the page. At the top of the one column with names, she saw in small print the words *slave owner*.

She picked up the box for the film. The small typewritten label listed the contents. The reel held slave schedules. She knew Missouri had been a slave state. How could she have been in such a hurry that she didn't think about that? She turned back to the reader and made her eyes focus even as she felt her stomach tighten like a closing fist. Like a person unable to look away from a terrible accident, she read the handful of names. Names familiar to her from the black community—Davis, Evans, Robinson. Names taken by black slaves from the white men who claimed to own them—Brock, Maxwell, Whitcomb... *Wesley Whitcomb.*

Emma Jean sat perfectly still. She shuddered and grabbed her briefcase. Her hands tore at the zipper and pulled out a thick sheaf of notes and papers. She shuffled through them quickly—too quickly. The newspaper article from Uncle Hank had to be there. It came in the mail yesterday just before she and Wes left for Madison. There hadn't been time to do much more than glance at the envelope before shoving it in her briefcase. Last night, Wes, not the information sent by Uncle Hank, had gotten all of her attention. She rifled through the papers again, then a third time. Almost at the top of the stack, the headline finally jumped out at her. *Local Man Turns 100! Former Slave, Cowboy.*

Her eyes darted back and forth over the article, *Winslow Whitcomb... worked thirty years in Milwaukee tannery... cowboy near Salinas, Kansas... born a slave in Missouri.* She checked the date at the top of the page—August 22, 1941. She turned her eyes back to the images on the microfilm screen and found the line for the one slave owned by Wesley Whitcomb—Male, 19. The ages matched—19 in 1860, 100 in 1941. She placed the newspaper article on the table and carefully ran her finger down the page. The line was there, the line she didn't want to be there, the line she had skimmed over a minute earlier: *Working in the tanneries is heavier than people think, not heavy like mining, but plenty heavy.*

The microfilm room, crammed with people and tables and readers and cabinets, began to close in on her. She jerked to her feet and started toward a bank of storage cabinets. She heard an "ooh" as she bumped shoulders with a white-haired woman walking back to another reader. Emma Jean brushed by without even an "excuse me." This time she carefully read the labels on the film boxes. She pulled out the roll holding Washington County, Missouri. Nothing mattered to her except that roll of film as she returned to her machine, loaded it, and cranked to page 246. The words were there—Wesley Whitcomb, age 24, occupation miner. It matched. It matched. It *all* matched. Winslow Whitcomb, her great-grandfather, took his surname from his slave owner, the great-great-grandfather of Wes, a man also named Wesley. There had always been a Wesley Whitcomb.

Something made her fill in a genealogy sheet for the Wesley Whitcomb she wished she had never found. She finished and bunched her papers together. She jammed them into her briefcase then stared down at the words projected on the screen. Tears flooded her eyes. A drop rolled down her cheek and landed on the reader. The teardrop picked up a few particles of fine dust and spread out in a faint circle on the white surface. Emma Jean rubbed away the mark with her thumb then wiped the backs of her hands against her eyes.

The microfilm room began to suffocate her. The banks of gunmetal gray cabinets, the sound of film squealing through the readers, the smell of dust on hot light bulbs combined into more than she could bear. She rose without turning off the reader. She took her briefcase and draped her coat around her shoulders. The simple act of fastening the buttons seemed too much for the moment. She had to get back to the hotel. Her watch read twenty-minutes-to-eleven. Wes would be finding his seat in the football stadium. She had to get back to the hotel. She had to be there when Wes came back. She had to make herself ready to see him.

Emma Jean pushed open the heavy doors of the historical society and stepped out into a cold November wind. As she rushed away from the historical society toward the hotel three blocks away, she felt herself running from a past she hated toward a future she dreaded.

CHAPTER 26

Wes opened the door to the hotel lobby, thoroughly reminded by the raw November wind why he liked going to basketball games a lot more than football. The excitement of a victory on a last-second field goal might have warmed the local fans, but he was looking forward to taking a hot shower and climbing under the thick blankets on the bed in the hotel room. He knew Emma Jean would be at the historical society all day. That left plenty of time for him to nap and then scout out a good restaurant for dinner as he had promised.

The short elevator ride to the fifth floor gave him a chance to ponder whether the hotel building was an octagon or a hexagon. He wasn't sure, but either way, it created odd, pie-shaped rooms very unlike the historic hotel where he and Emma Jean had stayed on their last trip to Wisconsin. The charm of this place was its location only a couple of blocks from the historical society. Still, the room and the bed proved to be perfectly comfortable. It was the bed he was thinking of as he put his key card in the door. He entered the room to the sound of water running in the bathroom sink.

"Wes, is that you?" Emma Jean's voice called.

"Emma Jean?"

The hotel maids had already done up the room, but he saw Emma Jean's closed suitcase and her black leather briefcase sitting in the middle of the bed. She emerged from the bathroom with her eyes red and her face freshly washed.

"What are you doing here?" he asked.

"I've been waiting for you."

"Is something wrong? Is it Shai?"

"No."

"Your mom?"

"No. Nothing like that. Wes, I want you to sit down."

Emma Jean turned around the straight chair at the desk and sat. He took a seat on the edge of the bed.

"I have to tell you something," she said.

Wes had seen Emma Jean scowl in frustration during tennis matches, flash with anger over a racist comment reported in the newspaper, turn away in embarrassment at some remark from her mother, and smile with anticipation as they walked hand in hand to her bedroom. He had never seen the look of sorrow she wore as she leaned back against the stiff wooden desk chair.

"What is it?"

"It's this trip." Her eyes glanced away in a far-off stare. "I had a surprise planned."

Wes felt his body relax. "If something went wrong, that's okay. It can't be that big a deal."

"No, I didn't mean that the surprise was for the trip."

"But—"

"You have to let me explain."

"Okay."

"I wasn't just working on my family's genealogy. I was doing some of yours, too."

"Mine?"

"You said there's always been a Wesley Whitcomb. I was going to find some of them for you. It was supposed to be a Christmas present."

"That's nice."

"No. It's not." She took a tissue from the box on the desk, dabbed her cheek, and drew a deep breath. "I found something I didn't know. Something I wish I still didn't know."

He started to speak, but she held up her hand and shook her head.

"No, I said that wrong. It's something I wish wasn't true." Emma Jean paused. "Your grandfather was named Wesley Whitcomb."

Wes nodded.

"So was his grandfather. Your great-great-grandfather had the name Wesley Whitcomb. That Wesley Whitcomb was from Missouri."

"Okay."

"Wes, Missouri was a slave state. He owned a slave."

"What?"

"There's more. The slave's name was Winslow Whitcomb. My great-grandfather."

Wes sat in stunned silence. He dropped his head. He tried to refocus his eyes as the carpet swirled in blotches of maroon, green, and navy blue. Finally, he looked up. "Are you sure?"

"I'm sure. I'm also sure it's why we have the same last name."

Silence enveloped the room. Wes slid his hand across the bed until it touched the soft leather briefcase. "That's why you packed?"

"I can't stay here with you. I'm going back to Iowa City."

"I'll pack," he said.

"I rented a car."

"But we have mine."

"No."

"We can drive back together," he said.

"No, we can't. I can't."

"At least let me take you to the car rental."

"It's already here," she said. "They dropped it off."

"But we have to talk."

"Not now."

"When?"

"I don't know."

"But what about us?" Fear crept into his voice. "The future?"

Emma Jean stood and walked to the window. She gazed out at the lake a block away. "I don't know if we have a future."

"I know we've never really talked about it."

"This isn't about what we have or haven't said. Futures aren't just the future. Futures have pasts. We have this past."

"I didn't have any idea. I swear."

"I know you didn't, but that doesn't change it."

Wes watched her staring out the window. Suddenly, she seemed taller, tall in a way he had forgotten during the past year. He stood. "So, we should just give up?"

"Do you want me to say it doesn't matter? Say we should get married? Say we should have kids? What if we have a son? Should we name him Wesley Whitcomb?"

"Emma Jean, that's not fair."

"No, it isn't, but it's a lot more fair than being a slave. And this is why we can't talk. I'll only end up saying things I don't want to say."

Wes watched her brush by him and pick up her suitcase.

"Since we've been together," she said, "I've come to think of you as the most color-blind person I've ever known. I told myself that was good, but it's not the way life is, Wes. It's not the way I am."

"There's nothing I can do?"

She moved across the room. "You can let me go. You can respect my feelings and not call."

"Ever? Because of some great-great-grandfather?"

"I can't look ahead to ever." She opened the hotel room door. "I think . . . I think I'll always wonder . . ."

"What?"

"I'll wonder . . . did he have your eyes?"

Emma Jean stepped into the hall, and the door closed behind her.

CHAPTER 27

No place had ever seemed so empty to Wes as the hotel room after Emma Jean left. It took him ten minutes to pack and three to call his parents and tell them Emma Jean was sick. He couldn't bear to talk to them longer, to tell them the truth, to tell them the real reason they wouldn't be meeting Emma Jean for the first time. The only thing he could tell them was that dinner tomorrow wouldn't be possible, that he and Emma Jean were heading back to Iowa City. He didn't tell them they were driving separate cars.

As he drove across the brown Wisconsin hillsides of November, he tried not to think about Emma Jean, but there was nothing else he could think about. Not some meaningless football game. Not the presents he had to buy for Christmas. Not even the gas gauge in his car. The low-fuel light clicked on just as he crested a hill overlooking the Mississippi River.

Dubuque sat in the valley below. He would have to stop there. Dubuque, the town another Wesley Whitcomb had come to from Missouri three lifetimes ago. The town Wes's father had left forty years ago with a family history in his wake that he either did not know or did not bother to carry with him. The place Wes's grandfather would come from on visits to Princeton and say, "There's always been a Wesley Whitcomb."

Dubuque was an old city, and as Wes drove along the expressway that skirted the edge of downtown, he suddenly hated all the old buildings that brought him closer to the past. Too close to the history that Emma Jean had discovered. Too close to the time when another Wesley Whitcomb had owned a slave. Wes stayed on the highway until it climbed a long hill out of old Dubuque to the south edge of town. He looked again at the yellow fuel light and pulled into a gas station.

Daylight dwindled earlier and earlier in the last days of November, and the temperature was dropping lower along with the afternoon sun as it disappeared below the horizon. Wes pumped his gas without bothering to put on a coat. *To hell with a coat.* He filled his car with $19.73 of unleaded and then walked toward the door of the station. He glanced at the sign in the transom that read "Food Shop." He realized he hadn't eaten since breakfast.

"I had nineteen seventy-three on the gas," he said as he approached the counter.

"Nineteen seventy-three," the clerk answered, punching the buttons on the cash register.

Wes handed him a twenty-dollar bill.

"And twenty-seven cents makes twenty," the clerk said as he gave Wes three coins.

"Is there someplace to eat around here?"

"What ya lookin' for?"

"I don't know. A diner or something. I own a diner in Iowa City."

"There's not nothin' out this way, but they got a couple good family restaurants downtown."

"Maybe I'll just get something here," he said at the thought of backtracking into Dubuque.

He walked to a bank of coolers across the back wall of the store and took a can of Coke and a packaged ham and cheese sandwich. He paid for his supper without another word to the clerk.

Wes settled himself in his car, opened the Coke, and took a long drink. He placed the can in the cup holder that slid out of the dash and started to open the sandwich. He worked at the corner of the package with the tiny printed words "Tear Here." The tough plastic didn't give. He twisted and pulled without luck. *Who the hell made these packages?* Finally, he yanked his keys out of the ignition and poked a hole in the package. With both hands, he ripped an opening large enough to take out the now misshapen sandwich. He took another long drink of Coke and started the car. He rolled out of the gas station and pulled back onto the road.

Wes took a bite of the sandwich. The edges of the bread were dry and tasteless. *How could something go stale in a package like that?* The meat was mounded up in the middle. *Too thick. Too salty.* He jammed his finger against the button for the electric window and heard a motor whir as the glass slid down into the door. He hurled the sandwich into the road. In a fury, he reached down for the half-full can of pop. A solid blast from a truck horn jerked his eyes up to the highway. His car had crossed the center line. The lights of a semi were on top of him. He swerved back into his own lane as the truck rushed by his open window. He lifted his foot from the gas and coasted to a stop on the wide gravel shoulder of the highway.

Wes slid his hands together at the top of the steering wheel and rested his head there. He closed his eyes and saw only the devastated look on Emma Jean's face in their hotel room. He replayed the scene in his mind. All he had been able to say was, "I didn't know."

Wes wondered what he did know. He remembered Sunday school in the little church where his mother was secretary, a place to learn that prejudice was wrong. But he had never learned enough of his own family's history to know the terrible truth in its past. He had grown up, gone to college, and lived his life certain that he knew racism was wrong. Now, at age thirty-five, he couldn't think of a single action he had taken because of that knowledge.

How many times in the last year had Emma Jean said, "You don't understand." Now, he knew how it felt to understand at least one thing and knew, also, that he had never worked hard enough to understand before. That there was so much more he still needed to understand. That maybe he never would or could.

Nothing he had done before he met Emma Jean had earned him the right to say, "I care." Now, how could he say, "I care because I love you." He felt no right to say the words "I love you" to Emma Jean, but only the words "I love her" to himself. Not words to offer Emma Jean with joy, but words of pain that silently burrowed deep within him.

He pushed the button to close the car window and drove back onto the highway. Drove into the darkness ahead.

CHAPTER 28

Shai pushed open the door to the girls' locker room and headed straight to the home bleachers. Her game had ended only ten minutes before, and the second one of the tournament was already underway. Early on a Saturday morning, ninth-grade girls' basketball didn't draw much of a crowd. She had seen Wes sitting by himself halfway up in the stands during her game. While the rest of her teammates fixed their hair or fiddled with jewelry, Shai had dressed as quickly as she could. Now that she saw Wes was still in his same spot, she slowed to a more dignified pace for a teenage girl. As she reached the bleachers and headed up the aisle, he leaned forward.

"Hi," he said.

"Hi."

They both looked down in a momentary search for words.

"Good game."

"I didn't play much."

"I thought you did okay."

Shai just shrugged.

"You wanna sit down?" Wes asked.

"Sure." She slid onto the bleacher beside him.

"So . . ." He turned and looked straight at her. "How've you been?"

"All right, I guess."

"And your mom?"

"Yeah?"

"How is she?"

"Who knows."

Shai's tone sounded more like *who cares.*

"You see her every day," Wes said.

"Barely. All she does is sit in her study and write."

"A play?"

"She says she's already got a producer."

"What is it?"

"A play!"

"No, I mean what's it about?"

"She's not tellin' me." Shai shrugged again. "She say's it's not time for me to know, yet."

Wes touched her hand. "Shai, I didn't mean for it to be this way."

"You didn't make it this way. She did."

"Don't—"

"Wes, you were my friend, too."

"Oh, Shai, I still am."

"It's the middle of January," she said. "I haven't seen you since Thanksgiving."

"That's my fault," Wes said softly. "I didn't know if I should . . . you know, if I should call. And then the games . . . I thought if your mom was here . . ."

"She doesn't come, either," Shai said. "I know she's afraid you'll be here."

"I guess this time she would have been right."

Shai turned her eyes to the court and stared at the players warming up.

"Shai, your mom—"

"It's not just about Mama!"

222

"I know. I really do. I care about what you think. It's your family, too."

"I don't care nothin' about that!"

Two women sitting below glanced back at Shai and Wes.

"I don't care nothin' about two old men lived uh hundred years ago," Shai said, lowering her voice. "My great-great-grandfather. How many greats you gotta go back 'til you ain't even related anymore? How many you gotta go back 'til everybody's related ta everybody?"

Wes rubbed his hands against his face. "Let's you and me go back."

"Huh?"

"Back to being friends."

Shai's eyes began to fill with tears. He handed her the napkin from the chocolate donut he bought earlier at the concession stand. She dabbed the tears before they fell from her cheeks.

"Prob'ly got frosting on your face," Wes said.

"Prob'ly."

"It's chocolate," he said. "Might not show."

Shai leaned over and hugged him with both arms around his neck.

"I feel stupid," she said as she let go of him. "I didn't mean to be a baby."

"Maybe this once, it's okay." Wes looked in her eyes. "Shai, I've never had a daughter, but if I did . . ."

"I know."

"Now, I'm sounding stupid."

"Yeah." Shai smiled.

"How about if I start coming to your games, again?"

"I'm not doin' that good."

"You looked good to me."

"I know the other girls are better."

"So, you need some coaching? I might be available."

"I think this is my last year. I actually like piano better."

"Nothin' wrong with that."

"Come to my recital?"

"Won't your mom be there?"

Shai nodded.

"I don't think she'd be ready for that," Wes said.

"She's not." Her smile faded, but this time her eyes stayed dry.

"You play again this morning?"

"Two games from now."

A buzzer sounded, ending the first quarter of the game on the court.

"Wanna go out to the stand and get a Coke?"

"Popcorn, too?" Shai teased.

"Why not?" The words touched an ache inside him. *Why not?*

CHAPTER 29

Even the tinted glass of the tall windows along the main concourse at the Cedar Rapids airport could not disguise the brilliant sunlight outside. That same beautiful sunny sky promised to make the day a hot one for late September. The cool of the terminal's air conditioning floated over Wes as he leaned back in his seat at the gate area and opened his copy of *Time* magazine. He found the short article he was looking for on page fifty-six.

An American Voice Returns

When Emma Jean Whitcomb assaulted America's race consciousness with her play The Black Hologram, *everyone expected to hear more from this voice of confrontation. The ensuing fifteen years saw Ms. Whitcomb turn her talents to the academic world as a professor, first at Howard University, and more recently at the University of Iowa. Her work as a playwright produced only a few minor notes in the world of theater—until now.*

   Last month, in Washington, D.C., Whitcomb's academic home for nearly a decade, her new play, Did He Have Your Eyes? *made a stunning debut. Charged with emotion unseen from Whitcomb* since *The Black Hologram,* her new play confronts audiences with stark truths from America's racial past and raises questions of whether that past can ever be buried.

Opening in a Midwestern university, the play unfolds as a summer of shattering discovery for two law students, a black woman and a white man, who have fallen in love. They embark on internships at a free legal aid office for poverty-stricken residents of western Tennessee. The pair leaves for Tennessee without sharing that each has distant family connections there.

Tim Crawford has no idea and little interest in why his great-grandfather left the state as a young man. Angela Franklin goes on the internship hiding her secret mission to learn more about a house fire set by the Ku Klux Klan that killed her great-grandmother, leaving three small children behind. When a forgotten cache of old records reveals that Tim's great-grandfather briefly belonged to the Klan, the full force of Ms. Whitcomb's sense of racial outrage takes over the play.

The playwright does not disguise her anger, even as she leaves room for ambiguity. Was the membership in the KKK extorted from Tim's great-grandfather in exchange for continuing his employment in a county job? Was Klan membership connected to his sudden departure from Tennessee shortly after the violence against Angela's great-grandmother? Whitcomb leaves the questions open, but there is no doubt about the playwright's fury against the depth of racial injustice and violence she sees in America's past and present.

Even with the exceptional elegance of Whitcomb's writing, Did He Have Your Eyes? is not an easy play to watch. The soliloquy from Angela as she imagines the pain of her great-grandmother's death in the horrifying house fire is not for the faint of heart. Still, the play is a must for anyone who cares whether the racial divide in America can ever be healed. Emma Jean Whitcomb's return to—

"Wes!"

The familiar sound of Shai's voice startled Wes out the pages of *Time*. He looked up to see her walking down the airport concourse a step ahead of her mother and her Aunt Lu.

"Mama didn't tell me you were comin'," she said as she approached. She turned toward her mother. "You didn't tell me Wes was coming."

"I thought it would be a nice surprise," Emma Jean said. "Hello, Wes."

"Hi." Wes rose from his chair and stood an arm's length from Emma Jean. He had not seen her in ten months, and now he had no idea what should follow the simple word *hi*.

"Well, Wes, don't I count?" he heard Lu say.

"Hi, Lu."

"It's good to see you," she said with a smile.

"You, too."

The passage of almost a year made Wes feel like he was seeing the three remarkably tall figures in front of him with new eyes. They stair-stepped down, Lu two inches taller than Emma Jean and Emma Jean another two inches to Shai, each beautiful in her own way. Even Shai, whom he had seen during the school year, looked different. The summer had been spent with her father. Had she grown again?

"Should we sit down?" Wes asked.

"Shai, we don't have much time before the plane leaves," Emma Jean said. "You want to get something to read? Maybe Wes would go with you."

Shai gave him a questioning look.

"Sure," he said.

Wes stepped next to Shai and they fell into stride with the familiar comfort they had regained through a springtime of the occasional Saturday morning visits she made to the Red Door Café. Still, Shai had changed during the summer spent out east. It wasn't her height.

She had passed Wes in that department several months ago. Now, Shai had begun to fill out, her body taking on the unmistakable contours of a woman. As they walked toward the airport newsstand, Wes was already missing the coltish girl he had shared his basketball with at The Manor two years earlier.

"Well?" Shai asked. "Are you glad to see me?"

"Of course."

"You're pretty quiet about it."

"I was surprised," Wes said.

"Me, too. What . . ." Shai paused. "I mean . . ."

"I don't know," Wes answered. "Your mom just called and asked me to go."

"So what did she say?"

"Just that the play was going to open in New York and I belonged there."

"That's all?"

"She bought me a ticket."

"Wes, she wrote the play. She can git a ticket for free."

"No, a plane ticket, goofy. And a hotel room."

"A room by yourself?" Shai raised her eyebrows somewhere between hoping and kidding.

"Shai!"

"I just asked. I'm not a little girl anymore."

"You're fifteen, and I can't tell you anything more about this trip. I didn't even know you and Lu were coming. Your mom and I barely talked."

"But you came."

"I did."

They turned into the newsstand. Shai stopped at the built-in display rack that formed a corner of the small shop. Wes watched as she flipped through the pages of a *Seventeen* magazine then put it back to choose a copy of *Glamour* instead. While she paid the cashier, he tried not to look at the caption about "Ten Things All Men Want" and wondered how the two-and-a-half months she had been in New York suddenly felt like two-and-a-half years.

"You stayed out east the whole summer," he said as they headed back down the concourse toward the gate.

Shai looked down and suddenly seemed more interested in the alternating light- and dark-gray squares of carpeting than she did in talking.

"Did you have a good time?" he asked.

"Yeah." She nodded.

"Well, that's good then."

"I know I stayed longer than usual . . ."

"And?"

"He's my daddy, Wes. I just wanted to spend more time with him." She hesitated. "It's not because of you and Mama or anything."

"That's not what I was thinking."

"Good."

"Of course, you could've written me. You know, even a postcard. The Statue of Liberty or something."

"You didn't write me either," Shai said.

"Didn't have your address."

"You could've . . ." she didn't finish her thought with the words *gotten it from Mama*.

Emma Jean stood staring out the windows toward the runway when Shai and Wes returned to the gate area. The sun glistened off her jet-black hair, and even with her back turned to him, Wes couldn't help but think about the first time they met. He remembered that night at City Streets and Emma Jean rising from the table, her hair worn like a black crown that only accentuated the exceptional height that set her apart from other women. He wondered if he had learned to love, or fallen love with, the things that set Emma Jean apart—tall and proud, black and proud, brilliant and proud. It hardly mattered now—now that some of those things also held her apart from him. He hung back as Shai walked forward and touched her mother's elbow.

Emma Jean turned. "Hi, Sugar. You find something to read?"

"Just a magazine." Shai pointed toward the plane pulled up at the end of the jetway. "Kinda small, isn't it?"

"It's only to Chicago, Sugar. We'll have a regular plane from Chicago to New York."

"I had big planes all the way when I came back from Daddy's."

"Well, weren't you the lucky girl," Emma Jean teased.

Before either could speak again, a young woman in a crisp white blouse and a blue skirt picked up the microphone at the counter.

"Good morning, ladies and gentleman. Welcome to flight 5867 to Chicago. We will begin our regular boarding process momentarily. At this time, we would like to offer preboarding to any of our Captain's Club and Platinum Card members, any families traveling with small children, or anyone else requiring a little extra assistance. Again, this is a preboard only. Regular boarding will begin in just a few moments."

"Captain's Club, that's us," Emma Jean said to Shai. Emma Jean picked up her black leather carry-on bag. She placed her hand in the small of Shai's back to guide her toward the gate agent. She glanced at Lu and Wes and repeated, "That's us."

The four of them converged on the gate agent with boarding passes in hand.

"Why don't you sit with Aunt Lu," Emma Jean said to Shai.

They walked in single file down the jetway, Lu, Shai, Emma Jean, and Wes, all four ducking slightly as they passed through the airplane door. Wes and Emma Jean stood side by side as they stowed their bags in the overhead compartment. He crawled into the window seat leaving the aisle for Emma Jean.

"Here we are," he said.

230

"Here we are," Emma Jean answered. "You have enough room?"

"I'm fine."

"Like Shai said, the plane's so little."

"Not a problem."

The boarding process grew into a hubbub of small women hoisting overstuffed bags into overhead compartments, human roadblocks rummaging for a pillow or blanket, and business travelers no doubt wishing for a plane with a first-class cabin. Wes sat quietly as the two flight attendants managed to restore order and finish closing the storage bins.

Emma Jean glanced to her left when a passenger's bag brushed her shoulder. She turned back toward Wes with a faraway look in her eyes.

"Thanks for inviting me," he said.

"Thanks for coming."

"I was pretty surprised."

"Me, too."

"That I came?" he asked.

"That I asked you," she said.

"At least you're honest."

The intercom spoke before Emma Jean could say anything more. "Folks, this is your captain speaking from the flight deck. I'd like to welcome you aboard this short hop to Chicago. We have the okay to push back from the jetway, and you couldn't have chosen a better day to fly, either to Chicago or wherever your ultimate destination might be. Right now, O'Hare Airport has a warm midday temperature of 84 degrees with fair skies. The National Weather Service reports indicate a thousand miles of blue sky in any direction. So, sit back, make yourself comfortable, and please give your full attention to the safety information the flight attendants will be sharing with you in just a minute or two."

"I wasn't trying to be harsh before," Emma Jean said.

"It kinda came out that way."

"It hasn't been easy for me."

"Me, either," he said.

"I know."

"So, why *did* you ask me to come?"

"I don't think I can put it into words," she answered. "It's what I said on the phone. When the play opens, I know you should be there."

He shifted in his seat and stared hard at her. "And after the play? What then?"

The plane gave a lurch as it was pushed back from the jetway, then began to turn and move forward under its own power.

"You're asking me to look into the future, again," she said. "I can't do that. Not now. I've spent the last ten months and all the creative soul I have trying to come to grips with the past. I'm not there yet."

"But we need to talk."

The plane began to gently bump and jostle its passengers as it taxied toward the end of the runway.

"Wes, we never flew anywhere together, did we?"

"No."

"I don't talk much on planes," Emma Jean said.

She closed her eyes and took a deep breath. Emma Jean reached toward Wes but pulled down the armrest between them. Their hands settled on each side. As the jet roared down the runway and lifted up into a thousand miles of blue sky in any direction, their hands stayed frozen in place—fingertips two inches apart.

Questions for Discussion

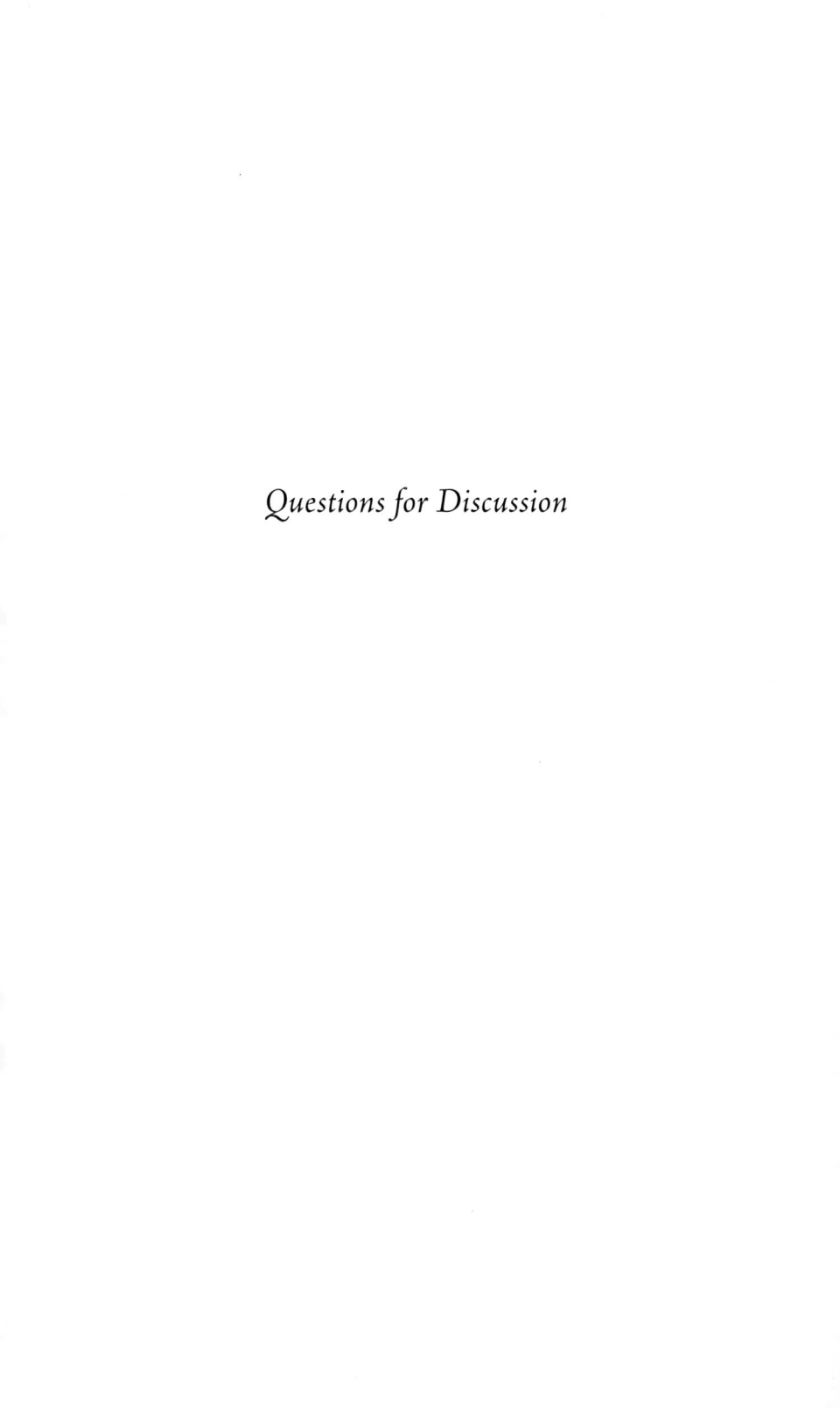

Tracy Williams and Tom McKay

Emma Jean's hiring by the university is a step toward greater diversity and inclusion. Does diversity alone lead to a sense of belonging? Are inclusion and belonging the same thing?

Do you understand Emma Jean's anger about race? What are some of her experiences that contributed to it? Do you think you can fully understand the experiences in Emma Jean's life?

What do you like most or least about the relationship between Emma Jean and Wes? What do you think Emma Jean and Wes find in each other that leads to falling in love? What role does Shai play in the relationship between Emma Jean and Wes?

Do you think Emma Jean has more reasons than she says to be against Shai playing basketball?

What does Wes learn about himself because of his relationship with Emma Jean?

Would you rather be friends with Emma Jean or Wes? Why?
How are the lives of Emma Jean and her high school friends Diane and Brenda different? Without a special talent like Emma Jean's, how hard do you think it would be to succeed when faced with discrimination? In addition to a special talent, did Emma Jean have any other advantages compared to her friend Brenda?

How does physical objectification of black and white people appear in the story? Does this include sexual stereotypes? If so, are some playful? Are some hurtful? Do you know about the role of sexual stereotypes in lynchings and violence against African Americans?

What societal challenges does Emma Jean face based on her physical appearance? Would she be considered feminine? Why or why not? In what ways have black women been physically objectified and exploited?

Are black women held to different standards of grace and beauty than white women? How might differences impact life outcomes? Do you think stigmas about body types as related to grace and beauty can discourage some black women from participating in sports and physical activity? Can this contribute to health disparities?

The novel begins in the year 2000. Is racial harmony and understanding better or worse today? Can you give examples?

The story ends with Emma Jean and Wes seated in an airplane with their fingertips only inches apart. What do you think happens next? Does this scene have a larger meaning?

Tom McKay is a museum consultant and historian. He received an Award of Merit from the American Association for State and Local History in recognition of dedicated service to local history museums in Iowa and Wisconsin. In addition to his chosen profession, he has written several works of fiction including the novels *West Fork*, *Another Life*, and *The Old Guard*.

Tracy L Williams is President and CEO of the YWCA of Southeastern Wisconsin headquartered in Milwaukee. She serves in her position with vision and purpose dedicated to matriarchal leadership while living, loving, and leading for justice. Prior to relocating to Milwaukee, she served in several leadership roles for diversity and inclusion at the University of Wisconsin.